SÁNGRE
The Color of Dying

By

Carlos Colón

HellBound Books Publishing LLC
Houston, TX

A HellBound Books Publication
Copyright © 2014 by Carlos Colon
All Rights Reserved
2nd Edition

Cover and art design by Keith Whalen/HellBound Books Publishing

www.hellboundbookspublishing.com

www.hellboundbookspublishing.com

Printed in the United States of America

To my wife Maria,
The light in the window
that guides me home.

SÁNGRE

The Color of Dying

"There have been a small amount of cases where victims retained a consciousness of who they were when they were alive, therefore carrying the characteristics, memories, intelligence and emotions that they've always had. Those are the ones that suffer the real horror—the horror of losing everything and everyone that they've ever loved."
– Dr. Teresa Gunder, Professor of Epidemiology, University of Pennsylvania

1

One of the few good things about being dead is making your own rules and not giving a crap. I do what I want, when I want and where I want to do it. And right now I want to feed.

Here at Rahway State Prison the blood of the prisoners is generally of the quality I need to be at my undead best. They eat well and they have nothing to do here but exercise, giving their blood the nutritional value that can last for about a week—much better than the crap running through the veins of the street scum I come across when I'm in *Charles Bronson* mode. In "Death Wish", Bronson drew muggers into dark alleys and blew their insides out with a .44. Me? I just drain them of their blood.

Being 5'9" and 160 lbs., I'm not the most imposing figure you'd find walking the streets, which makes me a tempting target for switchblade or pistol-wielding scumbags. And while I can't deny the enjoyment of seeing their expressions when my fangs rip into the bases of their necks, the feedings usually carry little nutritional value. Junkies aren't known for having the best eating habits so the quality of their blood might hold me for maybe a couple of days. It's our equivalent of junk food. I learned that back in my early predatory days feeding off a Bronx hooker I spotted at a seedy tenement doorway on 164th Street. She was succumbing to the toxic substances that were fighting for space in the thinning blood remaining in her arteries so I said fuck it. I dragged her ass out of sight, away from the street lights, and clamped my fangs onto her perfume-soaked neck as she drifted into the next world.

In the end, the effort was hardly worth it.

Not only did the sewage from her veins taste like shit, it barely lasted me into the next day. Who would have guessed it? The rules of proper nutritional feeding apply to the dead as well.

The prison allows me to enjoy a quality feeding with somewhat of a clear conscience. Yeah, that's right, a clear conscience. For most of my kind, conscience doesn't come into play; but me, I'm the less common of the undead species. The majority of us, when we become infected or turned, lose all of our identity and we become mindless, soulless, territorial predators. For others in the minority like me, it's different. We are burdened with a genetic resistance that retains our humanity and saddles us with conscience and emotions. Right now I would say that there are about two hundred of us walking the night throughout neighborhoods around every corner of the world. Out of that group, maybe fifty of us are genetically resistant. For me, that means a constant battle of emotions when taking a life in order to keep myself going—not the kind of quality you look for in a nighttime predator.

Dining in a place like Rahway makes things a little easier. Earlier this evening at the inmates' cafeteria, I walked unseen amongst the prisoners to catch the buzz on who is the biggest scumbag or who is due for a good *shanking*. Towards the end of dinner, I observed a pair of *goombahs* huddled together pointing at a large bull-like figure with a receding hairline and a forehead you could place a billboard on. I overheard them referring to him as Phillip Vernon, the piece of filth former high school coach that was recently convicted for sexual assault on a 14-year-old girl from his soccer team. It wasn't clear who was going to do the shanking from their conversation but it didn't matter. Neither of them is going to get the chance. He's mine.

The ability to control minds is a useful little trait that allows me to send any pain-in-the-ass corrections officer to rub one out in the bathroom while I dine on a selection from the Rahway menu. It might be immature but who gives a fuck? I'm dead. I could use a good laugh now and then. When I run into someone that is not so susceptible, usually some tough-guy corrections officer ready to shove his nightstick up my ass, I turn off the light on my presence. But going around unseen can be draining if you're lacking some good plasma.

#

The cell is cold, dark. Vernon's in the bottom bunk fast asleep. In the upper bunk, his cellmate, rustled by my sudden appearance, bolts up from his pillow. "What the f—?"

"Shh... just go back to sleep."

With no need for any of that Bela Lugosi *look into my eyes* shit, Vernon's cellmate compliantly falls back onto his pillow.

The commotion has stirred my intended. He groggily awakens to find a surly Puerto Rican stranger staring down at him.

The intruder is disturbingly calm. He gently places a hand on Vernon's shoulder. "Don't worry, I'll explain everything. For now, just be quiet and listen. I'll be quick, I promise."

The clammy prisoner rises from his pillow and leaves a profile of perspiration. The stranger kneels to look at him squarely in the eye (it's my preferable method of communication). "Vernon, I was walking around the cafeteria before and I heard some shit about you. It seems you like forcing little fourteen year-old girls to give you blow jobs after classes." His eyes are cold and detached, but they betray an unnerved acknowledgment that this isn't going to be a very good night for him. "I also hear, Vernon, that one of the girls tried to fight you off, and when she couldn't, she almost bit your cock in half." That must have hurt. "You then lost it and beat the girl so badly that she now has permanent brain damage." I have a daughter. Or should I say I had one when I was alive. The image of Vernon mercilessly wailing on that girl bothers me—a lot. "You see this shank, Vernon?" Vernon recognizes what was once a cafeteria spoon and mumbles some undecipherable gibberish. "This was hidden in one of the other cells. It was meant for you. Somebody on the outside wants you gutted." His fear is escalating. I smell it. "It seems you might have victimized the wrong little lady, my friend." He may be powerless to react, but it doesn't stop the sweat from escaping his brow.

"Vernon, my name is Nicky Negrón. And you might want to brace yourself for this one 'cause, believe me, I know how it sounds. But the fact is: I am a vampire." Even I still snicker when I say that. "Yeah, I know, it sounds like I'm some kind of nut. Believe me, bud, I wish I was. I'd happily take that over being what I am.

But unfortunately for the both of us, I am not. Instead I'm a predator that feeds on human blood …like yours. Now, as a human, you barely qualify. But you're going to have to do. Because that poor girl you assaulted is going to be stuck for the rest of her life with the thought of your filthy cock having been in her mouth. And that gives me reason enough to not only drain you of every drop of your blood, but to drag it out so that I can enjoy the essence of your fear as you realize that any one of the next breaths you take could be your last."

Enough shit talk.

Vernon's short muted gasp punctuates the slam of my fangs against his jugular. My tight embrace of the execrable coach is not one of affection, but of me not wanting to miss a drop as his blood springs festively onto my palate like the fountains at the Bellagio.

The desperate kicks are just reflex. At this point Vernon's mind is totally gone. His legs will give out, then start twitching along with the rest of his body as his life slowly drains away.

Hmm...

His blood tastes funny. I don't like it. It's thin, — especially for a phys-ed teacher. I wonder if he's on anti-inflammatories. You get a taste for these things after twenty-seven years. I better check the med facility, find out what the fuck I just ingested.

Loose ends first.

The 18" Filipino Ceremonial Blade I carry is the kind they use in the Philippine mountains to decapitate criminals. I use it the same way. It prevents my victims from turning. Don't need any other predators feeding in my territory. Theoretically, I could just leave Vernon here until morning and let him burst into flames. But who needs all the questions and speculations that come with spontaneous combustion? It's easier to just hack his head off and leave it and the shank on the upper bunk with his cellmate. I'll let him take the blame. He's in prison so he's probably scum too. Fuck him.

#

The squeak from the metal cabinet's "V" drawer echoes like the feedback from a Hendrix solo. The lights are out. I left them that way. Don't need any interruptions. With the half-moon only barely outlining the fern sitting on the window sill, the dancing beam from my iPhone's flashlight is the only hint that there might be some presence in the room as I search through the prison medical files. Next door, the resident doctor is enjoying some Internet porn in his office. The moan from Sasha Grey's fake orgasm should be enough to mask the metal grinding from the file cabinet.

Veglia... Velarde... Ventura... here you are, you piece of shit. Phillip Michael Vernon. The history doesn't seem that bad, just a little hypertension which they have under control with a prescription of Norvasc.

But here's a little something.

Just like I detected, he's taking anti-inflammatories. I always try to check things like this out so I know what kind of shit I ingested.

There's a sub-folder with some additional documents, they look new.

They are.

They're dated today.

His white blood cells have been monitored for the past month. He'd been coming in with fever, chills, and a loss of appetite. His weight had dropped fifteen pounds.

Shit!

Leukemia!

Cancerous blood that might last me for maybe a day.

I'll probably start feeling the pangs as soon as I rise. Looks like it'll be feeding time again in Nickyland tomorrow night.

2

Shut up, Othello!

Fucking cat. I can't stand this little bastard. And he obviously isn't much of a fan of mine either.

They're weird, cats.

I and the rest of my kind break every law of nature we've previously come to understand. We appear as we did when we died, giving the illusion of never aging, and we can remain unseen whenever we want to. Even Mother Earth is confused by us. We don't cast reflections, we have no shadows, and our images don't come out in photographs or on video. So why is Stefanie's black, long-haired, pain-in-the-ass cat hissing at me?

How can he see me when no one else can?

That being said, the little ass wipe is doing his job. He knows I don't belong here and he's spewing out his disapproval. It's as if his senses are telling him that I shouldn't be walking this earth, never mind snooping around on my widowed and remarried bride.

Stefanie always liked naming her pets after English

literary characters. During our days together we had a dog named Lancelot and a parrot named Romeo. The bird was my favorite. I used to get a big kick out of teaching him to curse in Spanish. Stefanie not so much; she'd blush every time he blurted out something like *coño* or *puta* in front of company.

Since he's only a couple of years old, Othello came into Stefanie's life long after my indecorous passing two-and-a-half decades ago, so his allegiance is to Stefanie and her husband of almost twenty years, Bill Rippey.

I don't know what I'm looking for when I come to Scarsdale to peek in on their quiet suburban life. Admittedly, there is some degree of comfort in seeing that a sense of order has been restored to the life of the woman I left behind. But it also comes with the price of realization that the only love I ever had has now been married to another man longer than she had been to me. Everything I'd worked for, every dream I ever had of sharing with Stefanie is now a part of Rippey's life, not mine.

It should be me curled up on that couch with her watching *Downton Abbey*, even though it would have bored the shit out of me. But for her I would have done it; even if I never understood how a Puerto Rican girl from the Bronx could like that crap.

Cozy as they are, she looks a little under the weather. She's got a cup of hot cocoa in her hands and a quilt wrapped around her (along with Rippey's arms). It looks like he enjoys this PBS bullshit too, a category where I fell short.

I knew this prick would win her hand the second she met him. The first six years after my disappearance for Stefanie there was nothing but despondency and mourning until she realized that she was still young and had a whole life ahead of her. And let's face it, as horrible as the circumstances of my death were, I didn't exactly leave this world very nobly, thanks to the newspapers that kindly emphasized that I died in another woman's bed. I mean, hey, they could have characterized me as the victim of a bloody crime. But nah, not the *New York Post*. They preferred to highlight the fact that there were traces of my semen on the bed sheets. Thank you for painting that picture for my wife and children, fuckers.

Stefanie was in her mid-forties when they met and she still had a smooth, soft complexion with only her eyes showing wear from years of crying alone in what was once our bedroom. Her hair was thick, wavy and still dark, showing little grey despite all she'd been through. She also still looked great in a dress, with those same shapely legs I fell in love with back at Hunter College. It made me seethe with jealousy whenever my unseen presence tagged along during her dates. Of her first suitors, the majority couldn't get past her attractiveness and they focused only on trying to get her into the bedroom.

Not Rippey. A calculus professor at Fordham University where Stephanie worked as a supervising librarian, appearance-wise, Rippey wasn't terribly impressive. He was about six feet tall with a thin build and wild, scraggly grey hair that matched his grungy beard, which looked like it smelled. He reminded me of a stoner that woke up from a thirty-year high at Woodstock.

As much as I wanted to dislike him, I couldn't. He treated Stefanie with total class. He was thoughtful, patient and completely understanding of everything she'd been through. His support was a key element in her working her way towards being her old self again.

Often, they just sat together on the couch, like they're doing tonight; watching movies with her leaning her head on his shoulder, the way she once did with me. Right in front of my eyes, I could see their bond intensifying as he gently stroked her hair, driving me nuts with envy. They ended up marrying two years later.

Othello continues to scowl and hiss while keeping a cautious distance away from me. You gotta admire his protective stance, although he's probably ready to shit himself. He doesn't know what the fuck I am but he knows I'm not human. I almost feel bad wildly, flailing my arms above my head to shoo him away.

My exaggerated *ooga-booga* gesture successfully freaks the cat out and his yowl draws attention from inside the house. Rippey rises from the couch and approaches the window.

He looks right through me, into the still night.

A couple of yards away out on the lawn, he spots his shaken kitty.

Because of my, okay I'll say it, supernatural condition, my appearance to everyone when I am visible is the same as it was when I went belly up twenty-seven years ago. The same can't be said for Rippey, whose long white hair now makes him resemble the professor in "Back to the Future".

Othello, at my feet again, meows at Rippey as if saying, "Hey, you blind bastard, can't you see what's in front of you?" For a quick laugh I could pick up Othello by the nape of his neck and dangle him in front of the window. Probably a bad idea; the sight of the floating cat would probably give the old guy a heart attack and make Stefanie a widow yet again.

"Bring him inside," she says as Rippey heads towards the front door.

Othello is drawn to the front door as he hears Rippey unlocking it and stepping out.

"Hey buddy, you want to come inside?" asks Rippey, who watches his cat scoot in with the obvious answer.

Looking out into the cool night, Rippey sees no sign of what might have stirred up his kitty as the answer to *that* question also slithers in past him.

Stefanie's looking thinner these days than I like to see her. It makes her face show her age more, even if her eyes still have the same sparkle that caught my attention in college almost fifty years ago. I can see the lines around them becoming more pronounced as she laughs at some line Maggie Smith spouts out on the TV. It's probably something that only Stefanie and the English would find funny.

Rippey picks up Othello and hands him over to Stefanie, who places him on her lap. "What's the matter, baby" she coos. Othello spots me. The anomaly from outside is now hovering in their living room. It's more than the little guy can handle; he frantically leaps from Stefanie's lap with a maniacal yelp, and dashes for the kitchen. "Oh my God," gasps Stefanie.

"What the hell?" says Rippey, following the cat, who wedges himself between the toaster and the cookie jar on the granite kitchen counter. "Come on, buddy. Get down from there," says Rippey.

Othello protests with an unearthly meow that even creeps *me* out. And I'm a dead guy.

Figuring the kitty's safe indoors, Rippey shrugs it off and rejoins Stefanie on the couch.

Here comes that knife in the gut again as he puts his arm around her and she customarily leans her head against his shoulder. Later they will climb into bed and she will sleep with her head again on his shoulder, just as she did with me during the seventeen years of our marriage.

During the early years of my disappearance I watched Stefanie sleep alone in the bedroom that I once shared with her, knowing that I couldn't join her and lie together in the spoon position the way we did for so many years. Instead I'd come up close and study her face, trying to read what was on her mind. Darkness had settled in under her eyes. Wrinkles had formed. They came from the strain of raising two children whose father not only died, but died in the bed of another woman. Not able to sense my non-breathing presence, as far as Stefanie was concerned, she was alone. Both of us were. Alone in the same room but in two separate worlds.

I should head back. It's getting late and I gotta make a stop before calling it a night.

#

It looks like the University Medical Center's O+ blood supply is a little lower than usual. Must be a lot of activity of late—even by Newark's standards.

Working here as a uniformed night shift security guard gives me the convenience of tapping into the blood supply on occasions like tonight where I need to compensate for Vernon's leukemia-tainted feeding. By sticking to the more common blood types, I feel a little less shitty about what I'm doing, a nagging, moral compass that most of my kind don't have to deal with. They wouldn't even think twice about guzzling down some AB-. But then again they wouldn't be skirting from feeding off live humans by going into the blood bank either.

It's my night off so rather than get caught up in any unnecessary chit-chat I roamed the halls unseen, though that can be draining when lacking a good feeding. As a security guard, I have the keys that allow me access to go where I please. Letting myself into the blood bank, I leave the lights off even if I'm cloaked from human eyesight. No sense in taking any chances.

Normally I'd pocket a few pints and take them home to enjoy during ESPN Sportscenter. Tonight, though, I'm thinking I need to take in a whole ten pints. The problem is that I'm pretty sure ten packets of plasma floating in the hospital corridors might get a little bit of attention.

If I were home right now, I'd be in the kitchen reaching for a can of Dos Equis in the fridge. Instead I'm pulling a packet of O+ from the hospital blood supply. That cancerous blood that I have in my system is playing games with my head. Rather than waiting 'til I get home, I'll puncture a hole in the edge with the pointed end of one my *pearly's*.

If I had a straw, I'd probably look like these kids today that suck from those packets they've been selling in the supermarket for the last twenty years that are 99% sugar and 1% juice.

The blood is cold, thick. It goes down nice and smoothly like a refreshing glass of tomato juice. My reflection on the refrigerator's glass door as it swings shut—it serves as an unfriendly reminder, one of the many cruelties of my curse that clings like a bad case of herpes. My projection to those around me is the handsome Nicky (if I may say so myself) that died twenty-seven years ago. To me that face is a memory from photographs. On the occasions when my projection is not present, like when I'm feeding or when my emotions take over, the only version I get to see of myself is that of my *death face*—the face that belongs six feet under. Dried, chalky grey-white flesh with cracked, darkened eyes and large black eyeballs floating in a blood-red pool where the whites should be. Not exactly the pretty face you see on those TV vampires that are always falling in love with the perky-titted cheerleader. It's also the last face seen by someone unlucky enough to be around when one of us needs a feeding.

Shit! Our hearing is extra-sensitive. I can be at the other end of Jersey in Atlantic City and still hear a Giants fan farting in the bathroom at MetLife Stadium. How did I not hear her coming?

The piercing scream from behind almost sends the packet of O+ splattering onto the floor. It's Juanita from the Environmental Services night crew. The poor cleaning woman was just exposed to something too unimaginable to process—unless she's accustomed to seeing cadaverous night-walkers raiding the hospital blood supply.

"Juanita, calm down." I gotta bring her down, reassure her. "It's me, Georgie," the name I answer to these days. As a little inside joke for my own amusement I go by Jórge Sangría. But since no one can say Jórge correctly (it's *hor-heh*, not *hor-gay*, you dumb fucks) everyone calls me Georgie.

"Georgie?" She gasps through trembling lips.

"Yes, Juanita, it's me." I gotta work fast. "Listen, any second now someone's going to come running over here wondering what happened. You're going to tell them you thought you saw a mouse or a prowler. Whatever, I don't care. As long as you don't say you saw me. You are going to totally forget that I was here."

Here comes the cavalry.

"Juanita, what's wrong?" It's Jimmy, one of the other third shift security guards. Sometimes he works with me, other nights we alternate.

"Oh no, I'm sorry Jimmy. I thought I saw something. I'm not sure. I don't know. I got scared. But it's okay. There's nothing." She's so frazzled that her effort to feign calm is nowhere near convincing. Jimmy's not even close to being fooled.

And now here comes the crowd. Fiona, the cleaning staff supervisor, Jose, the other security guard, Gladys from Admitting, and the supervising nurse, Taqualla.

Jimmy's quick to take control. "Okay everybody, just stay out here." He's going to scope the room out. "What did you see in there?" he asks Juanita.

"I don't know. I was confused." She knows she screamed. She's still shaking but she can't remember why. Mind control is a beautiful thing.

Jimmy steps inside, not realizing he's walking past the colleague he's always inviting out for a beer to watch the Knicks. I always turn him down. I can't stand basketball.

Jimmy flicks on the light and sees nothing out of the ordinary. Everything inside appears as it should. If I would have dropped that packet of blood, poor Juanita would have had some *'splaining* to do. As it is, Jimmy's satisfied enough to turn off the light and step back out into the hallway shaking his head. "Juanita, you sure you didn't see anything?" he asks her while locking the door to the blood bank.

Juanita's now more embarrassed than spooked. "No, I'm sorry."

"Then why'd you scream like that?"

"I don't know, Jimmy. I'm sorry. I'm just nervous."

"Nervous? Why?" Stop being a pain in the ass, Jimmy. Let it go.

Juanita just wants to get her shift over and done with. "It's okay, Jimmy. You can go back. I'll be okay."

The security camera in the hallway has got Jimmy's

attention. "Are you sure?" he asks Juanita. He's probably going to check the tapes. I got some erasing to do. The hallway camera will show a floating set of keys unlocking the door to the blood bank. It will then open and close by itself. And though I never turned on the lights inside the room, there should enough coming from the fridge to show a packet of blood making its way out before disappearing into the darkness. I better get to those tapes before Jimmy. These days, shit like that can go viral.

3

For the past couple of decades, the beauty of the Bronx has been buried under overbearing rusted signage, littered sidewalks and hip-hop thugs in pants hanging midway down their asses. Call me old school but I never considered the upper half of my boxers the most appealing part of my wardrobe.

In the early '60's, before its eventual deterioration, my beloved hometown still had some decorum and a mother could let her children accompany her to the *bodega* without hearing *shit* and *motherfucker* being flipped back and forth in loud casual conversation (I know, I should talk). Crime in our neighborhoods also hadn't risen to the barbaric levels that it would in the following years. Of course there were places to avoid, just like anywhere else, but when I was twelve, I was able to go wherever I wanted without being bothered. *Mami* and *Papi* didn't even give a second thought to letting me and my five-year-old sister Dani go to the playground at the Joyce Kilmer Park, across the street, unsupervised. They were comfortable enough to put me in charge of watching her with them peeking out periodically from the windows of our apartment.

Papi made a decent buck at a small clothing factory in the garment district. He came to the states after graduating high school in Puerto Rico, bringing no work experience but a decent head for numbers. The company's owner, Walter Reinhardt, quickly noticed *Papi's* affinity and took a liking to him, eventually pulling *Papi* out of the warehouse and putting him in charge of bookkeeping.

We were doing well. The building we lived in was on Walton Avenue near the Grand Concourse, which is a wide major boulevard not unlike Park Avenue. It was one of the nicer places to live in the Bronx, and while the residents in our area were not as well off as those living in Manhattan, they were comfortable and *white* enough to wonder how this Puerto Rican family became their neighbors. Eventually *los blancos* grew to recognize us as a hard-working respectable Christian family and their concerns began to subside, even if *la señora* played that Latin music too loud on the hi-fi.

With *Papi* making enough money to meet our modest expenses, *Mami* was able to be a stay-at-home mom raising me and Dani. Every night *Papi* would come home to a happy family eagerly awaiting his arrival before sitting down for some *arróz con gandules y chuleta*. On Sunday nights like every American family, we sat in the living room watching the Ed Sullivan show (*Papi* swore the Beatles were *maricóns*). During the week my mother would walk us to school in the morning while *Papi* would take the subway to work. On Saturdays we would either, go to the movies, take a family trip into the city, or maybe visit some relatives. Sometimes after work my father would join me and Dani at the playground, throwing a ball around a little bit with me and push Dani a couple of times on the swings. We would all then go upstairs together for supper.

In the pictures I saw from before I was born, *Mami* was pretty and surprisingly petite. I say surprisingly because by the time I was ten years old, *Mami* was anything but petite. It might have to do with the fact that she was an amazing cook and her own biggest fan. She *was* short, just under five feet, but she looked like a woman that never lost her pregnancy weight—that is, if she were carrying a linebacker. It didn't bother *Papi,* though. He was still as much in love with her as he was when he first met her in the city. Flowers every Friday, snuggles in the kitchen, and from the noises coming from their bedroom, I'm surprised that I only ended up with one little sister.

#

On Monday, May 9 1964 I was thirteen years old and it was a time when I'd get funny little feelings inside my pants when in visual range of a pretty girl. That afternoon, there was a group of Catholic school girls from Christ the King fawning over a portable record player while listening to the latest Beatles LP. I was a couple of yards away shooting hoops at the basketball court but I don't think I made even one shot. The girls were wearing those Catholic schoolgirl uniforms that seemed to have been designed by sexual deviants. I wasn't able to take my eyes off their legs.

Dani was over at the sliding pond playing with one of those light marble-colored inflated balls that they sell in those bins at the supermarket. She was throwing the ball up the slide and catching it on the way down. When it bounced away from her towards the entrance of the playground, I'd tell her to wait and let me get it but she would have none of that.

"I'm not a baby," she'd say, running after it on her own.

I had to be firm with her. "Stop!" The street was only a few steps away from the park entrance. There was no reason to take any unnecessary risks, especially since the ball sometimes went under the parked cars outside the playground.

Unfortunately for us men, sometimes the female anatomy can be a cruel distraction because at one moment, much to my visual delight, the pretty ladies started shaking their little asses and squealing as George Harrison rang out the opening chords to Fab Four's latest release.

I stopped dribbling.

The basketball, that is. My mouth was still dribbling. The lovely lasses then looked over my way and then started giggling the way girls do when they want to make you feel like a wart on a flea's ass. Sheepishly, I averted their eyes the way a baserunner would avoid his managers after being picked off of first base. I resumed dribbling; The basketball, that is. My mouth was dribbling all along.

Humbly landing back on solid ground, my attention was drawn back to Dani, whose ball was once again bouncing past the park entrance. I called out right away. "Okay Dani, I got it."

"No, I'll get it," she contested.

"No Dani, wait!"

The ball rolled out onto the sidewalk, wedging itself between a car bumper and the curb underneath. Behind the fence was a tree, which partially obstructed Dani's view of the sidewalk. Otherwise she might have seen that a few feet away, a man was walking a hulking, 120 pound German Shepherd.

Like many little girls that age tend to be, Dani was thick-headed and liked to pretend that she was tough and independent. But also just like other little girls, Dani had her share of irrational fears. One of them was dogs.

Dani happily skipped past the park entrance and the obtrusive tree to get her ball. Startled by her sudden presence, and perhaps with intentions of defending his master, the dog lunged aggressively towards Dani with a rabid bark that was clearly unnegotiable. The owner commanded the dog to stop and was able hold him back, but Dani was so frightened by the growling beast that she ran screaming between the parked cars, out into the street.

"DANI, NO!"

The sound of the screeching tires echoed through the entire neighborhood as the driver slammed on his brakes. I turned away covering my face. For a split second, with the exception of a surprisingly appropriately placed shout by Paul McCartney, there was a pause of paralyzed silence. The essentially happy pop record then took a suddenly dark tone, reverberating in the stillness of the street. To this day I still can't listen to those mop-topped motherfuckers.

Even the dog ceased to bark. It was as if he realized what had just occurred.

The silence didn't last long.

First came the screams of the horrified girls from Christ the King. Then came the cries from the other neighborhood women as they ran towards the scene of the accident. A crowd formed on the street as the driver tentatively opened his car. He never made it out of his seat. Holding on to the door of his 1962 Chevy to keep himself from collapsing, he heaved on to the street as his knees violently buckled. Somehow he didn't collapse on to the concrete.

The German Shepherd and his owner? As the crowd around Dani grew, they mysteriously broke away unnoticed.

I couldn't move nor make a sound. I was paralyzed. A damaged and devastated scream was building up inside of me that wanted to come out but it couldn't. I'm not even sure I was *breathing* at the moment.

Our senses as humans have a way of leaving permanent impressions. For example, there are sights, sounds, and scents that you can always associate with an experience from the past. The next sound that I heard while my mind was still trying to wrap itself around what had just happened, was one that I will always associate with death; the scream of my mother from our window across the street. Since that horrible afternoon I have seen lots of death, much of it by my own hand. But to this day, I have never again heard a sound as awful as that. Nor do I want to.

Despite *Mami's* crippling hysteria, she somehow made it down to the street, breaking through the crowd to see her daughter. Me? I still hadn't moved. I was trembling at the same spot where I was when the car struck my little sister. *Mami* then must have asked where I was because a couple of women in the crowd reluctantly turned towards me, with fear of what might happen next. Their fear was just. *Mami* sprang up and stormed in my direction with a ferocity that would normally have sent me running. And I did want to. Instinctively, that's what my mind was telling me to do. My legs were not listening.

"*Hijo de puta! Maricón! Te máto, maricón. Te máto.*" They were words that no child should ever hear from his mother, words that reeked of hatred. This was not my mother. It was a woman that I did not recognize. Surely this wasn't the woman that cradled me and comforted me in her arms in my younger years.

Run Nicky.

The legs were still not cooperating.

Say something dammit!

Cry, scream, defend yourself!

I couldn't even open my mouth to form a word or make a sound. Except for the involuntary shaking, I was completely still. Was it fear? Was it shock? I didn't know. I still don't. I was numb, unable to feel anything. Until that first fist crashed against my chin.

"*Hijo de puta!* I told you to watch her!" The blows felt like sledgehammers. "You were supposed to watch her! You were supposed to watch your little sister!" Dutifully, I took every hit until the neighbors realized the type of massacre that was developing in front of them. Once they did they quickly jumped in and pulled her away.

Somehow my legs didn't give out. I did. I was out on my feet, drifting away, distancing myself from the horror that had just occurred. When *Mami* was separated from me, I fell from the radar. No one showed any concern in seeing if I was okay. The attention went solely to my mother. Not a second thought went to the pre-teen child that just witnessed his sister's death and was assaulted by his own mother. Eventually one woman did turn away from the focus of everyone else's attention and looked back towards me. It finally dawned upon her that someone else was suffering. A boy, standing alone, just a few feet away, expressionless, suspended in another dimension away from this horrifying tragedy. Only the urine that soaked his pants served as possible acknowledgment that part of the child was hovering within range of reality. Sympathetic as she might have been. The woman never came over. It probably would have been an unpopular move. I was public enemy number one.

Papi was someone I had never seen cry before. It made the sound all the more gut-wrenching when he came home from work to find his baby daughter lying lifelessly in a pool of blood. Dropping to his knees, he cried alongside *Mami* almost to the point of suffocation. When they finally looked back to where I was still standing it became clear that my parents lost two children that day. Their numbed expression was one of confusion. They didn't know who I was or what they were going to do with me.

#

Doctor calls it tinnitus. I called it *Los Ruidos*, the Spanish term for noises. Tinnitus is a medical term for permanent ringing in the ears. For me it was the permanent effect of the walloping my head took, courtesy of my mother. When you have tinnitus the world is never truly silent again. The ringing stays with you, alternating with whooshing sounds. It's there throughout the day and it's especially loud at night when you're trying to fall asleep, a ceaseless, unwanted companion that you can't turn off the way you would a radio or a TV. It became the eternal reminder of the day that shrouded my family with darkness, an evil one-note tune with lyrics that sang, *"Los Ruidos estan sonando, Nicky. Your pain is calling. You can't hide. Your pain is what defines you."*

There was never any conversation at our apartment during that period. Outside of supper, it was even rare that two of us would be in the same room at the same time. And when we were, we barely ever made any eye contact. The air was thick with inexorable grief. We would never recover. How could we? How could any family? Was it even possible?

Our priest Father Gallagher did his best to help us come to terms with what had happened. It was a noble attempt on his part but the stench on his clothes from what he'd been drinking the night before made it difficult for any of us to lend him too much credibility. By the time my parents started making half-hearted efforts to reassure me that what happened wasn't my fault, it was too late. Their effort was forced. They couldn't even fake it, although I'm sure in their hearts they felt that they tried.

As we went on with our daily routines, doing our best to function under the same roof as *La Familia Negrón,* the closeness and the love that once lived within those four walls continued to seep out under the doors and the open windows. Most of my time there I stayed inside my bedroom reading Superman comics while listening to Cousin Brucie on my transistor radio playing the current popular tunes on WABC. In the living room (an ironic term considering that *Mami* and *Papi* sat like zombies watching Dean Martin, Red Skelton or some other variety show), the laughter from the TV audience only reinforced how all of the laughter and joy that was in our household had left with Dani.

A year or so later, *Papi* had all that he could take. He took off to Puerto Rico leaving us with assurances that he'd call regularly and come back once in a while to visit.

He did neither.

For a few months he sent checks back home to help us get by but that stopped as well. *Mami* tried making a few calls to track him down but in those days long distance calls to Puerto Rico were an expensive luxury that was out of our budget. She soon gave up and we never heard from him again. A buzz went around saying that he had committed suicide somewhere around Pónce but no one was ever able to confirm it.

We were now on our own, *Mami* and I, carrying on in the same morbid silence that had by then become a living, breathing part of our home. Even her *Hector Lavoe* LP's could do nothing to brighten the mood in our apartment. And with Papi's checks no longer coming around to lighten the load, *Mami* had to put herself back together and go back out into the work force.

In the late 1940's having just arrived from Puerto Rico, *Mami* had worked in the garment district like *Papi*. She was sewing dresses at a shop around the corner from where he worked for Mr. Reinhardt, they met at a sandwich shop that was on the same block; *Papi* used to go there to order his *cubanos*. Now it was over a decade and a half later and *Papi* was gone. *Mami* was desperate for some help. She put out a call to Mr. Reinhardt, who was obviously aware of our streak of misfortune, and he promptly hired her to get behind one of the sewing machines at the factory.

Once she was back at work, a different *Mami* emerged. The job appeared to be just what the doctor ordered. She met new people and her spirits seemed to lift, even if it was just a little bit. Her voice even softened whenever she spoke to me. Until then, her tone towards me always had an icy edge that pushed me deeper into solitude. And though her new tone wasn't of the *Mami* that once had an unconditional love for her little Nicky, I at least was feeling less like an unwanted border in the apartment I grew up in.

For my part, I was burying myself in schoolwork, doing well enough to graduate high school and enroll at Hunter College as a math major. Had *Papi* been around he might have been proud I'd inherited his adeptness at working with numbers.

On Tuesday, August 5th, 1969 I rushed back to the apartment after registering for classes so I could catch the first game of the doubleheader the Mets were playing against the Cincinnati Reds. Tom Seaver was pitching and I hated missing any of his starts, but as soon as I flicked on the television I saw that this was one I would have been better off catching the highlights (or should I say lowlights) on the ten o'clock news. The Reds were giving Tom Terrific a thorough ass-kicking.

That should have told me something.

Prior to that day I was starting to feel pretty good about things. I was on the verge of adulthood with college offering a host of possibilities that could lead to a path away from the bitter walls that stored our despondency.

Having seen enough, Mets manager Gil Hodges mercifully came out of the dugout to give his ace pitcher the hook. Shit! I ran all the way home to see this? When the skipper signaled the bullpen to bring in Cal Koonce, I went to the kitchen to make myself a sandwich.

The refrigerator was pretty lightly stocked. A trip to the supermarket was due. We had a few slices of Boar's Head ham and a couple of slices of yellow American cheese, none of which there would be any left after I made one of my Nicky specials. Some slices of salami would have been a great addition but it looked like we were all out. There was no mayo either.

I laid out all the components on the counter, ready to layer them between two slices of Wonder Bread but before the process could begin, the phone on the wall above the toaster rang. I figured it was *Mami* wanting me to pick up something at the store for dinner.

"Hello Nicky?" The deep voice on the other end

jarred me. It was Mr. Reinhardt. The somberness in his voice immediately alarmed me. I had met Mr. Reinhardt several times in the past at the Christmas parties. He was always very informal and very friendly. I could sense his hesitancy on the other end. Whatever he had to say, he did not want to say it. "Nicky, it's Walter Reinhardt."

I got right to the point. "What's wrong?"

"Nicky I'm so sorry but your mother's in the hospital."

"What? What happened?"

"I'm not sure, Nicky. She was fine..." Normally a well-spoken business owner, Mr. Reinhardt struggled in his attempt to convey something that he himself hadn't totally absorbed yet. "Your mother, she was working and then suddenly she just collapsed."

I learned from my parents to love and respect God but at that moment I wondered if He was ever going to cut our family a break. "Is she okay? Where is she?"

"Nicky, the doctors—"

"I said where is she?"

"She's at St. Joseph's—"

"Where at St. Joseph's?"

She was in ICU.

I'm not even sure I hung up the phone. As soon as Reinhardt laid out the details I rushed downtown in the opposite direction of those who were coming home from work. The doctor at the hospital informed me that *Mami* had fallen into a diabetic coma.

Diabetic coma!

I didn't even know she was diabetic! Apparently neither did she. It had been a couple of years since she'd gone to the doctor for any kind of checkup so she was completely unaware. If she'd known maybe she could have taken some precautions. Instead it had all accumulated to the point where she ended up collapsing at work and going into a seizure. By the time the ambulance got her to the hospital, all consciousness was lost and she remained that way throughout all the tests that were being performed on her.

I had never given up trying to regain the closeness I once had with *Mami.* Not even the bitter memory of the pummeling I withstood on the day of Dani's accident kept me from hoping that connection could once again exist. The doctor's expression made it clear that the likelihood of that coming to be was all but gone.

My hesitancy in entering the room was a futile attempt at trying to prepare myself for the sight of my prone mother. One would think that the emotional distance that had developed between us might have softened the blow, but it wasn't that way at all. I never blamed *Mami* for anything that happened after the realization that she had lost her daughter. Her heart may have still been functioning biologically, but it had lost all its ability to hold on to those around her.

I leaned over the bed and took *Mami's* hand, barely getting her name out. Not wanting to move anything hooked to the IV, I touched her as lightly as I could. There were no signs of any movement under her eyelids. It gave the strange illusion that she was at some kind of peace. Still denying reality, I nudged her gently to see if I could get her attention.

Nothing.

Reinhardt had done his best to prepare me over the telephone, as did the doctor when he walked me in, but even as I absorbed their bleak outlooks, there is nothing that can prepare you for the reality that your mother is slipping away.

In the end she wound up holding on for about a week. Any fight that she had left in her was probably lost years before. *Mami* died two months short of her 46th birthday.

The nagging pitch of my unwelcome guests, *Los Ruidos,* grew louder. Like any normal human being, I wanted to break out into a wail of frustrated despair but the paralyzing hum that roared between my ears wouldn't allow me. It was their cruel way of heightening anything I had ever suffered.

Once again all I could do was stare out into nothing. My own passing would come almost twenty years later. One would think that *Los Ruidos* would have died right along with me but they didn't. They're with me to this day. Apparently *Los Ruidos* are genetically resistant as well.

4

Jimmy likes busting my balls about Veronica. "I know you're hittin' that, Georgie. Don't even try to deny it."

There's a Veronica in every workplace. She's the one we guys like to step into a corner and share nothing but nasty, lascivious fantasies about. Like Juanita (who's probably going through a nervous breakdown right now), Veronica Rojas also works for Environmental Services during the night shift.

One can understand Jimmy's conclusion about me and Veronica when you consider the fact that she has been quite diligent in trying to lure me to her apartment. It's been pretty clear that she is very willing to be "hit" by me and his awareness of that, combined with the nightly reminder of Veronica's undeniable *hittability,* makes my lack of interest an unfathomable anomaly. Veronica carries a sumptuous medley of curves that any man would love to spend hours navigating his hands through. And though her dark roots betray her dyed-blond hair, it frames her nicely sculpted Mexican features, highlighted by eyes that promise an unforgettable time in the bedroom. On top of that she is also great socially. She is a devoted mother to her two boys and is also very giving to her friends, especially with food. For example; in my case she knows that I love her *chíli con cárne* so she's always bringing me leftovers from home. And I gotta say, her *chíli con cárne* kicks some serious ass.

So why in the world wouldn't I be interested? Why wouldn't any man? For Jimmy it will have to remain a mystery. I obviously can't share with him the risks someone would face having a sexual relationship with the undead. That being said, I also don't need the complication, especially with someone like Veronica, who loves to court the attention of other men despite being in a relationship with a trombone player from a local salsa band. She is a woman that feeds on the attention of horny males the way I feed on blood.

"I bet you had her last night, you dog," says Jimmy. "Look at her walking in here. She's got eyes on nothing but you."

Veronica's a safe enough distance away not to hear the lusty details of our conversation. She's got her ever present plastic Shoprite bag with her Tupperware container in it. And Jimmy's right. Her focus is only on me, making it harder for me to deny that there's anything going on between us. "Jimmy, you're wasting your envy. I am not sleeping with Veronica."

"I don't believe that shit for a second, but if it's true, then there's something wrong with you, bro."

Veronica's playful little sing-song call is that of a woman who knows how to tease. "Hi Georgie baby, guess what I brought for you tonight. Can you smell it?" Can I *smell* it? I was able to smell her chíli, her Victoria's Secret perfume, *and* the fact that she will soon be on her menstrual cycle before she even walked in the hospital.

"Yeah, I bet you smell what she's got for you every night," says Jimmy with a whisper. "And I ain't talkin' 'bout what she's got in that Shoprite bag. I'm talkin' 'bout what she's got inside her—"

"Stop Jimmy, she'll hear you." My smile as she approaches won't exactly make a great Facebook profile pic, but it's the warmest smile a guy who's been dead for twenty-seven years can give.

Unintentionally turning Jimmy into an awkward third wheel, Veronica continues to tease. "Ah, you *do* know what's in this bag, don't you?"

Now Jimmy wants to play. "Hey Veronica, any chance you can maybe one night bring what you got in that bag for me?"

"Of course, Jimmy. I didn't know you like chili. Why didn't you say so?"

"I'm saying it now. But listen, I want that good chili. The same kind of chili you give Georgie." Very funny, Jimmy.

"Oh, you want the special chili I make just for Georgie?" Her little wink at me suggests that she's in on the joke. "What do you think, Georgie? Should I make it for Jimmy the same way I make it for you?"

This is getting uncomfortable. "Hey Jimmy, shouldn't you be patrolling around the ER right now?"

"Uh, okay, so it's like that," says Jimmy, ever-so-slightly backing away. "I guess I'll, uh, leave you two alone." It would have happened anyway. Veronica always finds a way to get me to spend some alone time with her. The chili is her usual bait.

During the night shift, the hospital cafeteria is closed, except for the dining area where the employees take their breaks. I would happily enjoy her chili there amongst the other workers but Veronica likes things to be a little cozier so instead we go to the private waiting area near the Intensive Care Unit. There we can close the door and be *solito*, assuming Dr. Rothstein isn't in there *doggie-styling* Sabrina from radiology. And while that's what's probably on Veronica's radar for the near future, so far all we've been doing is eating and talking about her problems, primarily raising two boys on her own and the jealousy of Roberto, her trombone-playing boyfriend.

It's actually quite laughable that Veronica can't seem to comprehend Roberto's insecurities, considering that she's been trying to lure me into the sack since the first day I worked here. Not that she's been waiting inactively, during *that* time I can count at least four or five men she's probably slept with—two of them during the time she's been dating Roberto, which is about a year and a half. And then there's her sons. Each have different last names and neither of them are the same as hers.

Yes, we're talking about a woman with the libido of a major league baseball player on a road trip. It makes her both unpredictable and ridiculously desirable, but definitely not my type; even in my prior existence. If you're a half-way decent-looking guy at the *Los Chicos* lounge in downtown Newark, you would stand a shot by getting a couple of drinks in her and playing a little salsa or merengue on the jukebox. Call me old-fashioned but I, like Roberto, prefer a little more exclusivity.

I also keep my distance from Veronica for the same reasons I do with Jimmy. A nighttime predator that makes friends only creates problems for himself. Friends want to socialize. They want to see you in the daytime. Then what? How many excuses can you come up with before they realize there's something off about you?

The undead slurping of Veronica's fabulous chili resonates through our little private waiting area. I'd enjoy it a little more if she weren't waving her wrist in front of my face.

"¡Mira lo me que hizo ese hijo de puta!" She holds it out, waiting for a reaction.

Being that I'm devouring her chili the very least I could do is pretend that I give a shit. *"Que pasó?"*

"Look what he did to me, Georgie!" It appears that *Señor Roberto* got a little rough and took an extra firm grip of Veronica's wrist—another heated showdown about her weekend activities while he's out somewhere gigging. "What am I supposed to do?" she says. "Sit at home doing nothing? We're not married! I'm not his wife!"

I mumble through a mouthful of chili. "When did this happen?"

She rubs her wrist, pouting. "This morning, when I got home."

I know what she wants me to do but I really don't want to get involved. But then again, I *am* eating her chili. "You want me to talk to him?"

"No baby, thank you. I told him it was over. I don't want to see him no more."

Good, can I now finish my chili?

5

During my junior year in college I was in what you'd call *fuck-up mode*. I had pretty good grades as a freshman and sophomore so I thought it was time to coast a little bit. Professor Grossburg from my English literature class thought differently. He knew my capabilities from classes I'd had before with him. My going through the motions and copping some Z's while he droned on with his lessons about farty old authors was something he was not going to tolerate.

By that time, I had won the position as the starting second baseman on the Hunter College baseball team. And when our games ended, win or lose, some of our team members would wind down with a little vodka and orange juice before going home. But unlike some of my teammates, I never had to worry about tiptoeing past parents to hide my alcohol-soaked breath, so I started enjoying it a little bit too much and a little too often.

Something had to give.

I decided it would be Grossburg's 8:00 a.m. Chaucer class which, even without a six screwdriver hangover, would have been impossible to stay awake through. His monotone voice knocked me out quicker than a bottle of Sominex.

All that old English crap with Chaucer looked more like French to me and since I didn't sign up to learn a new language, I especially resented that we were not allowed to read a modernized translation. We had to read it as it was originally written. Well fuck that! Fuck Chaucer! Fuck the Wyfe of Bathe and fuck the Miller with his farts out the window!

"Young man, you are on a runaway train headed towards failure," said Grossburg. "To get you back on track I'm going to recommend you meet Miss Stefania Torres. She is a senior and one of my top former students. If I'm not mistaken, I think you have time to go introduce yourself to her now. She works at the college library over at the other building. Tell her that I'm sending you over for tutoring."

"What! I don't need no tutoring."

"Well spoken, Mr. Negrón, but I'm not asking." For a tweedy old bookworm, he had a surprisingly intimidating way about him. I decided not to challenge him.

In those days, the Hunter College library had the aristocratic, architectural ambience that inferred to me that I was not smart enough to be in there. The open contempt from the scowling silver-haired lady at the circulation desk asserted that as well.

"May I help you?" She sneered, fighting her urge to roll her eyes behind her cat-woman glasses.

"I'm looking for Stefania," I said, halfway expecting her to shush me.

Her air of superiority suggested *you're not good enough for her, spic boy*, but whenever I came across someone like that, I stepped my game up. Behind her, unloading a push cart full of books, was a slender-framed, dark-haired student in a yellow silk blouse and a suffocating pair of jeans. "Is that her?"

Cat Lady paused at first as if she was deciding before calling her over. "Miss Torres."

Miss Torres turned. Her eyes were warm and friendly, with a hint of playfulness. I was already thinking dirty thoughts.

"This young," Cat Lady paused with disdain, "*man* wants to see you." Her face suggested that the words tasted bad.

Fuck you, Cat Lady. Watch me work my shit.

I straightened up as Stefania approached, trying to look as cool as some clod that's flunking English could possibly manage. Taking into account my damaged past it wouldn't have been a surprise to anyone if it had taken a negative toll on my appearance. Instead, being on my own steered me towards taking better care of myself and seeking to accomplish everything I possibly could without resorting to any excuses. So Cat Lady notwithstanding, I wasn't unpleasant to look at. I also had a tangible air of confidence that came from being my own person. After *Mami's* untimely passing, I stayed in the apartment and took a full-time job at a tax preparer's office while also going to school full time. I had taken control. The rent was never late and I never missed a day of work or school. No one in that college was self-sufficient like that. I would have put money on it. Which made it all the more humbling to have to admit to this captivating senior that I was needing help to keep from failing English.

Stefania had an approachable smile. "Hi!"

"Hello Stefania, I'm Nicky. Professor Grossburg said I should come see you."

"Call me Stefanie," she said. "Everyone calls me

that."

"Okay, Stefanie," I paused trying to find the least embarrassing way to admit why I was there.

Sensing my discomfort, Stefanie cushioned the words for me. "Professor Grossburg already told me. You're having a little trouble with Chaucer."

I shrugged. "Well, it takes me about twenty minutes to try and interpret each sentence. I really don't have that kind of time between school, work, the baseball team... could the English language really have changed that much?"

Her eyes lit up. "You're on the baseball team?"

Being that I was five inches shorter and about thirty pounds lighter than everyone on my team (and every other college team in the city), many reacted with surprise that I was Hunter College's starting second baseman. I wasn't sure if Stefanie's reaction was surprise or excitement, but it looked like I found a hot button and I wasn't about to let go. "I'll tell you what. Tomorrow we play Bronx Community. Come to the game and afterwards we can go to the diner at Kingsbridge. Maybe there you can help me get started with this foreign language everyone calls Chaucer."

I hadn't really dated that much. Who had the time? It wasn't that I was uninterested. I had taken a couple of girls out here and there, I even banged the super's wife like everyone else in my building, but outside of that I just never had the time for a steady girlfriend.

Stefanie sized up the cocky *Boricua* before her—the one that was failing English. It was only a couple of seconds but it felt like an eternity. "Okay," she said with a shrug. "Why not?"

See that, Cat Lady? That's how it done.

#

When I was in elementary school *Papi* loved helping me with my math homework. He'd teach me shortcuts towards solving problems in my head and he'd show me how math would apply in things like life and sports. He was a big Mets fan (which I also unfortunately inherited) and he would talk about batting averages against right-handed pitchers and left-handed pitchers while watching the games on Channel Nine, long before those ESPN analysts started coming up with minutia stats like how a batter hits on natural grass against sinker ballers on Tuesday afternoons. "You see this fucking guy? I don't know why he's a switch hitter. He can't bat lefty. I've seen him bat twenty-five times lefty and he's got two hits. That's an .087 batting average. So why is he batting lefty?"

"I don't know, *Papi*," I'd say while reaching for the pretzels on the folding table next to his can of Schaefer. But along with his foul mouth, I also inherited *Papi's* mathematical skills and put them to good use at the tax preparer's office where I worked on Jerome Avenue.

Not the afternoon I met Stefanie.

That afternoon, I had no focus at all and completed only half of the tax forms I normally would have.

I was smitten.

When I got home that night I was in a complete fog while trying to watch an episode of *Columbo*. At the library, Stefanie had given me her number and, in my mind, I was desperately running in circles searching for an excuse to call her.

But what if I were to embarrass myself? What if she had a boyfriend—one that could read Chaucer? Maybe she was just being nice. Maybe all she cared about was helping me pass my class.

Peter Falk's voice echoed from the TV and bounced

off the walls inside the apartment. I was more alone than ever. School and work were good distractions that kept me from dwelling on the harsh realities of my past. But as the rumpled inspector interrogated his suspect on television, I looked towards the kitchen where *Mami* used to prepare dinner. The front door where *Papi* came home from work with the newspaper he read on the subway tucked under his arm. Dani's bedroom down the hallway, where she used to play with her dolls.

Even with me being on my own, my upkeep of the apartment never downgraded to the level where it could have been considered a dump. Yet with the lack of everyday conversation, errands and the presence of life in general, the air inside was overcast with forlorn shadows.

At first, when *Mami* passed, I had given thought to moving, but if I did that I would have thrown away a considerable advantage. Our family moved into that apartment in the early '60's. That made it rent-controlled. With the little life insurance policy from *Mami's* job and my modest part-time earnings while I was going to school, the monthly payment remained manageable enough for me not to have to make any additional changes in my life (although it might have been advisable). Was it hard living with the ghosts and memories within those walls? Yes. But there was also a comfort of familiarity which brought about a crazy notion that maybe someday, if I met the right girl, I could bring back the happiness that was once there.

I picked up the phone and dialed without knowing what the hell I was going to say. After the fourth ring, a soft hello cooed from the other end.

"Hello, Stefanie? It's Nicky."

"Hi!" She actually sounded happy to hear from me.

"Uh, yeah, I was thinking. Do you need a ride to the

game? I mean, uh, how're you getting there?"

She sensed my awkwardness. How could she not? "I'm only two stops away on the subway. I was going to meet you there. I figured you have to warm up before the game, right?"

"Uh, yeah, I suppose. But I was thinking, like, later that night, uh, I could drop you off at home so you don't have to take the train at night. So maybe I should pick you up, too." Of course that sentence made absolutely no sense whatsoever. I could still take her home even if she took the subway there. But I was reaching (and suddenly finding myself to be a stumbling idiot).

There was an awkward silence over the telephone. She was probably trying to make sense of the babble I'd sputtered (she probably never did). But then she caught me off guard. "Where do *you* live?"

Columbo was catching his suspect in a lie on TV (man, he was good). Stefanie probably sensed I was full of shit, too, knowing that all I wanted to do was talk to her.

I always kept the TV on in the apartment because of the painful silence, and especially to drown out the persistent chorus of *Los Ruidos*. But now there was another living, breathing voice, talking to me at the other end of the phone.

I answered her question about where I lived and proceeded to tell her how long I had been there and the events that led towards my living alone. It all just spilled out; the loss of Dani, *Papi*, and then *Mami*.

There was quiet on the other end.

"Are you there?" I asked.

There was a sniffle. "Yes, I'm here," she replied with a slight crack in her voice. Never had I gone that deep into my past with anyone. Not family, friends, counselors, no one.

The Nicky bio continued—total diarrhea of the mouth with her patiently listening. Before I knew it, two hours had passed. Johnny Carson was doing his monologue. We both had school the next day (and I had to be at that damn Chaucer class at 8:00 a.m.). We said good night. I hadn't said good night to anyone in years. But it was. It was a very good night.

Now I definitely had to pass that class.

6

What is it about women that make them think that everything they have to say is so damn interesting? Any man will tell you how he would sit through hours of insignificant babble without a woman taking a pause for a goddamn breath. It starts out with a nice dinner and a couple of sips of wine.

Then the chatter starts.

Ex-boyfriends, fights with their bosses, gossip at the nail salon, the story behind their shoes... holy shit! What a price to pay before you get down to what you're really there for! By the time the check comes you're having trouble deciding whether you want to fuck her or shoot yourself in the head! Being that I'm already dead, the latter really wouldn't help me much.

"I'm scared, Georgie." I don't think Veronica realizes that she hasn't shut up since she got in my car. "Now he don't stop calling me. And he says stuff like 'If I can't have you, nobody can have you.' He's talking crazy now like he wants to hurt me."

Apparently Roberto, her trombone-playing *amigo*, is

not taking kindly to being dumped by *la bella Veronica*. I assure her that nothing is going to happen. I'll drive her home from work over the next few days and escort her all the way to her apartment. As long as time permits for me to hop right back in my car and get myself home before the sun comes out, my chivalrous gesture should keep her safe from her jealous *salsero*. But it also means that during our rides I am going to have to endure the saga of the Rojas family tree from Tijuana through San Diego to El Paso and of course, Newark.

Like it or not, our little *chili con carne* sessions have formed a bond between us and I have somehow fallen into the role of protector. She's going to want me to come into her apartment, too, so I'll need to have an excuse ready before she invites me in for a cup of *Bustelo* while the boys get ready for school.

Hey, if things were different maybe I would have enjoyed a morning toss with Veronica. But obviously my current existence doesn't allow me to enjoy a morning anything—not even a little bit. I've seen shit in the movies or on TV where we're able to walk around in daylight as long as we're wearing a cool pair of shades. Damn, I wish. I've also seen where we can be out in the sun with a protective tarp over our heads to cover us. Yeah right. Or how about the fact that we can always be outside in the state of Washington because of its constant cloudiness? Where do they come up with this shit? And what's with the fucking sparkling?

The real rules? If any of us even *sees* daylight it will burn our eyes right out of our fucking heads. Hell, it'll burn our heads completely along with the rest of us. It can be the greyest day imaginable, with the sun being completely obscured by clouds. We can be *indoors with* the sunglasses *and* that tarp. The little light that gets through will *still* be enough to make us sizzle like burgers on a George Foreman grill. There's no more direct way of saying it, us and *any* kind of daylight, not friends. As for the whole coffin thing? Yes, we lie in coffins. And yes, it was a real pain in the ass getting one up to my apartment.

I suppose I can leave my 2008 Honda Civic here in front of the Martin Luther King projects while I walk Veronica up to her apartment. I must make a mental note, too. It's nice and dark out here. *And* quiet. Walls filled with graffiti, garbage lining the curb at the end of the sidewalk. On some other night this might make an appealing spot for a quick feed.

The smell of the urine coming from the hallways of Veronica's building is spearing through my nostrils. She smiles appreciatively as I open the passenger side door and take her hand. Her eyes expose a prone vulnerability: She's humbled by her surroundings. No one should have to live like this. The stench of the urine itself is enough to overwhelm almost anyone. Yet she doesn't even flinch as we cross the entrance and approach the elevator.

The numbers on the buttons inside the elevator are all scratched or chiseled out. Veronica presses the button to her floor, avoiding my glance. Well at least she stopped talking. But now I feel bad. And dammit, I'm feeling protective.

The elevator stops and opens to let us out on the third floor. A big glass window opposite us gives a view of the dark street below. My car sits in front of the project, unbothered, barely lit by a dim street lamp outside the building. Up the block there's another street lamp but it isn't working. Yeah, definitely have to come back here when I'm hungry.

The hallway's walls have holes scattered all over. And while the urine stench from the first floor has lessened somewhat, the air here still carries a stale foul odor. Maybe it's the muscular, pencil-thin mustached six-footer standing outside Veronica's apartment. He's wearing a baseball-style jacket with letters across the front reading, *Orquesta La Luna*.

The scent of Veronica's fear rises. I'm guessing this is *Señor Roberto*, the trombone player. It looks like I'm going to have to earn my *chili con carne*.

"Why you change the key?" His intent is to intimidate but outwardly Veronica only expresses contempt.

"What you doing here, Bobby? You're not supposed to be here."

"Who's this? Is this who you fucking now?" He's trying to draw a reaction out of me. He won't get one. But I also won't take my eyes off him in case there are any sudden actions. "What you looking at?" He still wants a reaction. Don't push it, amigo.

Veronica nervously fumbles through her purse for her keys. "Leave him alone, Bobby. He's my friend from work."

"Oh, your friend from work. So what, now you take him home to fuck? That's why you don't talk to me on the phone?"

"Stop it, Bobby. You going to wake up the boys! I told you, I don't want to see you no more. I could see who I want!"

A powerful hand takes Veronica's wrist, making her drop her keys. "Now you listen—"

I said, don't push it, amigo.

Roberto's next intended words don't make it past the vice grip around his throat. On TV they show us having all kinds of super powers or rising from the dead as experts in the martial arts. The truth is simpler than that. Our strength comes from having dead muscles with no limitations. Combine that with the adrenaline rushes that come from our steady diet of blood and it is understandable how I can take a six-foot trombone player with one hand and lift him ten inches off the floor.

"Pick up your keys, Veronica. Go inside the apartment."

She reaches down but can't take her eyes of her former trombone playing beau who's trying to wrestle away from my one-handed choke hold. Am I crazy or is she a little turned on by this? Or maybe she's just scared because Roberto's face is turning blue. Fuck it, I'll let him go. With the lack of oxygen going into his brain right now, he's no threat to anyone. My release sends him to the floor like a pile of dirty laundry. "Veronica, I said go inside." The door is open but she won't go in. She probably wants to see what I'm going to do next.

With Roberto seemingly unable to find his legs, I reach out to help him up by the collar of his jacket. Hey, nice material, I gotta pick one of these up—without the band logo, of course.

"Listen amigo, she never wants to see you again," I warn, as he desperately gasps for some air. "And *you* never want to see me again." His eyes are blank. He may be shivering with terror. But I think he's absorbing the message. "Now get the fuck outa here."

My shove sends him staggering, reaching for a wall to maintain his balance. I grab him by the jacket again and throw him a few feet further down the hall.

"You! You're a freak!" he yells. Tell me something I *don't* know. "This ain't over, man! You hear me? This ain't over! Freak!"

No need for me to reply. My point is made. I'll just watch as he turns the corridor and scampers towards the elevator.

Veronica's visibly shaken. Tears form in her eyes.

"Can you stay a little bit, Georgie? I'm scared."

Uh, no, I'm pushing my luck as it is. Daylight is approaching and I am a couple of miles from the comforting darkness of my coffin. This is as far as my chivalry can go. *"Lo siento, Veronica. No puedo."*

Her lips quiver. *"Por favór, Georgie, tengo miedo."*

My cold thumb catches a tear before it runs down her face. "Don't worry. I won't let him bother you again."

Shit!

Serves me right.

This is exactly the kind of thing I'm supposed to avoid. If I leave now, she will never forgive me and I'm going to look like the biggest asshole in Newark to her. No doubt everyone in the hospital will hear about it, too. But unless I want to turn into a pile of ashes here at the Martin Luther King projects, it's time I high-tail—

My back!

Fuck, what time is it?

I'm burning!

I don't believe this!

My head, it's starting to spin.

The end of the hallway, around the corridor, I can see it coming. The dawn! It's seeping in through the big window in front of the elevator.

Veronica can't help but see my sudden expression of panic and my legs buckling from under me. "Georgie, what's wrong?"

How could I have lost track of the time? Could it have been the company of a beautiful woman like Veronica (even with her babbling bullshit)? Was it the touch of her skin when I held her hand? Was it her eyes and the way she looked at me when I was protecting her? Or was it that all these things that brought feelings back from when I was alive, had gotten me so carried away that I forgot that I am dead? What am I going to do? If

Veronica was terrified before, imagine her reaction when her heroic work buddy suddenly bursts into flames.

The sight of my face slamming onto her hardwood floor, as I collapse into her apartment, sends Veronica into a panic. "Georgie, *que pasa*, Georgie?"

Can't tell you, *querida*. No way you'd understand.

A minute ago I was strong as a bull, lifting her ex off the ground with one hand. Now she sees that same bull writhing on the floor in the fetal position, inexplicably burning under his clothes.

The window behind her, in the kitchen, has the shade wide open with pending daylight piercing through. It's already barbecuing her undead *compañero*. "Oh my God, Georgie! What do I do?"

Her startled sons burst out of their bedroom to find a grown man crawling into their living room, looking like he's about to go up in flames (except there's no fire...yet).

"Get me out of the light!" A good thing Roberto's not around now or our confrontation might have had a different ending.

The sun is just minutes away from searing in through the living room window. Veronica is confused, frightened, desperate to help. But she has no idea what to do. How could she? "What do I do, Georgie? What do you want me to do?"

"Closet, get me in a closet." She stares at me quizzically. I'm not even sure she even made out what I said. It was barely above a whisper. "Now!" That time it wasn't a whisper.

Veronica snaps to attention.

"Ayudanme, muchachos!" She calls the boys to take me by the arms while she wraps *her* arms around my chest in an attempt to pick me up. It's agonizing. Their

touch against my burning, dead flesh is unbearable.

My pained shout startles the boys and they pull their arms away for fear of hurting me. The older one looks about twelve, the younger one nine. They shouldn't have to see something like this but there's no choice.

"No, don't stop!" I'll bear with the pain. Veronica's bedroom is only a couple of steps away. If they can get me close enough, I can stagger through the doorway and make a dash for the closet.

The TV in their living room is off. On the darkened screen is the reflection of a mother and her young boys trying to aid a man about to burst into flames. That means my projection is gone (which is no surprise). In this type of agony, we are unable to control our capabilities. So far, in their panic, they either haven't noticed or haven't reacted to my death face. Frightened as they already are, that's the last thing they need to see.

Veronica's holds the closet door open in her bedroom. I'm close enough to make a quick run and throw my smoking torso into what must be a pile of a hundred fucking shoes.

"Close it! Close the door!" I don't even feel the half dozen handbags that fall onto my head from Veronica's overly determined slam. I'm more concerned with the light bleeding in from outside underneath the door, a problem solved by yanking one of her dresses from above and tucking it under.

Veronica leans against the door, breathing heavily. "Are you all right, Georgie?" Damn, that was close. I'm so weak I'm not even sure I can respond. "Georgie?"

"It's okay. I'll be all right, thank you. Just please don't open the door."

"Georgie, I don't understand? What's wrong?"

What a strange turn of events. Now *she* is the one who is protecting *me*. "I have a condition. I can't be in the daylight. That's why I work at night." Wrap your mind around that one, babe.

"Daylight? What is it, like a skin condition?"

Please, Veronica, just go away. "Yeah, kind of..."

"But Georgie, we work in a hospital. Maybe they can do something."

Dammit, woman don't you have to get the kids ready for school? "No, it's incurable."

"How do *you* know, Georgie? Maybe there's like a new treatment or something." This woman isn't going to let go, is she? "Let me look it up. What you got, what's it called?"

"No, it's okay. I'll be all right. Don't worry about it."

"No, Georgie. I want to help. Let me look it up." Holy shit she's persistent.

"It's nothing. I'll be fine."

"So then I can open the door?"

"No! No! Porphyria, it's called porphyria."

"Por-what?"

"Porphyria."

"Por... por... what *is* that?"

"Please, please... I'll explain later. Just let me rest for a little bit. Please."

"Okay, okay. I'm sorry."

Silence.

Thank you.

She's off to the kitchen. *"Vamos, muchachos, limpiesen. Tienen que prepararse para escuela."*

Time for the boys to clean up and get dressed for school. Poor little bastards, I must've traumatized the shit out of them.

"Quien es ese hombre, Mami?" The older one's a little more curious as to who this walking torch is that's hiding inside her closet.

"That's my friend, baby. His name is Georgie."

#

An hour has passed. The boys have left for school and I'm well enough to fall into my inanimate state. That is, assuming Veronica can manage to shut up and leave me alone.

"Georgie? Georgie, honey, you okay?"

"I'm fine, thanks. I just need to rest."

"Can I get you anything?"

Dammit, woman! "No, no, I'm good. Just please don't open the door." It's not my coffin but it'll do, even with her four inch heels poking me in the ass.

"Okay honey, I'm going to go to sleep now but I'll be right here if you need me."

As a night shift worker her daily routine is similar to mine except that during the weekend she can spend some daytime hours with her boys. Hopefully she won't wake up before dark and check inside the closet. If she does she'll find her previously heroic friend bursting into flames above her shoe collection.

Being that we are not sleeping as we did during our living years, our inanimate state leaves us dangerously vulnerable. It's not like we're dreaming, snoring, counting sheep or any of that shit. We're dead, dead as your great-great-grandmother. You can blast *Uptown Funk* and throw a party with a hundred guests in front of our open coffin. We won't hear or feel a thing. That is why I lock my coffin from inside. Call me paranoid, but how else could I possibly rest in peace (pun intended) without any fear of being exposed to the daylight? What if some curious asshole finds the casket in the afternoon and tries to open it?

What's that noise?

Holy fuck, is that Veronica snoring? Man she fell out

fast. She sounds like a lawn mower. How can she fall asleep like that? I would think anyone would be completely wired and tense after a morning like she just had—not exactly the ideal way to end a work shift. The excess drama must have completely wiped her out.

But hey, at least she finally got me in her bedroom. Unfortunately for her it wasn't quite the way she imagined it.

7

Coach Nathan of the Hunter College Hawks baseball team used to get a great kick out of his starting second baseman Sticky Nicky. I don't know where he came up with that nickname. I hated it. It made me sound like I just stepped out of the bathroom with a copy of Penthouse. But to him it was a term of affection. He saw me as a scrappy kid that was also the team's most physical player. I stirred up the most action even though I was the smallest player on the field. My playing style involved diving for balls, sliding hard into bases, and barreling into catchers that were twice my size. He called me the Puerto Rican Pete Rose.

As a team we weren't that good, we always lost a few more than we won. But my constant harassment of star players on the better, opposing teams was a constant source of entertainment to our supporters in the bleachers. Even the girlfriends of our more talented players would single me out as their favorite.

My "scrappiness" often drew physical confrontations with our opponents and charged up my teammates along with our followers in the stands. They loved how I never backed down to anyone—even if it was the 6'2", 220 lb. All-City starting first baseman. Which is why, even with me not being the greatest hitter or fielder, I became the player everyone most enjoyed watching.

When Stefanie came to our game against Bronx Community, she witnessed this first hand and was able to hear some of the girls sitting in the bleachers, giggling about the *cutest* guy on the team. Apparently it was me. I couldn't have planned it any better.

Doing my best to impress my tutor, I stole two bases and slammed into Bronx Community's buffalo-sized catcher while trying to score from first on a single. I was out by a mile and the catcher never even budged. He flinched about as much as he would have if a fly had landed on his shoulder. Still, it was theatrical enough to get a good response from the bleachers.

When I picked myself up and dusted off, the catcher smirked as he threw the ball back to the pitcher. He couldn't resist stirring the shit. "Go sit down, *cucaracha.*"

I took the bait.

Ready to rumble, I charged him but was intercepted by our on-deck batter and the umpire before I could take a swing at him. The umpire then continued to fan the flame by throwing me out of the game, which incited from me a rant of ear-melting profanities.

Our bleacher supporters ate it up. Stefanie though, found my behavior a little unnerving—so much for impressing her on the baseball field. Now I was down in two categories, English class fuck-up and poor sportsman.

"Why do you play like that?" she asked later at the Kingsbridge Diner (a nice Italian dinner at an Arthur Avenue restaurant wasn't exactly in my budget).

Besides, in those days a greasy spic from the South Bronx probably wouldn't have been welcome there.

"Everyone on my team and all the other teams are like four inches and twenty pounds larger than me," I said. "That leaves me at a disadvantage. So everything I do, whether it's getting on base or scoring a run, I gotta fight for it."

Stefanie studied Sticky Nicky as he poured ketchup on his burger and fries. I wasn't stating my case too convincingly. "It didn't look like that. It looked like you wanted to start a fight just for the sake of starting a fight."

"Nah, that's just the way I play."

Apparently my aggressive style of play was more interesting than her tuna fish sandwich. "Maybe football is more your sport."

"Actually, I tried out for football. I just didn't make the team."

"Well, from the sounds of the girls in the bleachers it looks like you have a nice little fan section."

I laughed. "Them? Nah, they're all dating the good players on the team."

"You don't think you're good?"

"Oh, I'm okay. It's just that everyone else is better."

"Oh, stop it. You act like you're the worst player on the team."

"Hey, I'm only hitting like two-sixty. That *is* the worst on the team."

"It's not all about offense, you know."

That stopped me mid-bite. "Oh, so listen to the sports analyst over here."

Stefanie shifted the conversation back. "So you're not dating any of them?"

"What?"

"The girls in the rooting section."

"Oh, nah, don't have the time, too busy to date. I got school, work, and it's just me in the apartment so, you know, gotta pay the rent."

It was a reminder of the previous night's conversation. There was no mom in my apartment when I got home from school, no dad coming home from work, and no one to talk to about college, plans, or anything else. It was all up to me. No one checked my grades, no one paid my rent and no one from home came to the ball games to root for me. I was one hundred percent my own person.

"You must really miss your family," said Stefanie, again stopping me mid-bite on my burger. When she realized it wasn't the best point to bring up, she tried to retract. "Nicky, I'm so sorry. I shouldn't have—"

"No, no, it's okay. I just... I just don't ever really talk about it. I just..."

"Do you want to talk about it?"

We had already done so the night before, the sounds of my mother screaming, cries of my strong, proud father, my sister's blood spreading on the street in front of the car, the crowd gathering around her lifeless body, the fury of my mother's fists pounding against my face, my pants soaked in warm urine. "No," I answered quietly. "Not anymore."

There was no further talk at all that evening—no baseball, no Chaucer, no college, nothing. When we got back to my car, which was parked under the Jerome Avenue El, I awkwardly bumped into her while reaching for the door on the passenger side.

It felt electric.

Not the door handle, her body.

We had avoided making eye contact since we left the diner. It was if we thought it might lead to an impulse we wouldn't be able to control. Boy, were we right. Just as I opened the door we caught each other's glance. That was all it took.

We fell into the front seat on the passenger side, hungrily locking our lips together in a forceful embrace. We then paused for a second and looked at each other.

Oh yeah, we were ready.

It wasn't the ideal place, a parked car on Jerome Avenue with the Woodlawn Express roaring above us, but hey, these things happen when they happen. The mind goes blank and the bodies take over. I don't even remember how we journeyed our way to the back seat that night, but I do remember us sweating out the delay in her *time of the month* for about ten days.

I also ended up getting a "D" in English—nothing to brag about, but at least I passed.

#

The cloud was all but lifted. For the first time since I could remember, *Los Ruidos* had lost some of their grip and were allowing me to breathe a little freer. Tinnitus by definition never goes away but when you're able to tune it out, life can be a bit more agreeable. And with my mind always *being* on Stefanie, the presence of *Los Ruidos* was barely noticeable.

Our study sessions together usually began with all proper intentions at her apartment until her father's increasingly intrusive eye led us to seek solitude in mine—an obviously bad idea. It resulted in very little studying, a worn out mattress, a stained couch, and even a broken dining room table (we got a little carried away that afternoon).

My newfound high spirits, though, also had an effect on the Hunter College Hawks—and it wasn't a good one. Their gritty second baseman had mellowed. He had lost his aggressive edge. And since my other attributes were unspectacular at best, it made my spot on the roster virtually worthless. In my senior year I didn't even make the final cut.

Coach Nathan said it best. "You play like you just don't give a shit anymore."

He wasn't wrong. Being with Stefanie was all that my time allowed for. Nothing else mattered. Even Carmen, the super's wife, saw the difference in me. And though she was disappointed that I was no longer sneaking into her bedroom for our usual gymnastics while hubby went to Ace Hardware for maintenance supplies, she actually seemed happy for me. We had had our share of fun, but now it was nice to no longer have to look over my shoulder while her legs were wrapped around my ass. Besides, she had other playmates like the postal worker in apartment 3A and the pharmacist that lived on the fifth floor.

#

"There he is!" boomed Artie, barely acknowledging his own daughter.

"I'm here too, *Papi,*" laughed Stefanie, joining her mother in the kitchen.

"Yes, of course you are, baby. How was the zoo?"

"It was fun," lied Stefanie.

"That's what I like about you, my boy. You treat my little girl like a princess," said Artie, not knowing that for the prior two hours at my apartment, Stefanie and I had been knotted together like pretzels.

We had been dating three months and I was now regularly invinted to her family's apartment for Sunday dinners. Stefanie loved that her father had taken to me. He was one of those big, muscular dark-skinned

Boricuas that gave suffocating bear hugs to everyone that he liked. If my disfigured ribs were any indication, he *loved* me—especially after the string of *bums* (his words) that had courted Stefanie's attention before.

Artie was a hard-working guy that always smelled like dough when we came home from his job at a wholesale bakery on Castle Hill Avenue. When he learned about my story, he became such an admirer of mine that he'd regularly steal me away for a good part of the night to have a drink and chat. He had enormous respect for how I took care of things on my own and was working my way through college. And since by that time of the night he'd be working on his third glass of Bacardi and Coke, it would soon become bear-hug city. Artie was one of those *I love you, man* drunks.

"Dominic," he called out to his son. "Nicky's here!"

Dominic yelled back at us from the living room. "Hey, get over here, man. Duffy Dyer just hit another homer!" I couldn't resist. I had to check it out.

Stefanie introduced me to her older brother shortly after we started dating. Dominic and I immediately bonded over the Mets. He was one of those crazy, trivia-obsessed fans that you'd always hear on sports talk radio. He could tell you what after-shave Jerry Koosman was wearing the day he pitched a three-hit shutout against the Astros in 1968. Shit, he could tell you what time the game ended and how many people were in attendance.

"Sit down, man," said Dominic as I entered the living room. "Look at the replay." Artie came in behind me shaking his head at the two Met nuts in his living room. Not that Artie wasn't a fan, he just thought Dominic and I took it to another level.

"Two weeks ago, he's a backup catcher," laughed Artie. "Now, all of the sudden, he's Babe Ruth."

Dominic was big like his dad, even bulkier. He moved to the side on the couch to make some room. "Come on, Nick. Sit down."

It was a new scene for me, family fighting for my attention. But it was one that I was quickly getting used to.

By that time, all of my uncles and aunts had moved back to Puerto Rico. They all had done their best to get me to move in with them after *Mami* died. It was difficult for them to grasp why I would want to be alone and not seek comfort from his extended family. And while their point of view was not a difficult one to understand, the losses that I suffered were something I had to deal with in my own way, so outside of birthdays and holidays, I stayed to myself and avoided their sorrowful glances.

Tío Juan was the last of the older Negróns to move back to *la ísla*. And though he tried hard to sway me towards starting a new life in Bayamón among relatives, he just couldn't make the sale. Not even close. It's not that they weren't nice people. Quite the opposite, I loved my *tios, titis, and primos*. I just couldn't bear to be around them. Every moment I spent with their families reminded me of who was missing in mine.

With *la familia Torres* it was different. By the time I met them, *Los Ruidos* for the most part had been shooed away by their radiant daughter, which made me a much more pleasant person to be around. And just the business and the life that clattered around from room to room in *la casa Torres,* was a welcome relief from the stillness inside the walls where I resided.

Ramona, Stefanie's mom, was a traffic stopper. Happily, for me, her daughter looked just like her. Ramona was in her late forties, maybe even fifty. To this day, I don't think I've met a more beautiful woman. She had light brown, shoulder-length hair and a petite, curvy figure that looked like she hadn't gained a pound since high school. No wonder Artie was so happy.

Dinner was fantastic, *arróz amarillo con carne guisada, y aguacate,* man, that woman could cook. And though at first I thought they were all on their best behavior because there was a guest in the house, I quickly learned that the warm family atmosphere at their home was real—it was a feeling that for so long had not been a part of my life and was all but forgotten.

"*Mami,* that was fantastic," said Dominic reaching for another helping.

"Dominic, you have that police physical agility test tomorrow," said Stefanie. "Don't you think you should let up a little bit?" In those days the NYPD Physical Agility Test had a demanding obstacle course that applicants had to complete in less than two-and-a-half minutes to qualify as a candidate.

"What are you nuts, sis? You think me having one more plate is going to make a difference?"

Artie laughed. "You see, Nicky? That's why I have to work this hard, just to feed this guy."

I chimed in. "You know, Dominic. She could have a point. Those few extra pounds could make a difference."

"Oh, excuse me, Mr. Sticky Nicky, but who is the one that is always kicking your ass in one-on-one basketball?"

"Dominic, watch your mouth at the dinner table," said Ramona.

He was right, though. Even with that additional weight he was carrying, Dominic was a tremendous athlete. All sports, too; baseball, basketball, football, you name it.

I offered a weak defense. "That doesn't count. I suck at basketball."

Ramona slapped me on the hand. "Nicky!" This woman took no shit.

Dominic laughed. "Come with me tomorrow. I'll show you how I handle it."

"You *should* go with him," said Stefanie. "Maybe you can keep him from eating on the way there."

That brought a big laugh from Artie. The guy was always laughing.

"Alright," said Dominic, rising from the dinner table. "I'm gonna catch the rest of the game."

"Not before you take out the garbage," said Ramona.

"Don't worry, Mami, I'll take it out after the game," replied Dominic.

"No, you will take it out now," countered his mother.

"Call it a warmup for tomorrow's fitness exam," cracked Artie.

After dinner, Ramona rose and started to pick up the dishes. "Okay everyone, you all know what you have to do." Despite her almost childlike size, it was clear that Ramona was the no-nonsense leader of the family. She managed the household like an efficiently run office. Everyone in the family had individual responsibilities after dinner. Artie cleared the table, Ramona put away the leftovers, and Stefanie did the dishes. Dominic's part was taking out the garbage and she wasn't about to let him delay it. Knowing him, he'd probably forget later. I observed this all from the table as an amused guest, but not for long.

"Nicky, did you enjoy your dinner?" asked Ramona.

"Uh yeah, it was great, *Señora Ramona*," she liked when I called her that.

"Well good, you can now go help Stefania dry the dishes."

I didn't dare not comply.

I quickly took my position at the sink next to her

daughter.

As we stood next to one another, Stefanie looked over at me and winked. "Welcome to the family."

The next day, on the way to the NYPD Physical Agility Test, Dominic stopped at a nearby pizzeria and downed three slices while I stood by cursing the shit out of him. "You're never gonna pass, you fat fuck!"

"You don't want some?"

"No!" I refused to join him. "I can't believe you're doing this shit! Don't you want the job?"

"Relax, man. You're too up tight."

"You've done nothing to prepare for this. You didn't train, you've been eating like a maniac, what the hell is the matter with you?"

"Man, this pizza's good. There's no pizza like New York pizza. Am I right?"

Later at the site of the test, when his turn came to run the course, Dominic winked at me and took off, leaving behind a heinous, acidic fart. Barreling through effortlessly, he leapt each barrier, climbed the walls and trotted to the finish line with almost twenty seconds left to go. I still don't know how he did that.

They were my new family, Artie, Ramona, Dominic and of course, Stefanie. A family that accepted me and loved me as if I had always been a part of their lives.

Almost twenty years later, that same young man they welcomed into their family would die in another woman's bed.

8

The time on my cell phone reads 5:49 p.m. It's dark out, time for my kind to go out and play—or more accurately put, prey.

Veronica's bathroom is right behind the closet. I can hear the shower running on the other side of the wall. Thankfully she respected my wishes and left me undisturbed. Hopefully, if the kids are home, they are occupied enough so that I can sneak out quietly. Enough time has passed for my capabilities to be restored, which would allow me to walk past the boys unseen.

The squeaking of the closet door hinges should be drowned out by the running water in the bathroom. Actually the shower *is* the only sound I hear, no TV, no video games, nothing. The boys must be out. I don't know any kids that age that can be *that* quiet.

The sound of Veronica in the shower clearing her throat gives me that familiar little tickle below the belt. Dead or not, I'm still a horny bastard. Knowing that she's in there soaping that luscious body of hers is too good of an opportunity for me to not go in and sneak a peek.

My lack of reflection on the mirror above her dresser tells me my ability to project is intact, which means I can be a perv and take a look without being seen. But what if my lust takes over? What if I lose control and end up going to bed with her? After all, she's more than ready, willing and able.

Nah, can't risk it. Excitement like that could put me on a plane I can't control and result in some unsightly gashes on my pretty friend's neck.

The things I have to deal with.

Interestingly, Veronica's got a laptop on her bed that she's left open with a gyrating screensaver. It's calling my attention. Let's give her little mouse pad a tap and see what comes up.

No surprise.

It looks like the little lady's been Googling—a browser history with a string of misspelled variations of porphyria— close enough, though, to enable her to find a couple of articles about my *disease*. I probably wasn't thinking too straight earlier today with the prospect of going up in flames and such. My saying that I had porphyria was probably a good indication of that. It might have been the best way to get her to shut up but it also raised the potential of leading her to articles that identify it as the disorder that led to legends about vampires, centuries before.

Exhibit A.

One article she browsed through was about Phillip Peele, the dumbass biochemist that claimed porphyria patients avoided sunlight, craved blood, and that their gums recessed to cause the illusion of growing fangs. He also claimed that garlic had a chemical that was harmful to those that carried the disease.

What an idiot.

What we have is not a disease. We are dead! We are the living dead. We walk the night, we drink the blood of our prey, and sometimes we even like to eat them. And by the way, I *love* garlic. I like it with my rice, I like it with my potatoes, and I especially love garlic salt on my pizza.

Phillip Peele was a fraud. Hell, Bram Stoker was more accurate when he wrote Dracula (which I always wondered about). There was something up with that guy. Sure, some of it was crap. We don't turn into bats, for example. I wish we could, that would be fucking awesome! On the other hand, a lot of what he wrote was pretty close to fact. Yeah, Mr. Stoker, we sure do wonder about you.

"Oh, Georgie, are you okay?"

Busted!

I got so caught up in Veronica's browser trail that I didn't notice the water had stopped running. Surprisingly she seems more concerned about my condition than the fact that I'm snooping around on her computer.

"Uh... yeah... yeah, I'm good. Thank you. Thanks for everything."

"Are you sure, honey?" She approaches with no self-consciousness, drying her hair with a pink towel that matches her terrycloth robe. Underneath which she's wearing nothing. It's barely tied together, too. One slight turn and I get full frontal. Damn, this woman is sexy. "Let me see, baby." Her hand on my face activates my little undead friend. Hopefully she won't spot it. Knowing her, she might shut the bedroom door for a quickie before work.

Veronica's baffled, feeling around my face for signs

of damage from the burns I suffered earlier today. They are there, but she won't feel it past my projection which is tangible to the human sense of touch.

Her robe opens ever-so-slightly, drawing my eyes to her cleavage. She knows it, too. She wants me to look. Man, this woman knows how to turn a guy on. Look at those beautiful-

DAMMIT! NO!

"Oh my God, baby, you're still sick!"

What else can she conclude, seeing me back away in a panic, stumbling to the floor?

"No, get away!"

"Georgie, what's wrong?"

"You're right. I'm still sick. Back away, I don't want you to get sick."

"It's okay, honey. You're not contagious." What, so now you're an expert?

I can't face her. I have to look away. As long as that crucifix hangs on the thin, gold chain resting against her bosom, I'll be cowering away like a frightened little girl. "I'll be alright. I'm just a little woozy. But I have to leave. I have to leave *now*."

"Georgie listen to me," she says, taking me in her arms like a reassuring mother. "Honey, look at me." Fuck, no! She remains intent, turning me towards her. Thankfully her back is facing the mirror above her dresser. Otherwise she'd see herself having a firm grip on... nothing.

The Holy Cross is only inches away from me. Veronica, meaning well, is stroking my hair to calm me. "Georgie, there's no reason to be embarrassed. We can get you help at the hospital."

"No, no. I'm okay."

"But, Georgie—"

"No! I'm okay!"

I abruptly break away, out of her room past the burn marks on her living room carpet. I can sense her hurt. I'm such an asshole.

Being genetically resistant and raised in a Christian home, I and others like me, recognize ourselves as the unholy abominations that we are, causing us to fear the cross as much as we fear the daylight. It can even burn us if we come in contact with it. But if you pull out a crucifix on one us who wasn't Christian or even one of us that is not genetically resistant, then you could wind up with a cross being shoved up your ass while being drained of your blood.

9

"Honey, Dominic called," said Stefanie as I walked through the door from a day of collecting debits for Atlantic Indemnity. "He's got tickets for Friday's game!"

"He's got 'em? Holy shit! I love that fat bastard!" That was good news to come home to, tickets to see the Mets vs. Dodgers National League playoff game at Shea Stadium.

"It's going to be me, you, him and *Papi,*" she said, referring to Artie.

"No Patti?"

Dominic's wife Patti hated baseball anyway. They also weren't getting along very well in those days, which was pretty much the case for most of their marriage. Stefanie and I were the exact opposite, very rarely having the kind of Class A blowouts you saw over at their household. Most of their fights stemmed from Dominic's hours at the NYPD. His exemplary police work had gotten him a promotion to homicide detective in the city, making him a rare presence at home.

Whenever he *was* at home, a lot of that time would be spent arguing in front of their twins, Aida and Penny. So other opportunities to get out of the house were always welcome to Dominic, like bowling, poker night and of course, the Mets.

Sure Stefanie and I had bouts of our own, but usually they stemmed from me being a bore. I wasn't the most social animal and didn't care too much for jumpin', jivin' and wailin'. If it were up to Stefanie, every weekend I'd pick her up from work at Fordham U with the kids staying at Artie and Ramona's. She'd then want to spend the night clubbing and dancing until two in the morning. Not that the night wouldn't be without its rewards. The bumping and gyrating always got her in a frisky mood but truthfully, despite that appealing coda, I was more of the *what's-on-TV-tonight* type.

"The Case of the Fuddy Duddy Husband's Ass Print on the Sofa Cushion," was her typical reply.

But that was pretty much the worst of it. We were especially conscious of not fighting in front of our kids, pretty little Jessie and her destructive little brother, Davey.

"What about that sales meeting downtown?" asked Stefanie, concerned it might conflict with our night at the ball game.

"That's tomorrow, Thursday."

"So you're going to be out late tomorrow then?"

"Yeah, maybe."

"Oh, that's too bad. I really had some nice plans for tomorrow night after the kids went to bed," she teased.

"What's wrong with tonight?"

"Aren't you watching the game tonight?" That was true, and those damn nationally televised games always end after midnight.

"So what about after the game?" That was probably

the wrong thing to ask. I probably should have said something like, the hell with the game.

"Not tonight," she quipped. "I have a headache."

#

"I can't believe you said that," laughed Atlantic Indemnity's Bronx regional manager Greg Feldman after I displayed a brass pair at the monthly regional sales meeting.

I hated those meetings. They were an incredible waste of time. We'd have to drive to midtown Manhattan every month to listen to balding, overweight white executive types in the company pontificate about incentives, motivations, prospecting, and all other kinds of bullshit. Every month I did my best to duck them but this time I had to go. Not only was I going to get a plaque for outstanding sales achievement, but I was also going to receive a nice thousand-dollar bonus.

Three of us rode in together, me, Greg and my immediate supervisor Kenny Neglia, the manager of the South Bronx branch. My preference would have been to drive in by myself so I could break away as soon as I got my check, but Greg insisted we go in his car.

Other sales reps were starting to think of me as a big kiss ass because the bosses never bothered hiding who their favorite sales rep was. But I was their favorite for a reason, and at that meeting, I let them know why in a playfully brash sort of way.

"I would like to thank you all for this very nice award. And my wife, Stefanie, would like to thank you for the thousand-dollar bonus. Believe me, I won't see a penny of it." That got a nice little laugh. What came next is what made everybody's jaws drop. "I would also like to express gratitude to all you white pussies that are too afraid to take the debit routes in the South Bronx projects. It's those little debit life insurance policies that you don't want to bother with that have enabled me to set new commission and renewal highs every year."

It was meant lighthearted but my attempt at humor landed with a thud. It was only Greg's exaggerated Ed McMahon guffaw that broke the awkward second of silence that followed, effectively removing the stick from the asses of the blowhard executives posing for pictures next to me.

"Let's go to the Mick's," said Kenny after the sales meeting. He and Greg regularly went to dinner at Mickey Mantle's restaurant after the regional meetings because a) they were Yankee fans and b) it was only a couple of blocks away at the south side of Central Park.

I protested. "I'm not sitting in no Yankee restaurant."

"Oh, grow up," laughed Kenny. "The Mets are in the playoffs and the Yankees aren't. What the hell else do you want?"

"I want to not sit in a restaurant surrounded by pain-in-the-ass Yankee fans. Let's go to Rusty's instead." That was a restaurant owned by Rusty Staub, a former Mets All-Star. It was located on the east side around 79th street.

"Rusty's! That's all the way uptown on the east side," said Kenny. "By the time we get there with all that traffic, we'll starve. Mantle's is right here."

"Rusty's," I countered. "I'll buy."

That's when Greg, the top boss, stepped in. "No, Nicky, you made us both a lot of money this year, even if you do have a big mouth. Next meeting we're putting a muzzle on you. But anyway, you're not buying, we are. Mantle's it is."

Rather than waste the whole night debating I gave in to my Yankee fan superiors.

Once inside, much to the amusement of my ball-breaking higher ups, the host sat us beneath portraits of Babe Ruth and Joe DiMaggio. To add to their fun, they ordered the Yankee Pot Roast.

I gave it right back to them by ordering the Surf and Turf, the most expensive entrée on the menu. Fuck 'em! With what I earned them in bonuses and overrides, they could afford it.

From the bar we ordered two bottles of wine, a red and white, before launching into some *guy talk* about the current National League Championship Series. The Dodgers beat the Mets in Los Angeles to tie the series at one apiece, and yes, the game ended late and yes, just as she said, I did not get any from Stefanie afterwards.

Despite my resistance to anything Yankee oriented, the food at the Mick's was pretty good. But when dinner was over, I noticed that both bottles of wine were almost empty. Greg noticed it too because we both looked at each other in surprise. He and I had only one glass each.

"So you got tickets for tomorrow night's game," said Kenny. Not surprisingly his speech was already slurred. "I gotta tell you, Nicky, and I hate to say it. I got a feeling the Met's ain't gonna make it."

"Bullshit," I laughed. "The Mets played eleven games against the Dodgers this year and won ten of them. They practically swept the season series."

"Yeah but Nick, it's the playoffs now," said Greg, the other Yankee fan. "Anything can happen in a short series."

"Oh, screw the two of y— "

"Holy shit," said Kenny, a little louder than he should have. He was looking behind me towards the opposite side of the restaurant. Greg, who was sitting next to him looked in the same direction but couldn't make out what Kenny was reacting to.

"What is it?" asked Greg.

Kenny squinted his eyes. He then murmured "Is that... is that...? Shit, that's Orel Hershiser," said Kenny, claiming to see the Dodgers ace pitcher.

I wasn't buying it. "Get outa here!"

Greg then suddenly perked up and laughed. "He's right! That *is* Orel Hershiser."

I couldn't help but to turn around. "You two are so full of—oh shit!" It *was* him. The Dodgers' ace was sitting at a private table towards the end of the restaurant with two members of the Dodger bullpen that blew the game for him earlier that week. They were enjoying a nice quiet dinner before the series was to resume the following night.

"Hey man, tell him you're going to the game tomorrow night," said Kenny.

"What? What for?" I said. "What does *he* give a shit whether I'm going to the game tomorrow?"

Kenny got up and staggered towards Hershiser's table.

"Kenny what are you doing?" said Greg.

The check was already paid so it was time to leave anyway. Greg and I got up as well.

"Hey, Hershiser," said Kenny, approaching the pitcher like an old friend.

"Kenny, let's go," said Greg. From experience, he knew that his South Bronx Branch manager could be a little trouble when he was juiced like this. For their part, Hershiser and his teammates didn't seem too concerned at the slightly off balance New Yorker spinning towards them.

Kenny pointed his thumb towards me and addressed the Dodger ace as I tried to lead him away. "Listen, Hershiser, my buddy here is a Mets fan. He's going to the game tomorrow. I told him that they ain't got a chance against you guys as long as you get two more shots at pitching against them.”

Hershiser smiled politely.

“Kenny stop,” I said, before apologizing to Hershiser, who nodded graciously.

Kenny was pushing his limit. “Hey man, don’t apologize. It’s okay, right Hershiser?” The pitcher patiently remained quiet. “It’s the rest of these guys,” said Kenny, gesturing to the relievers that got their asses kicked by the Mets lineup. “They gotta hold up their end.”

And Greg thought *I* had balls?

Greg took Kenny’s arm. “All right, that’s enough.”

Kenny recognized Greg’s tone. “Okay, okay.”

I took Kenny by the other arm to help Greg lead him away. “A good thing *you’re* not driving.”

It was beautiful outside, a nice night to be out in the city. But really, my mind was on getting back home. It was a Thursday and we had to work the next day so I wasn’t too keen on being out late. Greg also seemed ready to call it a night.

Kenny had other ideas.

A quartet of stylishly dressed ladies sashayed past us swishing their perfumed little asses into the Ritz-Carlton. With his boner pointing the way, Kenny broke in their direction.

Greg was getting pissed. “Kenny! Where are you going?”

Kenny answered without breaking stride. “Didn’t you see what just walked in there?”

This was a regular occurrence with Kenny, be it at dinners, parties, or business road trips. Sometimes it was funny. Usually it was just annoying. That night I had already allocated more time to Atlantic Indemnity than I cared to; the commute to the city, the long, boring sales meeting, dinner at a Yankee restaurant, enough was enough. I had no interest in letting Kenny's hormones drag the night any further. "Come on Kenny, we gotta work tomorrow."

"Let's have some fun," he cackled. "Don't worry. We won't say nothin' to *wifey*. Promise."

"Let's get him," said Greg, shaking his head in frustration as he walked past the clueless doorman that allowed an obviously inebriated cad into the posh hotel.

"I don't see him," said Greg. "Do you?"

The main lobby was relatively quiet. It was just me, Greg, and a couple of people over at the front desk. At the far end, we saw a clear glass door to a bar called the Star Lounge that opened as a well-dressed couple came in to the lobby. The sounds from inside; people chatting, clinking glasses and sports on the TV followed the couple until the door swung back shut.

Kenny was inside.

We could see him through the glass, pouring his questionable charm on the ladies he followed in. He was known throughout the company as Kenny the Widow Banger, a reputation he had earned by insisting on handling death claims whenever an attractive widow was involved. By personally taking care of all the paperwork, he'd develop a bond with the grieving beneficiaries that would lead towards him alleviating their suffering in his own special way. To an outsider it may sound ridiculous and more than a little creepy, but I hate to admit it, I'd seen him succeed at it more than once. His wife Gail, who was married to the horndog for over twenty years, had her share of suspicions. It led to many nights of him sleeping on their couch. One morning I even found him sleeping on the couch in our break room at the office.

"I'll get him," said Greg, pulling the door to the Star Lounge open.

"All right," I said. "While you do that, I'm going to give Stef a quick call."

These days every walking person on the planet has a cell phone in his pocket. Back in the eighties it was, put a dime in the payphone. A few steps away, a row of them stood on the wall towards the back end of the lobby. I dropped a dime into one of them next to a woman whose back was towards me. Stefanie picked up midway through the fourth ring. The "Cheers" theme song was playing in the background from our living room console.

"You got the TV away from Davey? Congratulations!" Like every other nine-year-old in those days, our son always had to be pried from his Nintendo.

"I forced him to go read in bed," said Stefanie. "From now on he gets only one hour of Nintendo." She raised her voice a notch to make sure he heard the next few words. "And that's *after* he does his homework."

"What's Jessie doing?"

"What else? She's in her room listening to George Michael."

"One of these days, she's going to learn that guy is gay and it's going to break her heart."

"He's not gay."

"Not gay? Did you see those white shorts he has on it that video?"

"So? He's not gay!"
"Yeah, all right, he's not gay."

"So did you get your bonus?" Now we get to what was *really* on her mind.

"That's all you think about, isn't it? I bet you already spent it."

The woman at the next phone turned around to face me. The playful little banter between me and Stefanie caught her attention. Not wanting to disturb her conversation any further, I toned it down. That's how we did it in those days. We were considerate of others, not like these obnoxious idiots today yelling out their conversations on smartphones, Bluetooth or whatever the else they walk around with attached to their heads.

Being at the other end of the phone, Stefanie felt no need be subtle. "Actually I'm thinking about something else."

To avoid annoying the other lady, I played along quietly. "Oh really, and what might *that* be?"

Stefanie got to the point. "I'm wet. I am *so* wet." She knew I loved it when she played the aggressor. "Are you going to come home now? I can't wait, I'm already touching myself. God, you have to see how wet I am. Or maybe you want to feel how wet I am."

"Okay, stop right there," I whispered, conscious of the woman next to me. "You're going to make me have an accident."

"Ooh," she giggled. "On the road or on yourself?"

The woman on the other phone looked right at my eyes. It was if she heard what Stefanie said. Not wanting her to see the bulge developing below my belt buckle, I shifted slightly.

Nope, too late.

She looked right at it and gave me a suggestive smile.

The woman was stunning. She had straight Sahara-red hair that curled inward as it reached her shoulders. Her eyes were green and cat-like. On another woman, they might have appeared soft and vulnerable. On her they looked carnivorous. Her face was strikingly seductive, her figure slim and athletic, hugged eagerly by a silk red dress that ended above the knees. Her shoes were red too, with heels that made her an inch or two taller than me.

Stefanie, unaware of the awkward scene at my end, went on to describe the flimsy inviting nightgown she was going to be wearing, and the wicked, salacious things we were going to be doing behind our closed bedroom door. She always knew how to get me more worked up than a teenager at his first R-rated movie.

But this time I wasn't listening.

The woman next to me brought her hand down to her thighs.

Stefanie's voice became a distant echo.

The lobby, which was already a little quieter than any big city lobby should be, seemed to drift away in the distance.

The woman took hold of the hem of her dress and slowly lifted it to expose silk red undergarments (who would have guessed?). At the other end, Stefanie was still baiting me with erotic promises but she didn't stand a chance. I may have been fully cognizant of where I was and what was happening, but I was no longer the one pushing the buttons, they were being pushed by the woman reaching inside her intimates, doing exactly what Stefanie was describing on the phone.

I was no longer at the wheel. And Stefanie was no longer a factor in the equation. Nicky Negrón was now a passenger in his own body. Without saying a word, the woman gave me a knowing look and hung up the phone she was speaking into. Or was she? I'm not sure I ever heard her say a word. The woman was confident that I would follow her anywhere. And I did nothing to prove her wrong. I hung up the phone, cutting Stefanie off in mid-sentence.

We were in New York, the greatest cosmopolitan city in the world. You can't keep your eyes open for two seconds without spotting a beautiful woman. Not once had I ever been tempted. So how was it that this woman was luring me so effortlessly? With no feeling of interest, attraction, or any lust, I followed the woman towards the elevators perfectly conscious of the fact that I wanted nothing to do with her. I wanted to walk away. I wanted to help Greg collect Kenny and ride on home to my beloved wife's open arms. And yet I couldn't. I couldn't because I also wanted this woman more than I ever wanted any woman in my entire life.

When the elevator doors opened I held out for desperate hope that Greg would come out of the Star Lounge dragging a soused Kenny, saying "Come on, Nick. Let's go home." Instead I obediently followed the red-haired lady into the elevator.

When we entered the elevator, we waited until the doors closed before pawing at each other like two hungry beasts on the National Geographic channel. And with no thought of any danger we might have been putting ourselves in, we made the elevator sway on its cables by bouncing each other off the walls, groping at one another with nothing that resembled passion or lust. We were practically ripping our flesh off along with our clothes. When our faces slammed together, our mouths locked like links on a chain as our tongues probed for the other's tonsils. How lost was I? All throughout this martial exercise in foreplay I gave no thoughts to the inevitable marks that would be left on me and the troublesome conversation it would lead to when I got home.

When the elevator doors opened on the 14th floor, we rolled out onto the hallway, nearly tackling a refined elderly couple that was waiting to get on. Shaking their heads in distaste at the half-naked couple wrestling on the floor, they stepped over us and boarded the elevator.

Obviously my brain was in sleep mode. That much I could tell, though I was aware enough to be unnerved at how easily I was being thrown around, like a pillow in a sorority room.

The red lady pressed me against the door to her room, reaching for the card key in her purse (yes it was red). She unlocked the door while continuing to gnaw at me. Anyone who would have witnessed the intensity between me and this ravishing redhead would never have believed that my participation was completely involuntary. Even *I* was confused at how much I was matching her aggressiveness in disrobing her as we jetted towards the bed like two cruise missiles.

The panic was building. I wanted this to stop. I wanted it to stop immediately. But then again, I didn't.

Besides Stefanie and the super's wife back in the Bronx, there weren't a whole lot of notches on my belt. And none of the experiences I had resembled the steel cage match I was having with this lioness in red. On the bed, the ravenous redhead yanked my pants off and pounced, tearing at my Calvin Kleins to find a rod that made John Holmes look like a toddler. It was as if all the blood in my body was being funneled to that one specific area. It was seconds from bursting.

When her lips took hold, it sparked the early arrival that every man dreads. Normally that would have been completely humiliating, even as she eagerly ingested the results of her tenacity. Instead I was terrified because I was unable to rise and walk away from what was happening while this smorgasbord of conflicting emotions grappled throughout me.

It was already a forgone conclusion.

This was not going to end well.

A few seconds later she sat up and removed her matching red undergarments. I watched helplessly, still fully erect and still unable to move. When she mounted me, her eyes closed with pleasure and she made the only sound I ever heard her make—a deep enraptured groan of gratification as she rhythmically grinded her hips back and forward.

The red lady brought herself down closer to me, letting her breasts rub against my chin. Whenever Stefanie did that, it stirred me into a heated frenzy where I'd take charge and flip her over. Not here. With this woman, I could neither move nor respond in any way. Red hair, red dress, red shoes, even her bra and panties were red. What was with all the red? What the hell was going on?

She put her face up against mine. Our eyes met. I saw pleasure. Not the pleasure of sexual gratification. It was more like how I imagined my eyes looked when we'd go to Victor's Café and I'd take in the scent of the *lechón asado* as it was being served.

She kissed me. This time it was gently on the lips. When Stefanie kissed me that way and I felt her breath, I would let her essence envelop me. In this case, the tables were turned. It was the red-haired woman taking in my scent as her lips and tongue explored my shoulder. Scared as I was, it felt nice. It started to relax me. I was getting into it—the sensation of her mouth tasting my flesh. My eyes closed submissively as she licked and sucked at the base of my neck, drool oozing its way past my shoulders onto the bed sheets. Fixated on one spot, she sucked away like a newborn on her mother's nipple. The drool thickened. It had been a long day and a strange night. I was tired. The weight of my eyelids overwhelmed any effort of mine to keep them up. Red. So much red. The red lady lifted her head.

JESUS CHRIST!

I only had one glass of wine. That couldn't have been

it.

Was I drugged? Impossible. Mantle's was a reputable restaurant. How could any hallucinogenic drugs possibly make it into their food? And after that, I had nothing. Nothing that could have possibly made me see what was above me.

The sensual seductress I followed from the lobby was gone. The red hair was now dry and straw-like. Her eyes were now dark with huge black eyeballs and no white in the surrounding area. Her skin, which before was smooth and porcelain-like, was now pale and shaded gray.

Back at the elevator her tongue was dueling with mine as we explored every corner of each other's mouth. Now it was licking my red blood off her cracked, broken lips. A sick expression of happiness surrounded her venomous smile as she lowered her face to continue feeding.

There was no struggle, no fight. I laid there passively with echoes of my past clouding my consciousness—the cries of my parents as they knelt beside Dani's lifeless body, the emptiness of the realization that *Papi* was never coming back, the sight of *Mami* on her hospital bed, knowing that she would never rise again.

We often use colors for metaphors when describing situations in our lives. When we're scared, we're yellow. When we're sad, we're blue. When we're envious, we're green. My last moments were bathed in red—her hair, her silk undergarments, and my blood, which coated the lower half of her face. It's a color that humans connect with love—red roses, red cherries, strawberries, lipstick, hearts. It's the primary color of Valentine's Day, the color of love. But now everything that *I* loved was being taken away from me.

Again.

Stefanie, the woman that had brought me everything I had lost all hope for—she would never again greet me at the door after a long day's work. Her kiss, her smile, her voice, her love—never again to be mine. Having gone through the loss of Dani, *Papi* and *Mami*, the odds of me ever having a happy, normal life had to have been considered next to impossible. Somehow, Stefanie made it happen. Nothing but good came to my life after I met her. And now she was going to be left alone to raise our children Jessie and Davey. They would have to go on with their lives without a father.

In the years that would come I would be written off by many as another selfish prick that saw an opportunity to get some hot New York pussy behind his unsuspecting wife's back. And really, who could blame someone for thinking that? I have that same argument with myself all the time. Was I under the spell of her power or was I just under the spell of what was below her waist? Was there really nothing I could do to stop what was happening?

My heart was beating its last few beats. My lungs were struggling to take in their last few breaths. Across the room, the red high-heeled shoes that this woman maniacally kicked away before we got in bed were lying on their side by the closet. The red bra which held those delicious looking breasts was resting quietly on the tray by the ice bucket. On the carpet, her red panties were being approached by a growing pool of my red blood.

It's the color of love.

Happy Valentine's Day.

I knew we should've gone to Rusty's.

10

"Excuse me sir, please don't lock up yet. I just need to get something real quick for my friend."

The poor old bastard, a Black man in his late sixties, has already flipped the sign on the door. It reads "CLOSED". No Latino's going to turn up here at the last second before he can call it a night. It could only mean trouble.

"We're closed," he grumbles.

A couple of hundreds should get his attention. "I have cash, look. And I know exactly what I want. It's that little sapphire pendant right there in the window. I promise I'll be quick."

He's sizing up the *Porta Rican* waving cash at him in front of his jewelry store. Downtown Newark tends to shut down around six to avoid characters like this. Probably some dope pusher wanting to buy a gift for his trashy girlfriend, he figures. Still, cash is cash.

I'm in.

As a gesture I thought it'd be nice to bring Veronica a little "thank you" gift. She saved me from the worst type of destruction imaginable—the equivalent of being burned alive. And when it came to questioning the freakish symptoms she witnessed at her apartment, she also eased up and gave me some space, showing nothing but deep concern, loyalty, and generosity of heart. Sure, her appreciation for my chivalrous protection from her rejected paramour played a part in it, but I'd be kidding myself if I weren't acknowledging the obvious. Like it or not, I *am* in a relationship. It might not be a romantic or sexual one at this point, but it *is* a relationship. We have bonded. And it needs to be managed. Besides, hopefully this little token of gratitude will serve as a substitute for the crucifix, which will probably be exposed by a plunging neckline tonight.

We both happen to be off tonight so she thought it would be nice for us to get together while not in uniform (although she'd probably prefer not in *any* clothes). There is a little balancing act I've had to learn mingling with society over the past twenty-seven years and truthfully, I'm not sure I've figured it out yet. If I become too much a part of everyone's life, there's a natural desire from them to develop a familiarity that will put demands on me that I can't meet. On the other hand, if I stay too distant, curiosity could lead towards them seeking to learn more about me—also not good.

Let's see where tonight leads. Veronica and I still haven't gotten into any detailed conversation about our little "episode" back at her apartment. This might be a good chance to see what's running through her mind.

"With tax that's $263.94," says the old man, wrapping up the pendant in a little designer box. If I wanted to I could have put the old bastard under my spell and just helped myself to anything here at the store. But really, why should I do that? The old guy looks like someone who's been through a lot of shit over the years. With the economy being the way it's been over the past ten years and the big shopping malls in the nicer areas pulling away the majority of shoppers, how well can a little jewelry store on Broad Street in Newark be doing? Undead or not, sometimes it's best just to be a regular customer.

"Thanks for staying open for me."

He shakes his head at the four hundred dollar bills I've laid out. "That's too much. The total comes out to $263.94."

"I know. Like I said, thanks for staying open for me." I can sense him quietly watching me as I exit the store. The old guy doesn't know what to say. How about a "thank you"? That would have been nice, you old prick.

#

My judgment concerns me lately, especially since there is no alcoholic beverage more powerful, nor any drug on the street that can warp your judgment like sexual attraction. Some of the greatest minds of our times, many of them that even made our world a better place, still fell short when it came to making logical decisions when their hearts and genitals pointed them in obviously flammable directions.

One of the reasons for my concern is that I actually spent time deciding what to wear, laying out shirt and pants combos on top of my coffin before making a selection (looking in the mirror to check myself out obviously is not an option). After some deliberation I settled on breaking in a stylish pair of ankle boots I picked up at Kohl's the other night, complementing them with a black leather blazer, an aqua blue cotton shirt and a soft pair of charcoal slacks. Shit, who needs a mirror? I *know* I look good. The question is why am I even giving a shit? It's not like this is a date. Is it?

Women often like to point out how men regularly let their *little heads* control their *big heads*, even at the expense of destroying their lives. Not that they're wrong, but they should talk. How many times have you seen a woman turn blind when attracted to a man that was clearly no good for her? It's simple math. Love and sex, or the promise of either one, are responsible for 99% of all the questionable behavior and regrettable decisions made by the human species, making them say things *and* do things they would never even consider if their minds were in a clearer place.

#

"Hey, big guy, how are ya?"

Veronica's older son doesn't look too happy opening the door to the freak that almost went into flames the other morning in their apartment. Or maybe he's just sick of the cast of characters that have been walking through this door seeking his mom's favors. He leaves the door open for me but runs back to rejoin his little brother in front of the TV to resume some game on their X-Box. I guess I'll just let myself in.

"Hi Georgie, I'll be out in a minute." Veronica's little sing-song tone from the bedroom channels an air of starry-eyed giddiness. I don't know how I've kidded myself into thinking this is not a real date.

The boys are sitting right next to the burn stains I left on the carpet the other morning, thoroughly engrossed by some shooting game that fittingly pits them against (who would have guessed?) the undead. The younger one keeps turning back to sneak a peek at me. Yes, little man, one of those things on the TV is waiting in your living room to take your mother out on a date.

"Hi, Georgie!"

Veronica's dress is soft, floral-patterned, and red! Again with the fucking red! She is beautiful though, gotta say that. There isn't a man in the world who wouldn't want to be standing where I am right now as she approaches to greet me with a kiss (well, maybe not in the Martin Luther King projects).

"NO!"

"Oh no, honey, are you still sick?"

An understandable reaction, especially upon seeing your previously virile date fall backwards, knocking down a lamp from an end table like Inspector Clouseau.

"No, no, it's okay. I'm alright." The kids watch me pick myself up wondering who the fuck is this guy?

To any normal man the sight of Veronica's satin-smooth cleavage would be more than appetizing. For me it's a sight I cannot enjoy until we dispose of the crucifix that is swinging towards me as she reaches down to help. I must look like a complete dork facing away from her while analyzing her lamp for damage.

"Honey if you still don't feel good..."

"No, no, I'm fine. Here look, I got you something."

"Oh my God," squeals Veronica, yanking the nicely wrapped gift from my hand, inadvertently naming the cause of my strange behavior.

"Open it." Yeah, let's move it along so you can take that other thing off your neck. And take it down a notch, will you?

It's not like she isn't accustomed to receiving truckloads of baubles from previous *enamorados*. I know it may be a tad cynical of me but, to me, she sounds like she's mastered the gasp that's a little more impassioned than it should be. Is it sincere or is the reaction she thinks you're looking for? "Try it on." Let's get this show on the road.

"Here, hold this for me." No fucking way! "Nicky?"

She must really think I have issues (you have no idea baby). But no way am I taking that crucifix in my hands.

"Excuse me for a moment." A quick little dash to the bathroom, a grab at a piece of toilet paper, and some noises that I trust will pass as post-nasal drip, will hopefully have her set aside the crucifix while also pondering how much of a mess I am.

"So, how do I look?" So far I have to have been the most discombobulated spazz to have ever walked through her door. Yet somehow she still seeks my approval. But hey, no crucifix in sight so yeah, baby, you look fantastic.

#

You can't beat Newark's Hot Spot Diner for versatility. It's got a casual "diner" section, a finer restaurant section, and a bar area that features entertainment. Talk about an all-purpose location! My original intention was to eat in the casual dining area but when Miss Curves came out in that flowery red dress I figured the nicer restaurant section would be more appropriate. That's another red flag. What kind of a path am I headed on? Man, this shit is just building up and taking on a life of its own.

"Hello, my name is Felípe." The host holds out a pair of menus, ready to lead us to our table. He's a petite little fella with a pleasant Portuguese accent.

"Pero mira quien este aqui!" booms a voice from behind us, a large muscular *hombre* with a pair of hench-buddies beside him.

This apparent acquaintance of Veronica's leans over and kisses her a little closer to the mouth than I think appropriate. The fucking guy's acting like I'm not even here. I already don't like him. *"Y este, quien es?"* He finally acknowledges me, smiling politely but seemingly unimpressed.

"Este es mi amigo, Georgie," replies Veronica. *"Georgie, esta es Hector."*

I don't know who Hector is and quite frankly I don't give a shit but *he* seems to think he's *El fucking Exigente* or the world's most interesting man from those beer commercials. The hand he holds out for me to shake resembles a mitt that could handle a good Nolan Ryan fastball. I'll be cordial and extend my more modest paw. *"Mucho gusto, Georgie."* As expected he's gripping it much more firmly than necessary. If I were alive the excessively forceful clasp from this typical macho posturing probably would have hurt. Instead its implied subtext, that he could have Veronica if he wants her, is just annoying the shit out of me.

Unlike those TV vampires, we don't bend steel with our bare hands and leap tall buildings in a single bound, but being undead does allow us to use our bodies with an abandon that wasn't possible when we were alive. Our steady diet of blood enables us to concentrate all our energies into one area if we choose to do so. Right now I'm concentrating them on my grip. "The pleasure is all mine, *Señor Hector.*" *El Exigente* smirks at my *pathetic* little effort to match his brawn. Not impressed *amigo*? Okay, how about if I squeeze little harder?

His eyebrows creep downwards.

A troubled expression crosses his face. He tries to pull his hand away. Not so fast, amigo, I'm having a little fun. A little tighter maybe? "Veronica and I are going to have a little dinner. Would you care to join us?" Mr. Big remains stoic but he and I both know that his knuckles are about to break and his eyes are about to tear.

"Georgie, what are you doing?" scolds Veronica.

Uh-oh, I think I fucked up. I better let go.

The perplexed glare on Hector's face as he pulls his hand from my loosened grip is one that is familiar to me. It's the same one Veronica's trombone playing ex gave me outside her apartment. Felípe the host looks like he's afraid a scene might develop as Hector's buddies ponder whether they should step in. They're probably figuring, though, that it would be even more humiliating for him if they do. But I'm more concerned with Veronica's expression. For the first time since I've known her she is looking at me like I'm a turd on the sidewalk. She doesn't even know what to say to her amigo.

Señor Grande nods sheepishly, holding his aching knuckles. *"Disfrute, querida, pase una buena noche."* Veronica remains speechless, shaking her head apologetically as he exits the restaurant.

"What was that?" she asks, looking like she suddenly doesn't know me.

Yeah right. I'm sure this kind of crap happens around her all the time. But if she wants me to point out the obvious, I will. "Veronica, you know how dogs piss on trees to mark their territory? Well it looks like your buddy Hector felt the need to do a little marking."

"So what does that mean, I'm like territory to you?"

"Come on Veronica. Don't pretend like you're not used to that."

"What does *that* mean?"

Felípe dutifully stands by holding our menus wondering whether we'll ever follow him to our table.

"Listen, Veronica, I know the game."

"What game?" she asks through tightened lips.

"Oh, come on, the whole deal with guys tripping all over themselves to get your attention. They circle around you, trying to measure up. I mean, that's okay, that's who you are. That's the kind of attention you draw. Me, I'm not going to let—"

"So that's what you think I am?"

"Hey, so what if you are? It doesn't matter to me. Who am I to judge?"

Her eyes are tearing up. Nice going, dumb ass. Shit, now I feel bad. What the hell is wrong with me?

Veronica reaches above her chest and yanks off the pendant. "Take it."

My undead heart sinks as I slowly lift my hand and let her place it in my palm. The irony is that I should be happy. This couldn't have gone any better. My brutish behavior couldn't have disillusioned her more.

Veronica storms out of the restaurant, making me feel more of these feelings that I shouldn't be feeling. She rushes up the block attempting to catch up to her friend and apologize. It would now be perfectly understandable if she never wants to see me again socially, which is just how I should want it.

Right?

Right?

Hello, Nicky? This is what you wanted, right?

The pendant with broken clasp in my hand now has me questioning the intentions of my behavior. Was I trying to discourage Veronica from getting closer to me or did I really *want* to mark *my* territory? In other words, was I drawing a line in the sand and daring Hector to cross it?

I can see her out in the street, half a block away, talking to *El Exigente* and his *muchachos*. One of them opens the door to the passenger side of a white Cadillac parked across the street, holding her hand as she goes in. She's only gone a few seconds, not even a block away, and yet I find myself already missing her.

How did this happen?

11

The blurred faces above me made muffled noises that I couldn't comprehend. I was cold, shivering, with hazy recollections drifting in and out my mind, reflexively pushing away terrifying images. Teeth tearing at my neck. A stream of blood, my blood, forming a pool under me.

My head felt like a two-ton block of cement. Lifting it was an impossibility. And then there was the other sound, a distant one that wasn't coming from the two blurs above me. A minute or so passed before I realized it was coming from me. It was the sound of my own moaning.

The voices started clearing up—enough for me to determine that they were two male voices, more curious than concerned about my well-being.

Was I abducted by aliens?

"Take it easy, young man," said the one closest to me. His voice was thin, a little rough, like someone who had smoked too many cigarettes.

"He's resistant," said the second voice, which was

softer and higher pitched.

And though I remained lying down, motionless, it felt like I was falling into a deep wide canyon with no promise of landing, a sensation that led to nausea. I bolted up into a sitting position.

"Easy! Easy, young man," said the rougher voice as they both tried to ease me back down.

"He's strong," said the softer voice.

"Stay down, young man, you need to stay down," said the other.

The red, I started to remember all the red. And I recalled being scared, having no control. Again I fought to sit up. "Hold him down," barked the cigarette-worn voice.

Despite their efforts, I shot up and threw them back easily, like flicking lint off a sweater. As the two blurry figures picked themselves up off the floor, I noted that I was on a couch in someone's apartment. But whose? And where?

The room was spinning, not only left to right, but also over and under like those tunnels in Coney Island. As one of the blurry figures sprung forward and tackled me back down to the couch, images began to clear. Again I tried to fight. I was overpowered. The guy with the rougher voice straddled me and sat on my chest. Not ready to give in, I made another effort to rise but was halted by a hard sharp object that was pressing against my heart.

His face came into focus. It matched his voice, jagged, cruel, and unshaven with lines and scars of a life not spent behind a desk. His salt and pepper hair was greasy and combed in a spiky cut. He had a turquoise earring on his left ear but it did nothing to soften his appearance. The object causing the increasing pressure on my chest looked strangely familiar. Was it? Could it be...?

"Young man, I am leaning my body right up against this wooden stake which is pointed directly at the center of your heart," said the cigarette-ravaged voice. "Now the three of us have a lot to talk about. But if there is any upward movement on your part, this stake will pierce right through your heart and end any chance of us having a friendly little chat."

"Travis, he's scared," said the softer, more sympathetic voice. "He doesn't know what's happening." There was an understatement! I looked at my higher-pitched abductor. He was tall and wiry. I figure he was about in his early 30's, maybe twenty years younger than his partner. His hair was blond; his face was smooth. Dare I say it? He was actually pretty. "We don't want to hurt you," he said in almost a maternal tone. "Just try to calm down and listen to us. You've been through a lot. Okay?"

Travis took a little pressure off the stake. "What do you say, young man, can we talk?"Did I have a choice? I nodded cooperatively. Cautiously, Travis pulled the stake away and helped me sit up. Deciding that I was no longer a threat, he placed the stake on a coffee table in front of the couch next to a copy of the *Village Voice*. Guns n' Roses were on the cover. I remembered seeing that issue on a newsstand on the way to Mantle's. But I still was unable to latch on to any thought that could piece together what was happening. Yes, my eyes were coming into focus and yes, my hearing was starting to clear up; my mind though was lagging way behind. Mantle's, red, what was with all the red?

Travis and his friend sat down on a love seat adjacent to the couch I was sitting on. I looked at my surroundings. The apartment was neat and tastefully decorated except for the mess I made wrestling to break free.

Cigarette-voice had a way of sounding polite and threatening at the same time. "I'm Travis and this here is Donny. We looked through your wallet so we already know your name is Nicholas." Check. Wait a minute. There was a check, a bonus check. Was this attack all about the check? Travis read my expression. "If you're worried about your check, it's still in your pocket."

"You've been through a lot," said Donny. "Do you remember anything?"

Orel Hershiser, why was I thinking about Orel Hershiser? The Ritz-Carlton, the Star Lounge; I couldn't remember why but I was developing the suspicion that Stefanie wouldn't have been too happy about something that I did. A sick feeling set in. I reached for my neck. "NO!!!" The flesh was torn and jagged. Travis and Donny saw the panic and got up to try and calm me.

"Sit down, young man. Sit down," said Travis.

"NO! NO!" I continued to struggle.

"Nicholas, sit down," said Travis pushing me back down on the couch. "We're going to help you." Help? It seemed to me I was a little bit beyond being helped.

Donny placed his hand on my shoulder. "What's the last thing you remember?"

I felt the caked blood around the open gash above my collar. "That woman, who was she?"

"Her name is Simone," answered Travis.

"What! You *know* her?"

"You could say we have a history." Travis lowered his collar to expose a shredded wound similar to mine.

A halo of images circled above me, leading to the naked firm-breasted redhead straddling my hips. Normally that might be an appealing and arousing thought. Not so much when a piece of your neck is hanging from her teeth and your blood is spraying across her maniacally laughing face.

The wooden stake on the table, what's with that? This was all too fucked-up to believe. "What the hell is going on?"

"You don't have any idea what just happened to you, do you?" said Donny.

"Jesus! What time is it?" I ignored my queasiness and sprang up from the couch. "I have to get back to my family."

Travis gestured me down. "Young man, right now the last thing you need is to see your family."

"What do mean by that? What did you do to my family?"

"Nobody did anything to your family," said Donny. "Your family is fine."

"What time is it? My wife, she must be worried sick."

Travis came over and led me back down to the couch. "Nicholas, I can't stop you from doing what you want but right now you need to understand what is happening. You need to know your condition before you go back out and... Well, before you go out and walk among those that are not like you."

I stood up again. "What does *that* mean?" By that point I had determined that the two men gently restraining me were not a threat. In fact, as they were saying, it seemed like they wanted to help. Regardless of that, I was becoming more agitated.

Travis remained firm. "Calm down young man, you need to understand your current situation."

"And what situation is that?"

Travis took me by the shoulders and looked at me face-to-face. "You may be standing here, young man, talking and moving all about just like you have for the past number of years throughout your life, but the fact is you did not survive Simone's attack."

"What! What are you talking about? Where are we,

anyway? Whose apartment is this?"

"This is our apartment," said Donny. "We're on Fourth Street in Soho."

I was baffled. "What the fuck am I doing in Soho?"

"Never mind that," said Travis. "Tell us what the last thing you remember is."

"This is bullshit! I'm going home!" I ran for the front door. This time neither of them tried to stop me as I unlocked their door and bolted out.

In the building's corridor to the right of their apartment was a stairway leading to a small foyer at the front of the building. The sounds from the street outside comforted me. But they weren't the only sounds I was hearing. There was a couple on what I think was the fourth floor. They were screwing. On the floor below I was even able to hear someone flipping through the pages of a magazine while he was taking a shit.

"Aren't we going to go after him?" asked Donny from inside his and Travis' apartment.

How could I hear all this?

"He's going to have to realize things for himself," replied Travis. "Once he does, he'll come back for answers—if he survives."

On the first floor, through the glass door at the front of the building, I could see city life going on, business as usual. It brought the promise of restored sanity. But what about that remark Travis made, me coming back for answers? Whatever. I was not about to stop. If I could get back home to Stefanie, Jessie and Davey, once there, I could try and sort out what happened. I might not have the faintest idea of where to begin or how to even try to describe what occurred, but Stefanie had always been there for me in the past. Any chance of me putting my life back in order would have to begin with her.

It was early evening. Lights were coming at me from every direction as I stepped out onto Fourth Street. Streetlights, headlights, traffic lights, neon lights, I was overwhelmed like a small-town tourist from Idaho. The clothes I had on were the ones I wore that night at Mantle's. Since I was dizzily stumbling along the sidewalk, bumping into random pedestrians, they probably assumed I was some sleazeball corporate suit that just staggered out of a three-martini business dinner. The dried up splotches of blood probably passed for vomit.

A taxi came to a screeching stop as I spiraled out into the street. The driver stuck his head out, waving his fist and shouting a string of unpleasantries in Arabic. When I made it to the other side, I collapsed onto the steps of a brownstone duplex where a well-dressed mother shielded the eyes of her little kindergartener. The faint sound coming from my throat caught the child's attention.

"Help me."

They quickly scurried past me and ducked into their home. The mother was menstruating. I smelt it! I didn't know how I picked that up but I did. And it was making me...hungry?

A few minutes later I was able to pick myself up. My vision became clearer—enough so that I could see the typical New Yorker passersby avoiding eye contact with the wobbly spic in the filthy, wrinkled business suit. It was probably for the best. They were no longer fellow Big Apple residents to me. They were prey.

At the corner intersection, a pair of young ladies was looking into the display window of an art shop. They were students at the Metropolitan College campus on Canal Street. Though still weak and disoriented, I made my way towards them and pretended to admire the art in the window from a couple of steps away. The pretty little things were oblivious to any possible threat from the foul-odored stranger that was studying their reflections which were cast upon the glass. They were more interested in the abstract nuances of some local artist's painting, batting around bullshit analytical critiques that made them feel more discerning.

A delectable assortment of scents came from their direction. One of them had a nice floral essence while the other was earthy, yet sweet. The pangs were unmistakable. My body felt heavy, my mouth dry. Instinctively I tried to take a deep breath to soak it all in.

Nothing.

What the hell?

Again I tried inhaling with nothing making its way into my lungs. Okay, how about exhaling? Nothing! Nothing passed through in either direction. Yet I didn't feel like I was suffocating or choking!

"He'll come back for answers," said Travis when I left him and Donny back at their apartment.

He was right. I had to go back for answers.

But there was something I needed more. And it was only a few feet away.

All humans know the taste of blood, whether it be from cleanings at the dentist or from licking off a cut on your finger as a child. For most, it's not a taste that is particularly appealing.

The menstrual cycle of the woman in front of the duplex with the child had activated my senses. But why her menstrual cycle? And why did it stir up such a hunger?

I was craving.

Craving for my dry throat to be coated by what ran through the veins of the lovely little art admirers.

At the expense of their young lives.

I had to get home quick. There was something wrong with me, terribly wrong. Was it hallucinogenics? Was I on some kind of substance that was about to make me do something I could never take back?

To see if I was presentable enough, I looked at the glass for my reflection.

It wasn't there!

Where was it? The girls' reflections were there, where was mine? I raised my hand and touched the glass, searching for a sign of myself. The earthier student turned towards me. She let out a gasp. Hearing her reaction, I turned to look at her. The other one then looked at me. Her mouth opened as if to shriek but no sound came out. They just turned and fled. It was as if they had just come face-to-face with Death itself.

Not having a reflection, I couldn't see what they had seen because the cacophony of my emotions had not yet taken its toll.

"You need to know your condition before you go back out and walk among those that are not like you."

What did he mean by that?

"You may be standing here, young man, talking and moving all about just like you have for the past number of years throughout your life, but the fact is you did not survive Simone's attack."

That made absolutely no sense. Nothing was making any fucking sense!

I turned back to the window. This time my reflection appeared. They *had* seen Death! My face was hollow, cadaverous—the look of a man that... shouldn't be walking. I may have been above the earth, but I belonged under.

My face contorted. I sobbed loudly on the Soho street. Death was crying. Yet heavily as I wept, not one tear. I concluded that a dead man couldn't shed any.

A supportive hand took my shoulder. It was Travis. His expression conveyed no sympathy. Later, as I grew to know him, I learned that's how he was. His face remained the same whether he was happy, sad, or really pissed off. Donny was next to him. His face mirrored mine. Emotionally he was the exact opposite of Travis.

"Let's go back inside," said Travis. "It's going to be a different world for you from now on. You've got a lot to learn."

12

"Please be honest with us, Mr. Negrón. How is our daughter doing? What do you see in Myra's future?" Gabriella Crawford is a hard working mother of two that commutes ninety minutes every day to her job at a major publishing house. Her husband Horace, an equally dedicated family man, works extra shifts at Port Authority to help pay for their three-bedroom apartment in one of the finer high-rises in Flatbush. Their fifteen-year-old son Nate is a typical young man of his age that has left his chair at the dining table to catch the opening tip of the Knick game on TV. He is unaware that sitting beside him on the couch is the father of Davey Negrón, the substance abuse counselor enjoying a hospitable dinner with the Crawfords.

"She's making progress," answers Davey. "I am reasonably confident that she has a chance to straighten her life out in the not-too-distant future." My boy, you are such a horseshit liar.

Mr. Crawford can tell. "I'm sorry, reasonably

confident? What does that mean?" I feel so bad for this poor bastard. Horace Crawford is a burly bear of a man that always breaks down into tears at the family therapy sessions when his daughter goes into her hostile, disrespectful tirades about how overly strict he was in bringing her up. Gabriella also gets shredded by Myra for her disciplinary methods. She rants that her mother's corporal punishment drove her to seek refuge with neighborhood friends whose street activities were less than wholesome.

"It means that each day brings your daughter farther from the old Myra and closer to the new Myra." With a line of shit like that, Davey, someday you could run for office.

Why he bothers, I don't know. Personally, I wouldn't waste any time on a worthless little sludge like Myra Crawford. In fact, if it weren't for the heroin-tainted blood that's running through her veins, I would have no trouble feasting on her skinny little neck. The Crawfords, though, are exceedingly kind and generous of heart, which unfortunately has Davey extending himself far beyond the call of professional demand.

At all the sessions I have personally observed while keeping tabs on my boy, Myra has done nothing but throw trash-mouthed bile at the two people who are fighting the hardest to save her life. Why? Because they are trying to keep her away from Darryl, the heroin-addicted, gonorrhea-infected, twice-arrested piece of shit that has an inexplicable hold on her. Only for the vermin that treats her like an under-the-bridge crack whore, while spreading his venereal disease onto her, along with getting her addicted to heroin, does any warmth pass through Myra's lips. And that's with her knowing that he's been screwing around with some other junk-addicted skank from the same neighborhood. But hey,

Myra puts the blame for that on her parents too because they tried to distance her from him. Yes, *minor* flaws notwithstanding, Myra remains convinced that Darryl is the love of her life.

"I gotta take this." Davey's vibrating cell brings him a welcome reprieve from the doubting scrutiny of the Crawfords. He reaches for the phone in his pocket and steps away from the table.

Shit! That reminds me. I forgot to put my cell phone in silent mode. Luckily Veronica is still pissed off at me so I won't be getting any phone calls from her. But what if she or some telemarketer decides to reach out to me while I'm here? The whole Crawford family and my son will be wondering why the sofa cushion next to Nate is ringing.

By walking out of the kitchen into the foyer by the front door, Davey hopes to be a moderate enough distance away to be out of everyone's hearing range.

He is.

Except for mine.

Even with Knick announcer Mike Breen's animated play-by-play on the TV, I can hear the conversation clearly. Someone has "slipped out", and from the look on Davey's face and his glance over at the dinner table, I don't need to hear any further to know it was Myra.

Okay my boy, let's see how you handle *this*. "I'm sorry. I thank you so much for the nice dinner, but I need to tend to an emergency."

Gabriella's antennas are up. "Is everything all right?"

"Oh no, uh yeah, uh, it's okay. I just have to get back to the clinic." He's full of crap and the Crawford's both know it. They've been saturated with so many lies from their daughter over the past couple of years that they know bullshit when they hear it. But what are they gonna do? They've lost control of their daughter. Their only hope is to count on the help of those who have been there before.

Like Davey.

Each member of my family has had to grapple in his or her own way with emotions that have never been sorted out. Davey, now 38 years old, is the same age I was when my life was cut short by an involuntary tryst with a demon with red hair.

My disappearance was scandalous.

Painful.

Humiliating.

Having gone through loss myself, I had a clear understanding of Davey's suffering. Many nights after the Ritz-Carlton, I sat beside him in his bedroom, wanting to put comforting arms around my son. I wanted to tell him everything would be all right, even though I knew nothing could be farther from the truth.

As he grew older, Davey channeled his energy into becoming a promising athlete and focused all his efforts on becoming a professional baseball player. He delivered on that promise and was named the All City second baseman three years in a row, drawing the attention of the Pittsburgh Pirates scouting staff.

Uncle Dominic, meaning well, would regularly remind Davey of how his dad was a pretty good second baseman, too, and how proud he would have been to see his son not only follow in his footsteps, but also exceed him.

"I'm not following in his footsteps," replied Davey. "I'm staying *loyal* to *my* family." Thanks, I really needed to hear that.

The Pirates drafted Davey right out of high school, but through it all, he was hurting. Stefanie tried her best to give him all the support he needed and went to every game she could to cheer him on. But in the end, Davey missed not having his father there to share his proud moments with (even if he was a cheating scumbag). Dad, after all, helped him get his start in Little League and gave him pointers on how to play the position, so growing to be one of the most talented players in the city and not having his father there to see it took an emotional toll.

Talk about history repeating itself, the drinking parties with his teammates helped him to sometimes forget the emptiness. Also like his father, he grew distant. Strangely enough, his mother Stefanie, who was able to reel his father back into the world of the living twenty years before, could not do the same for her son. As it was, she was grappling with the same emotions, compounded by the heartbreak stemming from the nature of her husband's disappearance.

The excess baggage gradually took its toll to the point where Davey's skills began to diminish. Ground balls that he'd been gobbling up before had started elude him and pass through for base hits. Fastballs that he had been lining into centerfield were now turning into pop-ups to the catcher.

The scouts and the coaching staffs in the disappointed Pirates organization took notice and after observing Davey for a full season of Single A Ball, they began to suspect that he was no longer going to be the player they had signed. Equally disappointed by his sodden performance, Davey promised to regain focus and again become the player that they had invested in. He never got the chance. The Pittsburgh Pirates decided to cut their losses, releasing him before the next spring. And young as he was, with the promise that he once showed, the sad reality for Davey was that in the world of professional sports word tends to spread fast. No other organizations offered him a contract.

Much to his mother's heartbreak, Davey soon found himself working at odd jobs during the day while drenching his liver with vodka at night, making him a miserable lout to everyone around including his family. More than once, Uncle Dominic threatened to bash his nephew's head in for being disrespectful to Stefanie, but even that didn't stop Davey from spiraling downwards. Before long there were consequences.

They came on the night of a bachelor party at Tito Puente's restaurant in City Island where Davey and a friend were so loaded that they couldn't decide who the "designated driver" would be. It was a big joke to them as they boastfully debated which one of them was less fucked up. Davey eventually won (lost?) and took charge of the wheel. They didn't get far. The parking lot was on a pier and inexplicably, Davey wound up driving the car into the river below. Their more sober friends saw the disaster from inside the restaurant and ran to their rescue. Miraculously, they saved Davey and his friend before the car sank too deep into the water. Thankfully no lives were lost nor was there any permanent physical damage to Davey or his friend, but it could have been a lot worse had he driven any further.

The court had no sympathy for the young man whose father's murder had been a tabloid scandal just a few years before. They served him with a one-year sentence.

It might have been a blessing.

The year that Davey spent at Westchester County Correctional Facility became the turning point that he needed, though there were stumbling blocks here and there. Like any other prisoner, Davey had to deal with the little alliances, the internal predators and the general rot of our society. For the most part he handled himself pretty well—especially since he was the star of the prison's baseball team. The one exception was a bulky brown-toothed man-beast that roughed Davey up after he successfully fought off his sexual advances. Mysteriously, the slug ended up in the center of a circle of blood on the floor tiles in the showers with a huge chunk of his neck missing.

Anyone else want to fuck with my boy?

While behind bars, Davey began to study sociology, which he continued after being released. Shortly thereafter, he earned his degree and took a job at the inpatient rehabilitation clinic in Brooklyn where he works these days as a substance abuse counselor. And while I am proud of Davey for straightening his life out, I notice that he, like his undead father, also tends to keep relationships at an arm's length. Outside of a few casual flings, Davey has never let any woman become a regular part of his life and has basically shut the door to anyone that tries to get too close. Like father, like son. No one gets in. The ending result is that this pattern leads to him getting far too involved in his work.

#

Okay Davey, now this no longer qualifies as going above and beyond. Psychotic and suicidal would be a more apt description for walking by yourself into a neglected tenement on Nostrand Avenue (although he's really not by himself). What can he possibly expect to accomplish here? This dump is even worse than the project Veronica lives in.

The mailboxes he's sifting through mostly have broken locks with some of the labels scratched out so that you can't identify who they belong to. The door to the box he's looking at does have a label. It belongs to someone named Briggs in apartment 1C. There's nothing inside the box, although I have no guess as to what Davey's looking for.

Something smells bad.

And it's not just the stuffed sour scent in these hallways, where the paint on the walls is peeled and replaced by spray-painted, misspelled vulgarities.

Apartment 1C is a couple of steps away, the second door to the right. Davey calmly walks towards what I'm presuming is Darryl's apartment. What the fuck is he thinking?

He presses the doorbell.

No ring.

Knock! Knock!

Who's there?

The obviously suicidal son of the guy who had his blood sucked out of him at the Ritz-Carlton.

I can smell Darryl approaching the opposite side of the door. The guy could use a shower.

The door opens. It reveals a squirty unkempt punk in cornrows, wearing a stained *wifebeater*, jeans and no shoes. His image matches his scent.

Darryl sizes up my son with a disdainful sneer. "I think you got the wrong motherfuckin' apartment."

Davey is neither impressed nor intimidated. "Is Myra here?"

"What? Who the fuck are you?"

"I'm Myra's counselor. And I need to bring her back to complete her treatment program."

"I don't know what the fuck you talkin' about, nigga. Get the fuck outa here."

Darryl attempts to close the door but it's blocked by Davey's foot.

"How about I go inside and wait? Maybe she'll turn up." My boy's got more balls than brains.

WAIT! NO!

Quicker than a flash, Darryl swings the door open and

grabs Davey's collar, shoving a gun up against his throat. "How about I blow your fucking brains right out of your fucking head?"

Davey raises his hand with the intent of grabbing Darryl's wrist.

He doesn't get the chance.

An unseen force knocks the gun out of Darryl's hand. The same force also throws Darryl on the floor where he lands a foot away from the gun he just dropped (a miscalculation on my part). Both Davey and Darryl are now stricken by confusion but this is no time for anyone to stop and ponder.

That includes me.

Darryl spots his gun, which is easily within reach. Davey also goes for it but stops as he witnesses Darryl's head snap back before the dirtbag crumbles onto the hallway tiles.

Davey's dumbfounded. He has no idea what he just saw.

Never mind that! You almost just got killed, dumb ass. Get the hell out of here.

Now!

Good sense prevails. Davey backs away and scampers out of the building.

Man, that was a nice clean kick. Shit, I could play for the Jets. They're always missing their field goals, anyway.

Did it break his neck?

Let's see.

Well, there's a surprise. The fucker's still breathing.

Alright, how about a nice little quick twist like this.

Ah, there. That should do it.

His head is nice and wobbly now, like the Dwight Gooden bobble head doll on top of my refrigerator.

#

The front door unlocks. If Davey had gotten here just a little later, maybe he could have intercepted her. But how does she even *have* keys? No one in the clinic is supposed to have outside possessions while undergoing treatment.

It's dark inside her boyfriend's apartment. Myra reaches for the light switch. "Baby?"

The lights flick on to reveal a living room couch sodden with blood that's dripping onto the wood, mold-stained floor. On the couch, sprawled with the inners of his neck exposed, is her lifeless candy man, his wide-opened eyes staring back at her.

Myra opens her mouth to scream but a hand covers it and pulls her back before she can make a sound. The trashy skank makes no effort to break free. She's too paralyzed with fright.

"Listen you scummy little gutter tramp," says the voice behind her. "This is the only warning you get because personally I would be quite happy to see you rot right there next to that lowlife you call a boyfriend." A panicked squeal is smothered by the palm of the unknown voice's hand. "You have done nothing but break the hearts and ruin the lives of the people that love you and are trying to help you. For their sakes I am going to let you live. But if you ever take any more junk or behave with anything less than complete respect for those people who are devoting their lives to you, and you know who I'm talking about, right?"

With the hand over her mouth, she can't reply.

"Nod if you do!"

A tear streaks downward. Myra complies.

"Good! Because if I find out that you have been anything less than the sweet, wonderful daughter that they deserve, you will be reunited with your Darryl in the worst corner of Hell you could ever imagine. Do you understand me?"

Myra nods again.

"Good, because believe me, I know. I live there. And I would love to take you there with me."

13

"You may have trouble accepting what we've been telling you but you can't deny what you were feeling out there."

I remained stubborn. How couldn't I? All the evidence I'd faced pointed towards nothing that could make any kind of sense to someone who's right of mind. "I don't know what's happening to me. What the hell is going on?"

Travis did his best to be patient (not his strongest attribute). "We're trying to tell you but you're not letting us."

"No, this is like some bad dream, or something. She must've drugged me. This must be like some kind of drugged up nightmare."

"Oh, this is a nightmare, all right," he said. "And it can be a very painful one if you don't listen to us."

"Let me use your phone. I have to call my wife. I have to tell her where I am."

"Don't do that," said Donny.

"Why the hell not?"

"Young man..." Travis walked over to a coffee table and pulled a newspaper from under a stack of magazines.

"Travis don't," said Donny.

"Enough skirting around this young man's reality," replied Travis. "Putting him out there unprepared is not only a risk to him, but it is also a risk to us." He raised the newspaper and held the headline up to my face. "You're front page news, boy."

RITZ-CARLTON LOVER FEARED DEAD

The photo was from the prior year's Atlantic Indemnity Sales Leaders Conference. It must have been supplied by the home office. I wanted to say that I thought it was one of those gag headlines from the Coney Island boardwalk but it all looked too authentic. There was far too much detail. Besides an accurate, descriptive account of my disappearance, there were supporting and corresponding stories covering the case from other angles. There was also the usual gossip on Page Six about Cindy Crawford, Princess Diana and Michael Jackson. Even the sports coverage was complete. The Mets were down three games to two. It was too elaborate for a gag—and too expensive. And what for? Why would someone go through so much trouble and such cost? When was everyone going to come out of hiding to have their big laugh?

Something horrible had taken place. That much I was sure of. And if details were the part of the puzzle that was missing, the newspaper I held in my hands was more than thorough. "My God, I have to call Stefanie. I have to let her know I'm okay. I can't let this—"

Travis snatched the paper from my hand. "You will

call no one."

"Travis," said Donny, shaking his head at him.

"They need to know I'm all right," I insisted.

"You are not all right," barked Travis. "You are dead! I am dead! Donny is dead! That's pretty damn far from being all right!" Travis' patience was all but gone. "How much more do you need to see before you face the truth?" Travis pointed to the door where I ran out. "What happened across the street was not your imagination. It was real. You were thirsting to feed off those young little pretties across the street. You know it. You felt it. In fact, *we* felt it. We're able to sense when another one of us is ready to feed in our area."

"One of *you*? What does *that* mean, *one of you*? And what's all this stupid dead crap?"

"Stop and think, young man. We know how this all sounds and looks to you. But let's look at the facts."

"You were attacked at the hotel room. Can we agree that that happened?"

As surreal as everything was, I had to try and sort everything out so I went along. "Yes."

"Good."

Behind Travis, Donny nodded approvingly.

"Now let's continue," said Travis. "You woke up here with us. And you find yourself with torn flesh at the base of your neck. And you have a memory of this woman draining the blood out of your neck that night at the hotel. Correct?" I reluctantly nodded. "Across the street, you were overcome with emotion when you couldn't find a reflection of yourself on the window next to those little pretties. Then a reflection did turn up. Am I right?" I nodded again. "What did you see?" He knew damn well what I saw. I didn't need to reply. "And then the ladies saw the same thing, didn't they?" They sure did. Their lives were in danger and they knew it. They probably had no idea what the fuck I was, but then neither did I. All I knew was that I wanted to chomp on their little necks and draw every drop of their blood down my throat.

"You have a genetic resistance to what you are," said Donny. "When you are well fed and you are able to control your emotions, you are able to maintain the appearance you had before your death. But once you lose that control, you cannot hide what you are."

"And what is that?"

Travis shook his head. "Boy, how much more do we have to spell it out for you? It's all laid out. Your neck, the lack of a reflection on that glass, your thirst for blood, you can deny it for as long as you want, but at some point you are going to have to accept what you are."

"Do you realize how ridiculous you sound?"

"Believe it or not, we do," said Donny. "But you don't have time to gauge what's real and what is not. When the sun comes up—"

"Oh, what, now you're going to tell me that I have to sleep in some kind of coffin?"

Travis and Donny gazed at each other, deciding who was going to answer. They didn't need to.

"You gotta be shitting me."

"It's your genetic resistance that is keeping you from accepting what you are," said Donny.

"Yeah, what is that with the genetic resistance? Genetic resistance to what?"

"I'm going to come right out with it," said Donny. "You are a vampire, a vampire with genetic resistance."

Okay, they said it. "I gotta get the fuck out of here." I turned towards the door.

"Mouth off with your filthy tongue all you want," said Travis. "But know that we are real. And so are you.

Personally I couldn't care less if you walk out that door right now and shatter the hearts of your family more than they have already been shattered. But I am giving you a chance to think about it."

"Think about what?"

"What you've become. You need to understand the change that's come over you since that night in that hotel room."

Donny chimed in. "You really are free to go if you want. But first you should let us talk to you. We can help you. And maybe you can help us."

There were no answers anywhere in sight to the windstorm of questions flying around inside my head so I reluctantly agreed to listen. It was pointless to do anything or go anywhere until I could make some kind of sense of what was happening. I sat down and opened the floor. "Okay, go ahead. Tell me what you have to say."

Donny sat beside me and began to speak gently as if that could possibly make things more manageable to comprehend. "We had to take you out of there. We couldn't let anyone find you the way she had left you. We want as little evidence of these types of occurrences in our area as possible. Your case is already raising too many unanswered questions."

"And questions lead to investigations," added Travis. "We don't like investigations. Our business in this city is conducted without littering the streets with bodies. The rest of our kind aren't as careful. They tend to be nomads and don't care what kind of mess they leave behind."

I stuck my hand out at Travis. "Give me that newspaper again." He handed it back and watched quietly along with Donny as I read the witnesses' accounts.

I was last seen at the Ritz-Carlton with a red-haired woman in a red dress. That much I knew. After that night we had both been declared missing. The article then went on to describe the crime scene. It was determined that all of the blood splattered around the hotel room was mine. And with that amount of blood loss there was little or no hope of finding me alive. My red-haired lover, though, (yes, that's how they described her) was believed to be alive (how ironic) and she was wanted for questioning.

The cyclone of scattered recollections spinning above my head started falling into place. The blurs were coming into focus. I raised my head from the paper to find Travis and Donny staring back at me.

"You, me, Donny, we're all genetically resistant," said Travis. His tone was softer but he still sounded threatening. I would come to learn that that was just him. That's how he always sounded. "Being genetically resistant causes us to retain our human identity. It can be an advantage and it can be a disadvantage. In your case the main disadvantage is that it will give you problems feeding. And as you can see you will also have problems accepting what you are."

"If you were not genetically resistant you wouldn't even care who you were," said Donny. "You would feed off anyone, even someone that you had loved while you were alive."

"What we have is communicable like a disease," said Travis. "So a smart vampire—" Interrupted by a mocking snort, Travis glared as I shook my head before continuing. "A smart vampire always makes sure that when he feeds he doesn't leave any chance of his victims rising again. Our lady friend Simone has a pattern of not caring what she leaves behind. She also knows that this is our city and that we will destroy her given the opportunity. Like I said before, we can sense when another one of us is feeding in our territory."

"Territory?"

"Yes, territory," said Donny. She probably knew we were coming and left you as a calling card. She likes to taunt."

"Taunt!" I was waiting, hoping, for someone to break out into a big laugh. But there was no laugh, nothing but dead seriousness, a pun that I wish *I* could laugh at. "Who is this Simone, anyway?"

"She's the one that made you and me what we are now," replied Travis. "She's as savage as they come and with more power than any of us combined, which brings us to why you are here."

"Yeah, let's get to that, shall we?"

"We need to find her and end her existence."

"What's that got to do with me?"

"Simone likes to travel," explained Travis. "But her favorite place to be is here, right here in New York. So every now and then she likes to come around and rattle our cage. This was her city once and she'd like nothing more than to reclaim it. That means getting rid of us. There's no coexisting when it comes to our kind. It's either her or us. And *we're* not going anywhere."

"So... again, what is that you're looking for from me?"

"Is there anything that you can remember from that night that could help us find her?"

I shook my head. "The first time I ever saw her was at the hotel. I'd never seen her before and obviously I haven't seen her since."

"Are you sure?" asked Donny.

"Think," said Travis.

Much as I scrambled to get my decimated brain in order, nothing was coming to mind other than what must have been going on in Stefanie's. "Jesus, I need to call my wife."

Travis slapped his leg impatiently.

Donnie, while not as exasperated, reiterated that I should reconsider. "You may want to call your wife now but when you accept what has happened and what you have become, you might feel differently. This is not going to be the way you want your wife and children to remember you."

Travis grew more frustrated. "One more time, do you have any information, anything that could help us find Simone?"

"Hey man, don't you think that if I had anything I would tell you? With everything that had happened don't you think I would be the first one to want that Simone woman dead?"

"She already is," said Travis. "Just like the three of us."

"He does have a point," said Donny to Travis. "He would want her destroyed just as much we do. Give him some time. This is a lot for him to absorb. With a little more time, he might begin to remember some things."

After studying me for a moment, Travis put his arm under my shoulder. "Can you stand up?"

I pulled my arm away. "I can stand up on my own."

"Good, come with us."

They started walking towards what I figured was their bedroom. Not interested. By that time, I had seen enough of how they related to one another. These roommates were sharing more than just the rent.

"What's in there?" I asked.

Travis smirked and frowned at the same time. (How does he do that?) "Relax, young man. You're not our type."

Donny opened the bedroom door. "Go ahead, look

inside.”

Not having been the most enlightened person when it came to the homosexual population, I walked over cautiously, in no rush to see what went on behind their bedroom door. The events that had led up to the state I was in probably should have prepared me for anything—emphasis on the words *should have*.

If this was all a big practical joke they sure pulled out all the stops. Their bedroom was pitch-black. Even their windows were painted black like the Stones song. In the middle of the room, to no surprise, was a neatly made queen-sized bed. But apparently, it was there only for play because on each side of the bed were two high-end cushiony coffins. I looked at them like they were both insane.

“We don’t have a guest coffin,” quipped Donny. “So when the sun comes up you’ll have to go in the closet where there are no windows. That’s where you’ve been for the last few days.”

Their story, the newspaper, my lack of reflection, my thirst for the blood of the college students across the street, the coffins—even with all that facing me, I was still waiting for a punchline. “What lunatic asylum did you two break out of?”

“Young man, if you want to end this *nightmare* of yours easily, I can hand you a stake and you can drive it through your own heart,” said Travis. “Personally, I don’t care.”

Donny shook his head. “Travis, there’s no need—”

“Donny, however, appears to have taken a liking to you. For some reason known only to him, Donny wants to help. If I were you I would take him up on his hospitality,” continued Travis. “On the other hand, if you wish to end this *nightmare* in more pain than you have ever felt in your entire life, then go home. And make sure your wife and kids are up to see you when the sun rises."

Donny kept trying to have Travis lighten up. "Travis..."

"You *will* learn the truth. That much you can count on," said Travis, eyeballing me. "The only question is, whether it'll be too late."

A couple of hours later, when they retired into their bedroom, I remained on the living room sofa, afraid, weak, with no idea of what to do. By that point, since neither of them was stopping me from leaving, any theory of them being captors or abductors was out. And since they were in their bedroom entertaining themselves, I concluded that they had no interest in having me join in their little party. In fact, all they really cared about was that redhead they referred to as Simone.

My mind was clearing. The ugly images from the Ritz-Carlton were becoming more vivid. If I was on narcotics and they were wearing off, my current situation still couldn't have been explained in any sane kind of manner. The nightmare idea was out, too. I felt way too alert. Everything around me was too real. And if this all was real, how was I going to explain what was in the papers to my family?

It was a little bit after 6:00 a.m. when I first felt the burn. And with the enhanced senses that I was developing, I detected a faint smoldering scent. It was my flesh.

I ran into the bedroom where my undead hosts laid undisturbed in their closed coffins. Once I was inside the darkened room the burning subsided a bit. But there was no sense in taking any chances. I went inside the closet, taking a seat on the floor and shutting the door.

My hosts had been very hospitable. They'd patched me up to the point where I was somewhat functioning, though weak and in dire need of energy. If I was going to figure out what had happened to me, I needed that energy back. And there was only one thing that could restore it.

14

"Listen, you son of a bitch! I know you're in there with that whore. I saw your car around the corner!"

Jessie was only twelve years old when my human existence was terminated at the Ritz-Carlton. Despite that and the fact that I haven't been around in twenty-seven years, she apparently has inherited my mouth. "Come on out so I can cut off your puny little dick and shove it down your throat!"

Otherwise it would have been a calm, quiet November night outside the door of this nice little house in suburban Long Island.

"You have three daughters at home and you're sticking your dick in this whore! Come on out, you coward!" growls Jessie, wielding a knife from one of her kitchen drawers. "You too, you skeevy little cunt! Come on out so I can cut up those fake tits of yours!"

Inside the house on the opposite side of the door, Ross Nemeth, my daughter's husband, is listening quietly next to his tarty lover, Naomi Shannon. I never liked this bastard and if I were alive when Jessie started dating him, I would have done everything I possibly could have to keep her from marrying him. This prick, who is thirteen years older than her, in his early fifties, had already been divorced once before and he had been living with another woman for about six years when they met. But as the owner of the successful real estate business where she worked, Nemeth knew how to dazzle my daughter with his healthy portfolio and strut his fiscal capabilities in front of her adoring eyes.

Jessie was also on hand to witness his problems with the woman he shared his house with. She was his first relationship after his divorce and they ended up having a daughter who was four years old when Jessie and this piece of shit got together. When *their* relationship ended a fierce custody battle ensued, which Nemeth eventually won when she was declared unfit with a serious substance abuse problem. This was the kind of shit Jessie walked into when she married this ass. Stefanie begged her not to do it. Rippey too, but neither had any luck in dissuading her.

Keeping out of sight while being only inches away from this wretched slime ball is a major challenge for me, but I remain seething quietly while Nemeth shelters himself in his fuck-buddy's love shack with all the shades down. Both are unclothed, quietly waiting for tropical storm Jessie to pass so they can run back to the bedroom where Nemeth can resume enjoying silicone-enhanced Bronski's.

It's suddenly quiet outside. The ringing and the knocking have stopped—not a good sign. Nemeth knows it, too. Jessie's not exactly known as the type that easily gives up. If anything, she's the type that would do something outrageous or explosive. I already had a son go to jail. I better go outside and see what she's up to.

I'll leave the bare-assed lovers to ponder their situation while I sneak out the back.

Passing some frames on the wall on my way out, I notice no family photos. No husband, no kids, just pictures of Naomi throughout the past couple of decades. Well, I shouldn't say *no* family pictures. There's one with her parents and one at a younger brother's graduation, but no family of her own. I'm not making anything out of it—just an observation. The only conclusion I *can* make from the photo above the mantle, where Nemeth left the flowers he bought, is that her tits were purchased sometime around the late nineties.

Quietly closing the back door and coming around to the front, I see Jessie still in her car, parked in Naomi's driveway. Stepping to the front of her car, I'm getting the uneasy feeling that she's enraged enough to drive it into the house, although at this moment the engine is still off.

Calm down Jessie. He's not worth it. Just stay behind that wheel and take a couple of deep breaths.

She's a grown woman now. A grown woman but still my child. A father hates to see his child in any kind of pain. And it's especially grating to see his daughter sitting alone, dejected, staring through the windshield of her car at the front door of the house where her husband's lover lives.

The last time Jessie saw me alive she was upset at me because I wouldn't let her go on a date with Tommy Puccio. I had once passed that kid in front of a liquor store where I heard him bragging to his friends about feeling up a girl at the movies. It immediately crossed him off the list of potential suitors for my daughter. The only thing I was going to let that little prick feel was my fists walloping against his skull if he ever put his hands on my baby girl. That protective instinct never leaves you, living, dead or undead.

Jessie grips the steering wheel tightly as if trying to steady her trembling hands. Her chest is heaving, her pain worsening by the second.

It builds.

I know how it builds—especially if you have unwelcome guests like *Los Ruidos* sounding off in your head. It just builds and builds until...

... don't, Jessie, don't...

... it builds; it builds...

... until it erupts.

This is not what I expected.

I'm not sure if it is a scream, a wail, a cry... all I know is that it's awful.

It brings me back thirty years. As a little girl Jessie's mouth would contort into a wide, trembling frown before letting out a screech that would rattle the frames on the walls. The adult version is even harder to watch—an asphyxiated pause of silence that erupts into a torrential bellowing. Thick lava-like tears ooze out of my daughter's eyes which are shut tighter than a vault as she leans her head against the steering wheel.

All this while, inside, that worm she calls a husband seeks refuge in the store-bought bosom of Naomi Shannon.

That fuck. I want to kill that fuck right now. The two of them, I can kill them both. I can feast on their blood, maybe even...

Fuck, what am I saying? Control, Nicky, control...

A frightened shriek echoes through the neighborhood. Dogs are barking. Windows light up on both sides of the street. The scream, it was Jessie! Her head is up from the steering wheel, and though the tears are probably blurring her vision, whatever she saw has completely taken all the color away from her face. I don't see anything around that could have caused such a reaction except...

Me!

My reflection! It's on her windshield! It turns out Jessie isn't the only one to have lost control of her emotions.

As quickly as it appeared, I just as quickly regained control. My reflection is gone. She has literally screamed me out of sight. Still, I have to get away, although the damage has already been done. I can distance myself all I want now but I can't run away from the fact that I have just traumatized my daughter, irreparably.

Scrambling halfway up the block, I can hear Nemeth running out of Naomi Shannon's house. "Jessie! Jessie, what's wrong?"

Her voice quivers. "I just saw a ghost. It...it was my father."

Nice going, Dad.

#

Understandably, Jessie is now terrified of being alone. Her shaken condition even forced Nemeth to temporarily abandon Naomi's love hut to drive her home. He's been sitting on their living room couch for the last fifteen minutes feeling like the shit that he is, wondering what to do or say next. One thing's for sure, he's not going to get a clue from Jessie. Terror-stricken as she is, her anger hasn't subsided and she hasn't spoken a word to him yet.

After searching through the medicine cabinet for some pharmaceutical assistance, Jessie somehow managed to go to bed and fall into a numbed-out fog, even with everything she's been through tonight.

What could she have taken that would have knocked her out like that? And why is it in her medicine cabinet? I'm almost afraid to go to the nightstand and read the label on the prescription bottle.

The decorative lamp on her nightstand is on. She probably doesn't want to be in the dark right now. Who could blame her?

Her bottom lip is still quivering. Hopefully she won't open her eyes and see the floating prescription bottle.

Diazepam!

Just what I feared! From working in a hospital, my pharmaceutical vocabulary is better than average—my daughter is zoned out on Valium.

I hear Nemeth out in the living room sneaking into the garage with his cell phone. That scumbucket! He probably figures that with Jesse sound asleep he can carry on a conversation out there with his bra-busting screw-mate. Even from here I can hear her pick up on the fourth ring.

"Listen, Naomi. I'm sorry about all that. I have no idea how that happened."

His top-heavy sweetheart isn't having it. "I don't need this shit. I'm not going to have that crazy bitch wife of yours chasing me around with a knife."

"Wait, listen!"

The click on the other end seems to indicate Nemeth's days as Naomi's fuck buddy might be at an end. The dirtbag curses the shitty day he's been having, probably figuring it can't get any worse. It can.

Nemeth closes his eyes and takes a deep breath, shaking his head in frustration over the abruptly aborted phone call. His eyes open. He's about to exhale.

He can't. His heart does a two-step.

A Latino with more than a passing resemblance to his

wife magically appears before him. The shock sends Nemeth stumbling back, clumsily reaching for his tool shelf to maintain balance. It fails to do so. Apparently Nemeth's craftsmanship is as good as his fidelity. The shelf gives way, spilling hardware supplies all over him as he falls onto the oil-stained concrete.

Nemeth finally lets out a breath. "What the—?"

I feel no obligation to supply any answers. I'd rather let him wrestle with his sanity, like my daughter is with hers.

Nemeth crawls backwards on his elbows. "You...you're supposed to be dead."

Yes, prick, and you're supposed to be faithful to my daughter. "I *am* dead, Nemeth. Would you like to join me?" A pathetic little gasp escapes his throat. "Get up!"

He refuses to move. Perhaps he feels safer behind the tires of his Honda CR-V.

Nemeth's bottom lip trembles. "What are going to do to me?"

"Well, if you don't get up, I'll probably rip you apart with my bare hands."

Nemeth rises and backs away until he is up against the opposite wall of the garage. You're cornered now, fucker, no place else for you to go.

I love the smell of fear. We all do. But *he* probably doesn't appreciate my scent as I bring my face closer to his (unless, of course, he likes the stench of rotted flesh).

No need to be loud when up so close. I can speak in a whisper. "So, you know who I am."

"I've seen your pictures. But...you died like twenty-five years ago."

"Twenty-seven to be exact."

"Th-th-then...what..."

"Just shut up and listen, Nemeth." I'm not feeling real patient. "I'm hoping that when my daughter is over the shock about what happened today, she'll do the sensible thing and send you out on your ass. But if she doesn't, if she doesn't come to you first, I want you to approach her. It doesn't have to be tomorrow, or the next day, but soon."

"And do what?" His contracting vocal chords make his words come out like a squeak.

"Did I say you could talk?"

"I'm sorry—"

"Shut up!" My temper's getting the best of me. "It's very simple. I want you to dissolve your marriage."

"What?"

"Interrupt me again!" Hold back, Nicky, hold back. Whoops, too late. The reflection of death, it's in his eyeballs. Ugh! He's prairie dogging in his shorts. Unintentional as it might have been, my death face makes it clear that there is no discussion to be had. "She gets everything, Nemeth. You understand me? Absolutely everything. Whatever she wants, the house, the cars, the vacation home, the IRA's, the business, everything, without even a hint of protest from you. If she wants you to have nothing, then you get nothing. Understood?" His deuce works past his shorts and starts creeping down his leg. "I said is that understood?"

"But—"

"But what? There are no buts. Don't you get it? Any hint of you not doing what I say..."

His eyeballs no longer reflect the hideous anomaly that just stood before him. The monster has vanished. Was it real? Nemeth looks around desperately. He must wonder if what just happened really happened.

His neck hairs stand up!

A voice hums from behind. Nemeth gasps and turns. He's face to face again, with Death.

Death speaks. "The human body has ten pints of

blood, Nemeth. I feed on it." The scent of his fear heightens. It's a scent that makes feeding so much more satisfying. But I have to restrain myself. Jessie would be the obvious suspect if this scumbag were to be found dead. "Are you scared, Nemeth? Are you questioning your sanity right now?" No response. "Well, whether you are or not doesn't really matter. Just do as I say. Because until you're gone, I'm going to be reappearing in front of you just like this to remind you. And I'm going to keep reminding you until you are out of my daughter's life. After that I will give you thirty days to leave this part of the country. I don't care where you go. I don't even want to know. All I want to know is that you're not around here. Because if I ever come across you again... do I need to finish that thought?" No answer, but this time I want one. "Hey dirt bag, are you listening to me?"

"Ross?"

It's Jessie, calling from inside the house. How the fuck is she up after taking that shit she took?

"I'm in the garage, Jess." He's hoping his response will make me leave.

The door opens from inside the house. Jessie is wearing an off-white cotton robe. Her hair is tussled. She looks like shit. "What are you doing?" She looks suspiciously around the garage.

"Uh, nothing," Nemeth is relieved not to see me around. "I was, uh, looking for a client's folder in my car."

"I heard voices." My daughter's not stupid. "You better not be calling that whore."

"I'm not, I'm not." Yeah, like she believes you.

Jessie's shaking her head, wondering what she ever saw in this bastard. Join the club, honey. Her slam of the door shows her disgust at herself for ever having fallen for such a pig.

Nemeth, still in the garage, is breathing a sigh of relief that Jessie didn't press any further. He reaches for the light switch to head back inside but feels something blocking his hand. It's something he cannot see—even with the lights on.

That frightened little squeal again.

That's right, you son of a bitch, you can't see me but I'm still here.

Nemeth steps away, backing against the passenger door of his Explorer. For one last time I reappear, to remind him of the face he never wants to see again. Unable to back away any further, Nemeth remains still, waiting to hear what the ghoul has to say.

It's going to be a long wait.

I'm not going to say a word.

15

"That is one pretty little lady," said Travis.

Stefanie was dressed modestly in an old sweater and a pair of jeans. Her eyes were distant but still, the beauty of my not-yet-confirmed widow (I was still officially just a missing person's case) could still be seen through the cloud of heartache that accompanied her. Only a couple of weeks earlier this was my home. Now I was standing outside just a couple of feet away from the kitchen window and it felt like she was miles away.

By this time my new undead friends had taught me how to control my visible and non-visible projections. If Stefanie would have looked out past the kitchen window, she would have only seen the tattered November lawn.

The kids were helping out with the usual after-dinner routine that was passed down from Ramona. Stefanie was washing the dishes, Jessie was drying them, and Davey was clearing the table. It was a routine that taught the kids responsibility and kept the family close. Neighbors, friends, and visiting family members talked about the tangible love one felt whenever they walked into our home. Imagine how much worse that made the humiliation when reports came out of my blood being found on semen-stained sheets after having been seen with another woman.

Stefanie, Jessie and Davey went through their motions wearing loss and emptiness on their faces. A counselor probably recommended the routine as a way to deal with their grief, thinking the normalcy would be therapeutic. It wasn't working. They looked numbed, unknowing of where their lives would be headed.

From outside, my mouth pried itself open. I was searching for words. I wanted to go inside where I belonged. I wanted to do my part, putting away the dishes.

Travis put his hand on my shoulder. "You have to let them go, son. If they see what you are now, their lives will be destroyed."

Donny, the more empathetic of the two, was equally firm. "They're suffering now, Nicholas, but they *will* make it. She looks like a strong woman. The kids too."

"She's always going to think that I betrayed her."

"But you didn't," said Donny. "You know that. You now know how we can control the minds of others."

I pointed to my soon to be declared widow. "But *she* doesn't know that."

Donny took me by both arms. "Deep down in her heart I'm sure she knows. She knows how much you loved her."

"What are you going to tell them?" added Travis. "You know you can't be in the daylight. What happens when the press finds out about you? What are you going to tell them?"

"There must be some way," I countered, weakly.

"Like what?" challenged Travis. "Tell me. What

happens when you can't go back to work because the sun will turn you into ashes? Or even your son's little league games, how are you going to explain that? Are you going to tell your family what you are? Do you think you can hide this from them? You don't think your little girl's not going to notice you're never at the breakfast table? And what about the Mrs.? How will she feel about having a coffin set up in the master bedroom? Or having her husband go out for a midnight stroll so he can feed off one of the neighbors while she's watching David Letterman?" I wanted to come back with something that would shut him up but I had nothing.

"Don't make their lives any worse than they already are," said Donny.

Travis emphasized his seriousness by bringing his face close to mine. "To the rest of the world we don't exist. And since we feed on the primary species of this planet it needs to stay that way. Up until now we've been keeping you going on blood that we've had stored away. But now it's time for you to start feeding on your own. That means taking human lives." He knew my genetic resistance made that a challenge. "Like I said before, what we have is communicable. If we don't decapitate or stake our prey, they become one of us. Right now there are probably no more than two hundred or so of us walking around on this entire planet. Some of us are several centuries old. The last thing this world needs is more of our kind. The more of us there are, the less we will have to feed from. The more of us there are attacking the population in our vicinities, the better the chance for awareness of our existence. What happens then? Well? What do you think? It then becomes a matter of survival because they will start seeking us out." Travis paused to study me. "Am I getting through? 'Cause if you're going to continue as one of us, you are going to need to feed. And to feed you are going to have to kill. And make no mistake about it. You will enjoy it, even resistants enjoy the kill. It just takes a little longer for you to get used to it." Travis' lip curled into an Elvis sneer. "So go ahead. Tell *that* to the Mrs."

I glared back at Travis but lost the staring contest. Instead I chose to turn to what was once my kitchen window. Davey finished helping in the kitchen and darted off to play Nintendo. Jessie was still next to Stefanie, helping her out. They were always very close. She was now starting to develop some of her mother's features. An authoritative figure would soon be needed to keep his eye on the young men that would be seeking her company. The position was now vacant.

As for Stefanie, Donny was right. She was always strong. But now I had broken her heart twice—not only by dying, but by dying after a sexual encounter with another woman. She was going to have to suffer grief, betrayal and humiliation, all at the same time. In the following years I would return regularly to visit them without being seen. Eventually I would reluctantly accept that as one of nature's anomalies I had no role there anymore.

Travis saw that the truth was setting in but being the hard son of a bitch that he is, he showed no sympathy. I looked one last time through the window. Davey was back in the kitchen. Stefanie had called him away from his Nintendo. It was now his job to put away the dishes.

#

"It's time to cut the cord, young man. We can't go on feeding you our leftovers much longer." Travis wasn't one to be subtle. He spoke loud and clear so he could be heard over the loud Euro-disco playing at the

Hindquarters, a Soho nightclub he owns with Donny. Judging from the packed dance floor it looked like business was going quite well for my nocturnal mentors. By its nature, you couldn't find a more convenient occupation for our kind. Night life, nighttime predators, you do the math.

Donny was with us on the balcony leaning over the railing watching nymphs in shoulder-less tops and camel-toe jeans grinding with hairy-chested "studs" trying to look tough in skin-tight Picasso-patterned polyester shirts.

Travis continued to babble his bullshit. "You need to decide if you want this new existence because if you do, you will need to feed off the living. (The guy was like a fucking broken-record.) It's the only blood that will do. If you're thinking maybe animal blood will do the trick, it won't. You were human, you were not an animal. You will need human blood. The more and the better quality, the stronger you will be, making your capabilities like mind-control and projection sharper. And remember, when you feed, it is your responsibility to make sure that the victim never rises."

"How do you suggest I do that," I asked, while Duran Duran blared over the sound system.

"Decapitation," he replied. "That's generally the best way."

"What about that wooden stake you were pressing against my chest when you found me?"

"That works too. Whichever way you prefer, as long as it gets done."

"So is that what you do every night? Drink blood? Cut people's heads off?"

Travis pointed his finger at me. "How we feed is our business and our business only. How you feed is yours. As long as you properly dispose of your prey, what you do is no concern of mine," he said, coldly glaring at me before walking away.

"What's *his* problem?" I asked Donny, wondering if he was targeting his prey below on the dance floor.

Donny turned to me and shrugged with his usual sympathetic look. "Believe it or not, he really *does* like you."

"Bullshit," I said. I turned and took the steps down to the main floor.

"Come on, Nicholas. Where are you going?" said Donny, following me through the shaking asses and the thrusting pelvises.

At the exit, the bouncer offered to stamp my hand for re-entry. I waved him off and stepped out into the crisp November air. Outside, young Generation X-ers were lined up waiting to get in. Some were couples, nuzzling and kissing in the slight chill of the late fall. I looked at them, wondering how I was going to do this. How was I going to choose whose life I would end to keep myself going? They were all young, happy, unsuspecting and having fun. Some were in love. Some were just out looking for a piece of ass. Whatever they were, I became ill at the thought that one of them could end up not coming home that night. Only weeks before I was a doting husband and father making a comfortable living. Did I really have it in me to become a serial-killing predator?

Halfway up the block I heard the pattering footsteps of Donny coming up behind me. "Nick, what are you doing?"

"You know what? I have no idea."

"Well come back then," said the lanky, undead pretty-boy. "Don't mind Travis. He just doesn't like being asked questions like that. He can be an asshole sometimes, you know that."

"Not that I give a shit, but why does he have such a bug up his ass about me?"

Donny sighed. "When we found you, it was because we sensed Simone feeding. We were trying to catch her so we could destroy her. But by the time we got there she was already gone. It was just you in that room. Normally we'd have just decapitated you so we wouldn't have another one of us in the area. But I told Travis to hold off because I thought maybe you might have known something that could have helped us."

"So it was *you*, then."

"Me what?" asked Donny.

"You," I repeated. "You're the reason I'm still here."

"What do you mean?"

"I mean; you should have let him do it. You should have let him cut my head off!"

I turned to walk away again but Donny pulled on my arm to stop me. "Listen, you can't just go out there yet."

"You, it's on you. I have to kill people for blood now? Guess what? Every life I take now is going to be on your head. Not that you give a shit with that nice line of fools lining up in front of your club to be your supper."

Donny cocked his head to the side like a shamed puppy dog being yelled at for pissing on the carpet. "I thought maybe we could help you get started. You know, somewhere else outside the city. I mean, if you don't want this, we can always, you know..."

"That's not the point, dammit!" I confronted him Travis-style. "Let me ask you something. Have you ever killed anyone? Because according to the two of you, you're both genetically resistant. So tell me. How do you do it? Does taking someone's life away give *you* any problems?" Donny remained quiet. And then it occurred to me. "Wait a minute. You never killed anyone, did you?" His eyes drifted towards the line I front of the Hindquarters. "So what then?" I asked. "How do you feed?"

Donny thought for a moment then shook his head. "We never told you how Travis was turned, did we?" I didn't answer. I just waited for him to continue. "During the prohibition era, Travis ran a speakeasy here in the city for the Capelli family."

"Prohibition Era!"

"He doesn't look too bad for a 100 year-old, does he?" said Donny, trying to lighten the mood. "I worked for him there. And of course back then, relationships like ours were not something you wanted to have known, especially when you were involved with someone like Capelli. So we did our best to be discreet."

"So what's this got to do with—"

"Easy," said Donny. "You're so impatient. You remind me of Travis sometimes."

"Never mind that. Where's this story going?"

"Well, if you stop interrupting me..."

"All right, go ahead."

Donny shook his head and continued. "Simone was Capelli's *goomar*. And she was a manipulative, horny little bitch that everyone in the boss's group had had a little time in bed with. And though he always suspected something was going on, he was never able to prove anything."

"Was she already—"

"Oh yeah," said Donny. "That tramp goes back centuries"

"So what's that got to do with you? I'm sure neither of *you* were screwing her."

"Let's put the sarcastic quips aside, shall we?" Donny continued. "I don't know how, but someone found out about me and Travis because Capelli went ahead and put out the word on us. I think his exact words were, "*I want that pervert and his faggot boyfriend* dead."

"So what happened?"

"Well, I guess he forgot that Travis had done a few jobs for him in the past because he sent only one man to take him out."

"Travis was a hit man?"

Donny beamed. "Travis was never someone to be messed with." He went on to describe how Capelli's goon was found at the back door of the speakeasy with his throat slit. After that Simone mesmerized Capelli with either her mind control or her lady bits and convinced him that she could handle Travis. But after she left, one of Capelli's other men secretly put a tail on her because he never trusted the hold she had over the boss and wanted to see what she did when no one else was around.

"Was that when she got Travis?" I asked.

Donnie nodded. "Well, you already know what a horny wench she is. And though she isn't necessarily his type, she had him under the same spell that she had you."

I hung my head. "That doesn't make me feel any less responsible for what happened a couple of weeks ago."

"I understand, but it wasn't your fault," said Donny. "Travis didn't want this either. And who knows? Maybe Simone didn't even want him to turn because if she was planning on staking him or removing his head, she never got the chance. While they were lying naked together and she was feeding off him, the doors burst open with three of Capelli's men spraying machine gun bullets at them."

"Why didn't she attack them?"

"Well Nicholas, even though we're dead, those bullets can be pretty painful. And they leave permanent damage underneath our projected appearances. Once our skin is torn, it doesn't heal that well. Our projections only give that illusion. I don't know if you've seen *Simone's* skin without her projected appearance, but I can tell you for a fact that Travis' body is full of bullet holes."

"Let's leave Travis' naked body out of this. What happened after that?"

"They were on the fifth floor of a hotel. Travis had been hiding there after killing the man Capelli sent after him. When those other guys went in that room and started shooting, Simone jumped out of that bed and dove right out the window."

"Shit, they must have wondered how the hell she did that."

"You're right about that because when they looked out that window, expecting to find her naked body splattered on the concrete, she was gone, nowhere in sight."

"What about Travis?"

"They stuffed him in the trunk of their car to deliver to Capelli. But when they got to Capelli's house and opened up the trunk... well, let's just say that Travis always has had a taste for Italian food."

"He turned that fast?"

Donnie nodded.

"But isn't he genetically resistant?"

"Yes," said Donny patiently. "But as I just explained, Travis had no problem killing before he became victim to Simone, so taking lives after his change was never an issue." Donnie then giggled.

"What's so funny?"

"I was thinking about Buffalo Johnny."

"Who's Buffalo Johnny?"

"He's the only one of us I know that doesn't actually kill anyone."

That got my attention. "What? How?"

"Donny!"

It was Travis pushing through the line waiting in front of the Hindquarters. "What's going on?" he asked as he approached us.

"Nicholas wants to leave," said Donny.

"Then let him go," said Travis. "Feel free to go on if you wish, young man. There's really not much more to teach you at this point, so as long as you're not feeding here in the city, you can go wherever you want."

"Why do you want me out of New York? This is a big city," I asked.

"Two reasons; first, this city is ours, three of us are too much for one city. Second, you're a dead man, a dead man whose face has been all over the local newspapers. You can't be here."

He had a point. The risk of running into people who knew the living Nicky Negrón was much too high. What if it got back to my family?

Regardless, Donny's Buffalo Johnny story piqued my interest. "Donny says I might not have to kill anyone to feed."

Travis gave Donny an incredulous look. "What are you talking about?"

Donny giggled again. "I was going to tell him about Buffalo Johnny from Upstate."

"Buffalo John—" Travis looked at Donny like he was crazy.

Now they really had my attention. "Who's Buffalo Johnny?"

Travis shook his head at me. "Johnny's a rare case. It's not the best way to—"

"To what? There's a way for me to get by without having to kill anyone and you're not going to tell me?"

"Well, if you can find someone willing to..." For the first time Travis seemed a little awkward in trying to express himself. Donny giggled some more.

I started to lose my patience. "Why the hell are you laughing? Who is Buffalo Johnny?"

Donny shrugged as if saying, why not. "He owns a night club like we do, near Niagara Falls."

"So?"

Donny raised an eyebrow suggestively. "Well, he has some ladies that come to him once a month for a feeding."

"I don't get it. I thought we have to kill them. What aren't you telling me?" I then thought for a moment. "Wait a minute. What do you mean monthly?"

Donny giggled again. "Johnny is very popular with the ladies."

"Are you telling me—?"

Travis nodded. "The blood is of good quality, too. It's been known to hold some of us up for close to a month. And it's true," Travis admitted. "You don't have to kill the woman if you can wipe her memory. But there lies the problem. Menstruating women tend to be difficult to hypnotize."

"But that's kind of like rape, isn't it?"

"Well you *could* find yourself a girlfriend," scoffed Travis. "But you're probably going to want to avoid close relationships with humans. It creates a lot of problems. Questions, explanations, it goes on and on."

"So then my choices are rape or murder?"

Travis gestured Donny to join him back at the club. "Whether you violate or kill your prey is your business, just don't do it in our city."

16

Back when Veronica started work here at the hospital as a part-timer, she had another job during the day as a waitress in the Ironbound section of Newark, stacking up a massive amount of work hours to support her two boys on her own. The other females here at the hospital paid no mind to that side of her and only thought of her as the local *puta*. It was more jealousy than anything else, but that being said, there was no question that Veronica enjoyed watching men trip all over themselves to get her attention.

When Veronica lost her job at the diner (after slapping a regular that copped a feel of her ass), she started working here full time and became intrigued with the mysterious (and devilishly handsome) security guard that everyone called Georgie, especially since he showed little interest in her.

At first she began playfully singing his name out whenever she'd pass him in the corridors. Such flirtations had little effect on her undead target until one night in the cafeteria she opened up a Tupperware containing her homemade *chili con carne*. The smell was so good, so fresh, he made a passing comment on how he missed the scent of old-fashioned home cooking. Not one to miss a beat, Veronica took that opportunity and ran with it.

Ever since then Veronica would regularly bring in leftovers to share with me. And since my species isn't exactly known for restraint or will power, I was not about to turn that food away. Human blood may be what I need to survive but my taste buds still love to savor the foods I enjoyed during the living years. Even in my death I can still taste those warm, home-cooked meals *Mami* used to prepare. And talk about torture, there is none worse than when I check in on Stefanie and smell the meals she used to prepare during the years of our marriage—except now it's Rippey that gets to enjoy dinner time with her.

So yes, recognizing a path that could lead towards developing a bond, Veronica jumped on the old cliché, "the way to a man's heart is through his stomach." Now that she's been here a few years, she's made a couple of friends at work. When she started sharing her meal breaks with me, they teased her about how she was wasting her time. Georgie's a lost cause. He just likes to keep to himself, they'd say. But the more they told her I was a hopeless case, the more she wanted to pursue me.

Now *she's* not talking to *me*.

It shouldn't matter. I shouldn't give a shit. It gets me out of her line of vision. Well, guess what. Now *I'm* the one that's missing our breaks together. I'm missing her smile, I'm missing her singing out my name and most of all I'm missing her *chili con carne*.

My behavior at the Hot Spot turned her off completely. Prior to that, I never openly judged her. She loved that about me. But on what was in effect our first date, I threw her a curve ball and barely resembled the person she thought she was getting to know. Since then she has built a wall of ice around her that I have been unable to penetrate. She goes out of her way to avoid me and refuses to make eye contact anytime we pass each other. Why does this bother me? I don't need any relationships. This is what I should want. To make it worse, now even my predatory libido is disrupted. Since my change, I have only acted out my carnal desires with women that I feed from or know that I am never going to see again. And since I don't want to kill Veronica nor leave my job, boning that hot little *Mexicana* is out of the question. But now I feel like I want her and it is disturbing my equilibrium. Why? Because it doesn't feel like the desire of a predator. It feels like the desire of a man. I know it's not love. If my heart still had a beat, it would beat for my very much alive and happily remarried Stefanie. But having grown accustomed to Veronica in my undead existence, I find that her current indifference is affecting me in ways it shouldn't. Suddenly it feels wrong sitting alone in the cafeteria with just a newspaper and a cup of coffee from the vending machine.

Her entrance into the cafeteria with her familiar little container gives me that little twirl below the ribcage— the one you get with rejection from someone you care about. Care! Did I just use that word? I'll bet she's got *chili con carne* in that container, too. Not above rubbing it in my face, are you, babe?

Shooting for my own personal low in levels of lameness, I have my own little Tupperware. I'm planning to use it in an attempt to break the ice. Even in high school I never resorted to these sorts of cheesy tactics. Suddenly I have no game.

"Veronica!" She does a 180. Really? "Come on, Veronica!" The other workers taking their break look up. I have everyone's attention but hers. In fact, she's even picking up her pace back out to the hall. No way, you're not outrunning me, sweetheart.

"Veronica, stop!"

Not appreciative of the fact that I've jumped out in front of her and blocked her path, Veronica clenches her teeth, refusing to make eye contact. *"Georgie, déjame quieta!"*

"Come on, Veronica, don't do this." Who is this person speaking? It can't be me.

"Georgie, don't make me call somebody. Leave me alone."

"Veronica, who're you gonna call, security? That's me! Come on, let me just apologize. I behaved very badly the other night."

"I don't want to hear it."

"I know, but I feel terrible about what I did. I want us to be friends. Will you give me another chance? I miss you." I did *not* just say that. "You know, us. I miss us, you know, like, talking." Somebody please shut me up.

Too late.

That last line worked. I can see it. She's quiet. That means she's thinking. Boy, I really did it now, didn't I?

Our eyes make quick contact before she catches herself and diverts them away.

"How are you feeling?" Ah, she still cares.

"Me? I—I'm fine." Am I stuttering?

"You didn't get sick again?" She cares and I'm liking it. Boy, am I in trouble.

"No, no, I'm okay. I just miss you. And I'm sorry. I was totally out of line, the way I acted." Man, am I hating myself right now.

Our eyes meet again. This time she doesn't turn away.

She's even tearing up. "Why did you act like that to me?"

Change the subject, Nicky. "Look, I made my own chili." Yeah, real smooth, guy. But hey, what the fuck? I haven't dated since college. "It doesn't taste anything like yours." That's no lie. "You want to try it and tell me what I'm doing wrong?"

She covers her mouth to suppress a laugh. A tear rolls down the side of her face. She probably wanted to make me work a little harder but her stifled laugh, along with her involuntary tear, has given her up. She'd been hurt and now she's struggling to play hard-to-get, but we both know the battle's over. I can be an irresistible prick when I want to be. And that was with no hypnosis, either. Maybe I *do* still have some game.

Veronica takes my arm and so help me it feels great. I follow submissively. She's probably leading us to our favorite waiting room. Hopefully Dr. Rothstein and Sabrina haven't beaten us to it.

Or maybe not, it appears we're headed in a different direction. The newly constructed North Wing? That's not scheduled to open until the end of the month.

"Where are we going?"

She's feeling playful again. "I found a new spot where we can be *solito*."

"We're not supposed to come here, you know. This part of the hospital isn't open yet."

Some player from New Jersey Devils donated some money to make this new addition possible. It just passed inspection yesterday and they are planning on opening it before the holidays after a little picture-taking ceremony.

"It's okay," teases Veronica. "I have a friend who works for Security." Her eyes, I know that look. Her tone of voice, I know it too.

She wants it!

The air in this section is clean, untouched, with the scent of fresh paint still dominant in the new waiting area on the second floor. Interestingly Veronica knew right where the switch was to turn on the light. Kind of makes me wonder about her familiarity with this unused section of the hospital. But I better not jump to any conclusions. That already got me into trouble earlier this week. Instead I'll be a good boy and go along for the ride, cooperatively sitting beside her on the couch while I open my half-assed container of chili.

I hand her a spoon. "Here, I want your honest opinion."

Her forced smile betrays a certain lack of enthusiasm but she gamely scoops up a spoonful of *Chili a la Georgie* and gives it a taste.

"Mmm," she lies after swallowing. "Good!"

"Yeah, but it's not like yours. Something is missing."

She wrinkles her nose at me. It's love, baby. I make mine with love."

Oh, boy, I know where this is going.

Historically, self-control has never been much of a problem for me, even when my hunger was at its worst and my temptation was at its highest. But now Veronica is pouring out heat with every word and every look in my direction. And her scent has been dancing through my nostrils from the second I spotted her at the cafeteria. This is going be a losing battle. The combined scent of the North Wing's fresh paint and my not-so-succulent chili are doing their best, but they are not even close to curtailing my hunger. And it's not my crappy chili that I'm hungering for.

Travis made clear many years ago that the quality of the blood we consume directly affects our capabilities, which is probably why mine are so erratic. A steady diet of undesirables such as thugs and junkies makes it often difficult for me to maintain proper control until I steal some healthy plasma from the hospital. In this instance, control would be the operative word, because that is exactly what I am lacking right now.

How else to explain behind my current behavior around Veronica? Hell, it's probably the only reason I'm giving her so much attention to begin with. Poor feeding impairs everything; our projections, our strength, and our ability to control the minds of others. Hell, if we can't control our own minds, how are we going to control others? Knowing that, it is probably safe to say that a genetically resistant vampire would have even more trouble controlling his emotions and his impulses when not properly fed. And right now, my impulse tells me that I need to feed. Real bad. And my chili, hell, not even Veronica's chili is going to cut it.

Our faces draw closer. "No Veronica, there's something else. There's something else that you put in that chili that I'm not able to figure out."

"Oh, so now you want my secret recipe." Veronica bats her eyes playfully before closing them, anticipating the meeting of our lips. Surprisingly, even after tasting the rankness of my chili, her breath remains lusciously sweet.

"So you're not going to tell me the secret ingredient?" I feel like I'm reading off the script of some cheesy Rock Hudson movie.

"No," replies Doris Day.

"Why not?"

Her scent grows stronger as she tilts her head, licking her lips as they zero in on mine. "You're going to have to earn it."

My better judgment is fading. I want to feel and taste the softness of her lips in my mouth. That being said, right now, that kiss is not going to happen.

"WHAT? Georgie, what are you doing?" I bet she didn't see *this* coming. "Georgie, stop!"

Sorry babe, Georgie's not listening. You can take his nosedive towards your lap as official notice that chili is now off the table. And you can also presume from his undoing of your work uniform that what he's really hungering for is somewhere in there.

Veronica pushes with both hands against my shoulders but she's overmatched. Her uniform pants are already below her knees.

"Georgie, are you crazy?"

Off with the shoes.

"Georgie!"

And the socks.

"Georgie, no!"

And down with the pants.

You've been trying to get my attention all this time, wondering when I was finally going to come around. Well, I'm sure you didn't imagine it would be like this but here I am, baby.

Veronica tries to hold on to her silk, white panties as I pull them from her grip. ""Georgie not here. Not like this. I can't! Not now!" Georgie? Who's Georgie? Sorry baby, but your scent has awoken Nicky, and Nicky ain't listening. "Oh, my God, you are crazy! Can't you wait?" She's almost laughing in disbelief as I pry her panties off. "Georgie, I can't do this now! Can't you see?" Yes, I see, sweetheart, but that little hanging string is not an obstacle for me.

Veronica gasps in shock as I pull out the blood-soaked mass of cotton and throw it on the floor. "Oh my God, Georgie, are you a freak?" You have no idea, baby. Another gasp as my head lands down on her lap. "Georgie! Oh, my God, what are you doing?" You know perfectly well what I'm doing. You just can't believe that I'm doing it now. "Georgie, stop it! Not here! Georgie!" I give her credit. She's putting up quite a battle. With her promiscuous history, I'm actually kind of surprised. But her arms are now tired and they're dropping to the side. "Georgie, this is crazy." She's out of breath. "Georgie, you have to stop. We can't do this here." Hey we came to the North Wing for privacy, didn't we? "Georgie please, not like this, Georgie. Not..." Her breath's turning heavy. "Oh, my God, Georgie..." My energy is rising. It is easily gauged by the obvious reaction that comes with a feeding of fresh, healthy blood. A reaction that is ready to pierce through my pants. "Oh my God, Georgie, you feel so good." She's settling back, closing her eyes, clenching the fabric of the couch.

A jolt! Her body stiffens, almost as if electrocuted. I must have hit a spot. "Oh, my God! Georgie, don't stop! A*y Dios mio,* Georgie... Georgie... GEORGIE!" I'm not sure what I'm doing right, but whatever it is, I'm not about to change it. "Oh my God, Georgie. Don't stop! Oh, my God! Oh, my God! Baby! Oh, my God, Georgie. Baby, you are so beautiful. Baby, I love you so much. Oh, my God, Georgie, I'm gonna come! Oh, my god, Georgie, I'm gonna come! Georgie! Georgie! OOOAAAHH!!!"

I know *that* sound.

The tables turn. Veronica is now the aggressor. "Fuck me Georgie! Fuck me now! I don't care, Georgie! Fuck me!" You don't have to tell me twice.

A terrified shriek echoes through the halls of the North Wing!

She saw it! She saw Death! Careless dumb fuck that I am, I lost myself and forgot how I have no projection when feeding. This poor woman just looked down between her legs and saw a cadaver staring at her with blood dripping from its fangs. It was probably just for a flash, as the second she screamed it snapped my projection back into place. But, still, she did see it.

"What's wrong?"

With my human appearance restored and her head still in a whirl, she's probably not even sure of what just happened. "Huh? Oh... I... I thought I saw something."

"What?" I gotta play the part, even though I know damn well what she saw.

"Forget it," she says, grabbing the back of my head and slamming my face back down between her thighs.

17

"Well, look who's here," said Donny, dressed in a silk maroon-colored bathrobe, cheerfully opening the door to his and Travis' apartment. It was 1992, Bill Clinton had won the election, Kurt Cobain was smelling like teen spirit, The Toronto Blue Jays had won the World Series, and the Mets sucked.

Accepting Donny's welcome, I stepped inside and saw Travis coming out of the bedroom tying the belt of a matching bathrobe. I instantly wiped away the thought of what went on before I arrived.

"Well, well, it's the Jersey boy," said Travis. He actually looked pleased to see me. "What brings you to town, young man? Still checking up on that lovely little family of yours?"

Acceptance had set in by then. I was now an established member of the living dead society. That being said, letting go of the ones I loved was pretty much not an option. I wanted to remain close without upsetting their lives any further while remaining in compliance with Travis and Donny's territorial boundaries. That's how I wound up in Newark, where I worked out my routine of feeding on worthless rejects that didn't conflict with my fanged neighbors' borders.

Maintaining a territory isn't easy. You need to respect the daytime life that you're not a part of, while also tending to your own nocturnal needs. That means not creating too many missing persons cases and not leaving a trail of headless corpses in your surrounding area. To date I've been successful in not stirring up anything above the norm in our community. Even the nomads of our undead population have steered clear, understanding that North Jersey is mine the same way the five boroughs of New York are Travis and Donny's.

Back during their little turf war in the prohibition era, when Simone failed to finish off Travis, he rose again knowing that Capelli's men would go after Donny. Fearing that it might have been too late, Travis rushed back to his apartment to find his mate lying on the living room floor with six bullets in him. Without any hesitation, Travis clamped his fangs into Donny hoping to turn him before his life slipped away. When Donny joined the ranks of the undead, he also turned out to be genetically resistant, although his transition suffered some bumps in the road like mine did. That's probably why he was more sympathetic about my conversion. Once Donny's transformation was complete, the happy couple went hunting after Simone together, eventually finding their frequently unclothed maker gorging herself on another bedmate. This time it was a pretty music hall dancer.

The ensuing confrontation was a fierce one but ultimately, not yet having developed the dominant traits that she currently possesses, Simone found herself overmatched by the two-on-one lover boy advantage. A few more epic rematches followed over the next few months but Travis and Donny held their own, forcing

Simone to concede the city and become the intruding nomad she currently is today, regularly returning with more capabilities and heightened powers. This war still isn't over.

"What's going on with Teresa Gunder?" I asked, slicing the mood of our friendly reunion like a sword-wielding Ninja.

Travis immediately transformed into the Travis I am more familiar with. "What do you know about Teresa Gunder?"

"The same as everyone else who reads the papers. But there's more to her story and I don't think I know everything there is to know. Don't you think I *should*?"

"Yes, you should know," said Travis with an edge to his voice. "She is a very dangerous woman to us, dangerous to us all. But if you've come across any knowledge about her it needs to come out now."

I lied. "I haven't. I know about her from her report and the media coverage but that's *all* I know. That's why I'm here to see you." It wasn't a complete lie. I did know about The Gunder Report and a little bit about her history, but when I came across her name on Dominic's desk at the police station, the picture changed completely.

Earlier that night, Dominic, now an NYPD sergeant, was at his desk looking through his old files unaware that his undead brother-in-law was reading over his shoulder. He was going over my case—a case that never made any sense to him. Why would his brother-in-law suddenly just ditch his bosses without warning, to go with what most figured was some high-priced, redheaded call girl?

When Dominic's shift ended, I was bored and looking for something to do so I swiped the files and took them to a Chock Full 'O Nuts half a mile away.

There, I settled into a booth, wishing I had a Bustelo, and laid the files out on the table, reading them at my leisure.

Dominic wasn't allowed to work on my case because he was a close relative, but that didn't stop him from staying informed on any developments. Knowing first-hand how much I loved Stefanie and how proud I was of having her as my wife, there was no way in his eyes that what happened was consistent with any part of my behavior. He repeated this many times to his devastated, heartbroken and humiliated sister. He just didn't buy the official story. Not Nicky. Nicky would never do that. I wish I could believe that Stefanie shared that sentiment, but it was difficult to tell if the pain in her face was from the mourning or the betrayal.

Dominic was regularly reprimanded for interfering with the officers' investigations regarding my case. When the time came that I was officially declared dead, he became even more consumed, putting additional strain on his marriage to Patti, which wasn't the storybook kind to begin with.

The waitress brought over a corn muffin I had ordered and shook her head at the mess I had made. Files were spread all over the table; newspaper clippings, crime scene photographs, witness reports, and documents from similar disappearances throughout the country. There had to be something that was overlooked.

Who was this redhead? She was the only one who might have had any answers. Yet she was missing as well. At first they thought maybe she was also a victim, but that changed when the forensic reports revealed that only traces of my blood were found in the room. If she was abducted, then why was there no demand for any ransom? And why wasn't anyone looking for her?

Even stranger was the fact that there were witness

accounts of her entering the hotel without anyone seeing her leave. They went through every security tape over and over without finding any trace of her. Me, I was all over the tapes, talking to Greg, going to the pay phone and then sticking my tongue out, doing spastic Joe Cocker gyrations alone in the elevator (Thankfully those tapes were never released to the public. These days that shit would be all over YouTube). But with no videotape or photographs to identify her, all the police had of Simone were sketches that were made from witnesses' descriptions of her. And since the room where I was found was not registered in anyone's name, that added even more to the mystery.

But there was something else that bothered Dominic, and he couldn't let go of it—the case of Ronnie Gunder's disappearance near Syracuse University. It happened three years prior to my disappearance and the circumstances were too similar to ignore.

Ronnie had spent a night bingeing with some SU buddies at an upstate bar before leaving with an attractive older woman that had long, red hair. He was found the next morning in a motel room after a maid had heard a smoke alarm go off. When she saw the smoke coming out into the hallway, she banged loudly on the door and got no response. The room was finally unlocked by the hotel manager who heroically burrowed into the thickening smoke, only to find Ronnie's body lying on the bed, engulfed in flames. The workers at the motel quickly got together and put out the fire, but when the smoke cleared, they were stricken by how quickly the body had burned. Only blood and ashes were left. The night before, a couple of the male workers remembered envying Ronnie when he came in with this sumptuous looking redhead. But in the morning she was nowhere to be seen.

When the investigators arrived they were completely baffled, as would be expected. They looked everywhere for evidence that could tell them how the fire was started. Yet nothing was found that they believed could have sparked an inferno that would burn someone to a crisp so fast. No matches. No gasoline. Nothing. And as far as anyone could tell, young Gunder was wearing no clothes so there was nothing *on* him that could have gone up so quickly in flames.

Ronald's mother, Dr. Teresa Gunder, was a professor of epidemiology at the University of Pennsylvania. When she learned what happened to her son, she was naturally devastated and drove to Syracuse to find answers. But as the investigations went on, she became more frustrated and agitated that the police, nor the fire inspectors, could provide any answers. The frustration then turned to obsession. She wanted to know who was to blame and more importantly, where the hell was this red-haired woman? With no developments coming up after she had returned to work, her behavior at the university became increasingly erratic and distracted. Her superiors at the university tried to convince her to take some time off. Anyone who had suffered such a loss couldn't possibly have been expected to function normally without some time to heal, especially since she was alone, having been divorced for over fifteen years.

Caring little about anything else, the doctor continued her own personal investigation, looking deeper into any information that had anything to do with her son's death. Tired of receiving well-meaning advice discouraging her from being so fixated, she withdrew from everyone around her and shut herself away from the outside world.

Without anyone to steer her away, Dr. Gunder spent all her time studying newspaper accounts and making constant calls to the Syracuse police, the fire department, and the medical examiner's office. Her superiors at the university, having seen enough, as her emotional condition continued to deteriorate, finally demanded after a few weeks that she take some time off.

Initially she resisted but then came to realize that she could use that time to return to Syracuse and look deeper into the case. Her first stop was the motel. With the investigation still going on, no access to the possible crime scene was allowed, but using the motel manager's sense of guilt, Dr. Gunder exploited his sympathy and gained entry to the room despite orders to the contrary.

In her notes, the doctor described how she walked in and was still able to smell the smoke from the fire. When it occurred to her that the smell was that of her son's burnt flesh, she was overcome with tears. Considerate enough to allow the doctor a moment of privacy, the motel manager stepped out into the hall.

It was the break that she needed. Dr. Gunder took advantage of the motel manager's courtesy and knelt down on the burnt carpet to fill a small jar with some of her son's ashes. She also took a knife out and cut a one-inch square out of the blood-caked mattress, sealing it inside a zip-lock bag and stashing it in her purse along with the ashes.

With the little time that she had, and the prospect of the motel manager returning, there was nothing else she could come up with. The sheets were already gone. They had been taken to the lab by the police. What she had was going to have to do. Hopefully they would turn up something.

When the doctor returned home she convinced her superiors that working on a limited basis would be therapeutic for her. Unknown to them, she would be using that time to run her own tests with the evidence that she had collected.

Her first findings showed nothing out of the ordinary. From the dried blood on the piece she cut out from the mattress, she determined that Ronnie's blood alcohol content was a little over 0.05—no surprise there since the reports already established that he had met the woman at a bar. It was a couple of tests later when something strange turned up from the results. It was a micro-organism—one that she, nor anyone, had never seen before. Was it a disease? Was her son sick and she didn't know about it? To check heredity, the doctor ran tests on herself. The results showed that whatever that micro-organism was, it did not come from her. But comparative tests to other results raised another question.

A very odd one.

The doctor double-checked the declared time of death. Now she was really confused. Before these events, Dr. Gunder was considered one of the best in her field, yet her findings made hardly any sense. She ran the tests again. The results were the same. There was no one she could turn to. Everything Dr. Gunder was doing was unauthorized and there was considerable debate as to whether she should have been working even on a limited basis. And since the organism was one that was never scientifically documented, there was nowhere that Dr. Gunder could look for further research. It also bothered the doctor that there was no mention of any such findings in the coroner's report. How did they miss it? Were they incompetent? Were they covering it up? Perhaps it was arrogant of her, she thought. Having once been considered one of the leading epidemiologists in the nation, was it fair for her to expect a coroner to have the same expertise?

In the eyes of those involved in the investigation,

Ronnie Gunder burned to his death. There was no biological cause to speak of. But if they would have run the same tests Dr. Gunder did and had gotten the same results, one question could not have been ignored. How was it possible that the organism that she found was still alive almost four hours after her son's death?

#

"The good doctor has accumulated a lot of knowledge," said Travis with eyes of self-preservation.

Dominic had files on Dr. Gunder that could fill a milk crate so I hadn't yet completed reading them. I had to bring them back to his desk so they wouldn't be noticed missing. But I did make it over to Staples to run copies of what I lifted from his desk including:

THE GUNDER REPORT:
A SCIENTIFIC ANALYSIS OF VAMPIRE
MYTHOLOGY.

"To date she has been discredited and is considered a tragic source of pity," said Travis.

"But ever since Simone killed her son, she's gone everywhere doing research," added Donny.

"What do you mean everywhere?" I asked.

"The doctor found a biological substance in her boy's remains that was not, well, it wasn't human," said Travis. That much I knew but I played dumb. Travis continued. "She researched for well over a year, neglecting her responsibilities at the university, and as I mentioned, losing her credibility and the respect of her peers. But she didn't care. She wanted to know everything there was to know about her boy's death."

"I'm not trying to make a joke here," I said, about my

upcoming pun. "But this should have been a major *red flag* to anyone investigating my death."

"It was, young man. The police are not blind to the fact that a similar woman was at the site of two similar deaths but there are so few answers, they don't know what to do with the information that they *do* have. Our opinion is that young Mr. Gunder turned while she was feeding on him and he fought her off."

"What? How is that possible?"

"It's rare but it does happen," said Donny. "We think he put up a fight with her and she fled. And since he was weakened from the fight and probably confused, he probably stayed in that room long enough to get hit with the sunlight coming in through the window. She was probably smart enough to give up the fight and let him burn on his own."

"So when the doctor learned what she did from the results of her tests," added Travis, "she looked everywhere to see if anything similar turned up in any medical reports around the world."

"Did she find anything?" I asked.

Travis shook his head in grudging admiration. "She found traces of what was in her son in lab readings from a 15th century meteorite."

"Meteorite? Are you fucking with me?" I looked at them both but, by then, I already knew that sense of humor was not one of Travis' strong suits.

"And that's not even the best part of it," said Donny.

"What do you mean?"

"The meteorite was from Cluj County in the Mocs-Palatca region."

"Where is that?"

"Romania," replied Travis.

"Romania? What are you gonna start telling me, some Vlad-the-Impaler shit now?"

Donny smiled nervously. "The fact is that the doctor began researching mysterious deaths from that era and traced the beginning of our existence to that point in time."

I was waiting for them to burst out laughing.

I waited a little more.

Nothing.

"C'mon guys!" They had to be pulling my leg.

Travis made it clear they weren't. "What do you know about Teresa Gunder?"

"You're afraid of her, aren't you?"

Travis clenched his teeth. "Again Nicholas, do you know where she is?"

"No!" I snapped back. "What is it about this woman that's got you all worked up? Nobody believes her anyway."

Donny explained a little more patiently than his partner. "Dr. Gunder has made a lot of progress in her research, and that's with no one taking her seriously. But now she knows how we began, how we evolved, and just about everything else there is to know about us. She's looked back through history, police investigations, and scientific findings. And while she remains out of sight and difficult to find, we think she is well on her way to developing a way of identifying us while we're out in public."

"In other words, she is taking significant steps in learning everything she needs to know to eventually destroy us," said Travis.

Oh, so *that's* the problem.

"So, where is she now?" I asked.

Travis was never the easiest to convince of anything. "You *really* don't know where she is?"

"No!"

"She's gone into hiding," said Donny. "But if you

read her report, you'll see that she knows our strengths and our weaknesses. Travis is right. She will soon know enough to be able to destroy us."

"So what is she waiting for?" I asked.

"Well, obviously the woman needs people to help her," said Travis. "This is not a battle she can win on her own. The second that one of us finds her, she is finished."

"But no one believes her. You said it yourself."

"She knows about genetic resistance," said Donny. "She thinks that she can find one of us with a conscience that can help with her research."

"In other words" said Travis, with his threatening eyes, "if she gets one of our kind on her side, we're as good as done."

18

"Oh my God, Georgie, you are so crazy," says Veronica, still catching her breath, barely having landed from her cloud.

We'd be quite a sight if someone would venture into the North Wing right now and peep into the waiting room. She's lying halfway off the couch with her uniform and undergarments down to her ankles and I'm beside her with blood dripping from the bottom half of my face.

"I'm crazy? Look at you." I'm feeling myself smile— a real smile, one from within. I can't remember the last time I did that, actually *feel* a smile. When I deal with people here at work or outside and a situation calls for it, I usually have to remind myself to smile. But here with Veronica it's different, I'm actually enjoying myself. I'm enjoying the company of the person I am with. The smile just came out. "You think you might want to pull those pants up before somebody comes by here and sees you?"

Veronica naughtily laughs and rises to wiggle her curvy ass back in her pants. Man, we're actually having a moment.

"Hay Dios mio!" My little undead guy has caught Veronica's attention. He's bloodied from where he's been over the last few minutes but still locked and loaded. "You can't get enough, can you?"

We're both satisfied customers and should really get back to work but it looks like *Señora Veronica* wants a little snuggle time. She nuzzles up and reaches for some napkins on the table next to my half-assed chili. Her attempt to wipe my face clean isn't working. The blood isn't coming off. Her solution? Licking the blood off my lips. "You see, baby? I'm a freak, too."

#

Although we are both single healthy adults (the healthy part applying to her, being dead I wouldn't exactly call myself healthy), Veronica and I did our best to avoid being seen when we snuck back from the North Wing together. Having a little rendezvous during work hours wouldn't be something the hospital administrators would smile upon.

Speaking of smiles, the look on Jimmy's face speaks volumes. "Damn, man, I knew you were hittin' that. I cover for you on break so you can ride that Mexican wonderland in the North Wing?"

What? My shirt isn't hanging out, my zipper isn't open and I maintained a considerable degree of quiet. Did Veronica's vocal range reach out all the way to the main part of the hospital? "What are you talking about?"

"Don't try to deny it. I can smell the pussy on you from here."

"You heard?" No surprise since Veronica sounded like she was auditioning as a backup singer for J Lo.

"Did I hear? Who *didn't* hear? You could hear that

shit in Hackensack."

"Then why didn't someone come over and stop us."

"Stop you? You kiddin'? That shit was better than HBO! You got every woman in this hospital wantin' to fuck you, now. What you packin' in there, boy?"

#

Thanksgiving at the Rippey house seems a little quieter than usual. Rippey, Davey, Artie and Dominic are talking sports while on the 65" inch plasma, the Eagles are struggling to mount an offense against the Lions. Let's make that, Rippey, Davey and Dominic are talking sports. Artie appears to have nodded off, which is understandable, the guy after all, is 87 years old. That doesn't stop him from insisting that he drive, though. Dominic always offers to pick him and Ramona up. But no, "I can drive on my own," he insists. Aging means never having to admit you're too old.

In the kitchen, Jessie and Ramona are helping Stefanie prepare the turkey. Noticeably absent is Nemeth, who by now should be somewhere incognito in the caves of Afghanistan.

Accompanying Davey is his latest excuse for a girlfriend. From the *tramp stamp* and the pink highlighted hair, I'm guessing, recently rehabbed stripper that he met at the clinic. Far as I can tell she's also not much of a football fan. She looks considerably bored sitting alongside Davey, leaning her head against his shoulder. But then again it's not much of a game with the Lions up 31-7. That's probably why Dominic's taking the floor with his usual rant about the Mets.

"Jesus, bring some fucking bats to the World Series, why don't you? I've never seen anything so fucking pathetic. I'm telling you, as long as those Wilpon's own the Mets they're never going anywhere."

"C'mon Uncle Dom," gestures Davey towards his lady friend—one that hardly anyone would think would be offended. Davey shakes his head as Dominic reaches for his Budweiser on the snack tray.

Rippey isn't much of a follower of sports but he gamely tries to get in the conversation. "Well, at least they made it to the World Series, right?"

Dominic shoots him a *shut-the-fuck-up* look and addresses the stripper. "Sweetheart, what's your name again?"

"Amber."

"You like baseball, Bambi?" Either his hearing isn't what it used to be or Dominic's just fucking with her. Knowing Dominic, I think it's the latter. I love that about him.

Amber doesn't bother to correct him. "No, not really,"

"Well, if you ever decide to root for a team, don't let it be the Mets. They'll make you want to shit."

This conversation's making *me* want to shit. And I don't even shit. I'd rather hang out with the ladies, even though being this close to Stefanie without her knowing of my presence is something I can never get used to.

Rippey rises up from his chair, following me into the kitchen. It's almost as if he jealously senses me in the area. I even have to move aside so he doesn't walk right into me.

He nudges up behind Stefanie, putting his arms around her and kissing her on the back of her neck. Go ahead. Put my heart through the meat grinder, you prick.

"How are you feeling, honey?"

Stefanie nods her head without turning.

There's a somberness in the air. I don't know what it is but it is definitely here, and no one is saying anything that would indicate why.

Still feisty at 86, Ramona appears to be irked at Rippey's presence in the kitchen. Like Patti, Dominic's ex, Rippey has always been an outsider. The difference is that Patti was a bitch. Rippey, as much as I hate to admit it, is a good guy. He actually deserves to be treated better.

Dominic ambles into the kitchen over to his mother. "*Mami*, why don't you go sit down? The girls got it."

"You sit down and watch your football," answers Ramona.

Dominic persists by taking his mom by the shoulders and turning her around towards the living room. "Come on, Ma. Go sit next to Pop. Food will be ready soon." Dominic turns to Stefanie. "Ain't that right, sis?"

Stefanie forces a smile. "Right! Are you good and hungry?"

"Oh yeah, sis, bring it on!"

Yeah, there's something wrong. It definitely doesn't feel right in here. The mood is forced, not celebratory at all.

Reluctantly, Ramona heeds her son and slowly paces back to the living room, taking a seat next to her snoring hubby.

In the kitchen, Jessie tears up.

Dominic quickly notices and strokes his niece's hair "How you doing, baby? You alright?"

She wants to reply but she looks afraid to.

Rippey answers for her. "She's still a little shaken up by everything."

Dominic nods and puts his arm around Jessie's shoulder. "Hey, forget about that asshole,"

Stefanie scolds her brother. "Dominic!"

"It's not that, Uncle Dom," says Jessie.

Dominic nods his head and rubs Jessie's shoulders. "I know, honey. But look, we're all together. We're gonna have a nice turkey..." Jessie shakes her head. Her uncle is barking up the wrong tree. Dominic turns to Stefanie and Rippey, looking for a clue. "Well, what is it then?"

Dead silence. The only sound is from the TV where the Ford Field fans are cheering another Detroit touchdown.

A film of tears coats Jessie's eyes. "He seemed so real." A blink of her eyelid pushes a tear down her face. Stefanie puts down the salad and hugs her daughter who weeps on her mother's shoulder. Rippey looks over sympathetically.

"Honey, you've been through a lot," whispers Stefanie.

"You've been under a lot of stress," adds Dominic.

"I know what I saw," responds Jessie, quietly, but with emphasis.

Dominic, Stefanie and Rippey exchange sullen glances. They think Jessie's wheels are coming off the tracks.

Rippey gently tries to reel her back in. "Jessie, you know that's not possible."

"I saw his face," says Jessie. "I know what my father looked like."

Davey comes in from the living room, leaving his little sex pet staring blankly at the television. "Hey, dinner almost ready?" His sister is in her mother's arms, crying. Davey nods for Dominic to follow him back into the living room.

Davey whispers. He doesn't really need to. With the Ford Field crowd cheering the extra point on the TV, no one could hear anyway. "You know about that drug dealer that got killed in Brooklyn?"

Dominic's troubled by the oddly timed question. "Yeah..."

"I was there."

"*Pero que carajo!* What do you mean, you were there?"

"I was there outside his apartment. I got into a fight with him."

"What!" Dominic struggles to keep his tone down. "What the hell were you doing there? Did you—"

"No, no listen, that's not what I'm trying to tell you. Listen."

"*Pero mira, Jesus Crísto!*"

"Uncle Dom, please listen. That thing that happened to him, I don't know anything about that. I was there trying to help a family find their daughter. But when I asked him about her, he pulled a gun out on me."

"A gun!" Dominic's eyebrows meet at the center of his forehead.

Davey nods. "I went after it and tried to take it from him, but when I reached for it, the guy just flew back like someone grabbed him and threw him against the wall." Great! Now my son too, is questioning his sanity. On the other hand, what if I wasn't there? Davey could have been the one dead instead of that Darryl. "When he hit the wall, he dropped his gun," says Davey. "I wasn't sure whether I should go for it or not. But then he *did* go for it. And when he did," Davey can't believe what he's about to say. "His head snapped back. It snapped back like he got kicked in the face." Dominic's eyes narrow, making Davey feel the need to assert his clear-headedness. "Uncle Dom, I'm not crazy. It felt like someone else was there."

"What? Someone like who?"

"Look, I don't know how to explain it other than, have you ever been in a room by yourself and felt like there was someone else in there watching you?"

Dominic's eyes open into widened glare. His breathing intensifies. He's practically blowing smoke

out of his nostrils but he doesn't answer.
    He doesn't need to.

19

"Dominic, are you seriously going to order that shit?"

"Fuck you, you scrawny little bitch. At least my sister makes nice warm meals for you when you come home from work. Patti won't even microwave me a TV dinner."

Dominic was twice my size and easily could have broken me in half, but he let me get away with shit that no one else could say to him. "Look at you. Who the hell eats a twelve-inch sub all by himself? What are you 300 pounds? No wonder Patti won't have sex with you, if you get on top of her you'll kill her. If she gets on top of you, she'd be banging her head against the ceiling."

"You're up," said Dominic. "Shut your fucking face and bowl."

It was only our close bond that enabled me to be such a merciless ballbreaker. And on our bowling nights at the lanes on Tarrytown Road in White Plains, he was a captive audience. We participated in a league there with some of his buddies from the NYPD and every week our team would witness Dominic's gluttony when he ordered from the sports bar attached to the bowling alley. His sub would be loaded with ham, provolone, salami, turkey, lettuce, tomatoes, oil, vinegar, and whatever else they could get their hands on in the kitchen. By the time they finished with his sandwich, not only was it twelve inches long, the fucking thing was twelve inches thick. On top of that, he would order two liters of beer so the food chunks could float around his guts like dead rats in a sewer.

One night Dominic's order came in while he was taking his turn bowling. He was completely focused on the lanes because he was working on a 200 game. Unable to resist, I took the waitress who brought in his sandwich aside and paid for it without him noticing. I then hid it underneath my jacket. Our other two teammates and the opposing team played along. They laughed quietly as Dominic came back to his seat, looking towards the sports bar, wondering where his sandwich was.

On his next turn when he was again in deep concentration aiming for another strike, all of us feasted on Dominic's sandwich, leaving him with maybe three inches of the former foot-long monstrosity. At the lane, Dominic threw a particularly impressive hook to get his sixth strike of the game. He strutted proudly on the way back to his seat but noticed there was still no sign of his sandwich. Our other two teammates and I couldn't hold back any longer. I presented him with the mangled remains of his sub.

"Hey Dom, your sandwich is here."

He lunged at me but I quickly leapt out of his reach. "Come here, I'll kill you!"

"You see, you fat bastard? If you weren't so overweight you could have caught me," I said from a safe distance.

"You can't stay away forever," said Dominic, pointing his finger at me. "When it's your turn to bowl, I'm gonna kick your ass."

Dominic was a good-natured guy, though. He cooled off quickly after seeing his cop buddies double over in laughter. He couldn't help but shake his head and join them.

Later after he reordered the same glop, I took a seat beside him and watched him gobble it down. "Pretty good sandwich, ain't it?"

Dominic glared at me, chewing slowly before swallowing. "You're a prick, you know that?"

#

Dominic and his *esposa* Patricia, met while he was on duty at a car show at the Coliseum. She was tall, attractive and blonde, just the way he liked them. Patricia Giuliana Vargas Ledesma was from Argentina. And for some reason, she would get extremely offended whenever someone would pronounce her name *Patrisha.* She would correct you, *"se pronuncia Pa-tree-see-ah,"*. It didn't matter anyway, we called her Patti.

The first few years of their marriage went pretty well and often they would double-date with me and Stefanie. When their twin daughters, Aida and Penny, were born we did more of the family type stuff like barbecues, weekend trips and even vacations together.

But Dominic's first love was police work, and when the NYPD began demanding more of his time, his marriage to Patti became increasingly antagonistic. The more time he spent away from her at work, the more incensed she would become. Eventually that resentment spilled over towards the rest of the family. Whenever we defended his work ethic she would say that we were taking sides against her.

Once she began to feel isolated from the rest of us, she ultimately morphed into a nasty, sour battle-ax and by the sixth year of their marriage, they could barely stand the sight each other. Somehow they managed to drag things out another eleven years before finally throwing in the towel with a quickie divorce.

Dominic let her have whatever she wanted. "Just get her the fuck out of my life!" Oddly enough, when he talks about her today, he insists on how much he misses and is still in love with her. Hey, don't ask me.

After the divorce Dominic moved into a one-bedroom apartment in Co-op City, where he spent nights staring out the window at the passing cars on the Hutchinson River Parkway. The night after I asked Travis and Donny about Dr. Gunder, I snooped through the files in Dominic's apartment while he gazed at the traffic outside with a can of Schlitz. By that time, I had mastered the art of quiet, unseen presence with someone else in the room. It's unkind to make someone you care about hear *things that go bump in the night*. Without even rustling a sheet of paper, I looked through Dominic's desk for anything else that could shed a light on his unsanctioned investigation. I was especially appreciative that his window was open and the cars on the parkway were noisy enough to cover any sounds coming from the desk.

Or so I thought.

A little bell from Dominic's computer broke the silence. It was an e-mail from *tg48*. Soft as the bell was, he heard it and walked over to his desk. With no mercy to the tiny office chair whose wheels were about to snap off, Dominic planted his size 46 caboose and opened the message.

"We have still not resolved the critical effect that the

MV-12 Detection Serum has on the human condition. Until then, I cannot accept your offer to volunteer as a test subject. I will remain the only test subject for now. The serum contains several known carcinogens and as a doctor I cannot in good conscience test it on a healthy human being."

Healthy? Obviously this person didn't know Dominic too well, even though it was apparent this was not their first communication.

"The serum has shown great promise, however. It has succeeded in enabling me to trace one of the infected by penetrating through his projected facade. This was confirmed in the daylight when we found the domain where he had retired into his casket. We exposed the room by opening the curtains and blinds that were covering his windows. When we pried open his casket, his torso almost immediately went into flames. If it were not for the colleague that I had working with me seeing the same thing, I might have questioned my own sanity as so many others have already. Instead, we will now be able to soon understand what happened to my son and your brother-in-law. To this day, these types of deaths are still being foolishly described as spontaneous combustion. But now, for the first time, I was able to trace and identify one of these beings—a creature that in the past had been written off as legend or superstition instead of reality—one that grows more frightening with everything I learn. This is a danger that cannot be ignored. The nature of this infected species is predatory, and humanity is their prey.

I thank you for your support and your assistance. I will continue to inform you of any further developments. Teresa Gunder"

Holy shit!

No wonder this woman shook Travis like no one else

could. She *is* the biggest danger our kind has ever faced—a real life Von Helsing! But what was MV12? Obviously it was dangerous to humans too, so why was Dominic volunteering to put that shit in him? And how did these two become pen pals? Self-loathing vampire or not, I still have the self-preservation drive that keeps us from ever wanting to face death—again. Knowing how bad it was the first time is incentive enough—and that's not even taking into account that my unholy existence destines me to eternal flames.

I think I'll stay here.

When Dominic took his beer buzz to bed, it allowed me to log on to his account and read his e-mail history with *tg48*. It went back almost two years when she saw that Dominic had taken an interest in her son's case. She began her correspondence anonymously before identifying herself as Ronnie's mother five months later, eventually trusting him enough to share details about her research.

The doctor had travelled as far as Central Europe, where she listened to local stories about mysterious deaths similar to her son's. Like here in the States, most of the stories had already been laughed off by the local authorities, who refused to give her access and permission to study these cases further.

In Romania, the doctor met an 86-year old woman whose husband's death in the 1930's had some parallels to Ronnie Gunder's five decades later. The woman, who was totally devoted to her husband, was never able to accept his death and she remained a widow ever since, singing an old Romanian love ballad to his ashes at her bedside.

Ashes!

The old woman resisted at first but Dr. Gunder worked hard to convince her that giving access to just a trace of those ashes would allow her to compare them to her son's and use what she learns to prevent similar deaths in the future. It would bring something positive from the losses that they suffered. From there, with her scientific background, medical knowledge, and whatever-the-fuck lives inside the brains of these analytical types, the doctor was able to see patterns and similarities surrounding many other unexplained deaths throughout Europe, and North and South America.

Inside Dominic's desk I also found a VHS tape, which I took home with me. It was labeled "DR. GUNDER 8/20/90". Once I got home, I slipped it in my VCR and sat down with a bag of Lay's sour cream and onion chips and a can of Dos Equis (maybe I'm the most interesting *undead* man in the world). The tape was of some local access cable interview out of Syracuse University, where her son attended. The interview subject was Dr. Gunder. She had granted time to some smug college student at the university studio.

The doctor was in her early fifties but the lines of pain on her face made her seem older. Still, she was doable, like Kenny Neglia used to like to say. I'm sure the doctor detected the skinny, bespectacled interviewer's skepticism but she was probably used to that. She spoke patiently with the young man, understanding how difficult it was for a normal person to wrap his mind around the outrageous claims she was making. But to the interviewer's credit, he handled the conversation with respect to the surviving mother of one of his fellow students. He gave her free reign. The doctor went on to describe how the unexplained deaths she had researched around the world were raising whispers of the supernatural.

In those days there was, what I like to call, decorum. In deference to the suffering mother, the tape was probably never shown outside of the local cable access channel—until now. Now it's all over the Internet. Anyone who'd seen that interview back then probably took it as the ramblings of a broken woman who had lost her child. Me, I was shocked at how much she was actually able to learn.

"The reason they have these capabilities that for so many centuries were dismissed as folklore is because they are literally not from this world," said Dr. Gunder.

"What do you mean?" asked the interviewer.

"In my visit to Central Europe, I had found fossilized organisms on a meteorite that matched some of the remains found at the scene of my son's death."

The student tried to word his question carefully to not come across as if he was mocking the doctor. *"Are you saying that not only do vampires exist, but that they are also actually an alien life form?"*

The doctor forced a miniscule smile. *"The viral organisms located at the site were brought there by that meteorite. It was not an organism that came from this earth. I have even found remains of this organism in the ashes of those infected. And let me make this clear, no organisms associated humans can leave remains. You can find elemental compositions in human ashes but no organisms. The remains of this organism were not human. And yes, I have traced the source of the mysterious deaths and the symptoms described by the local town residents to that meteorite. It is a virus that kills and reanimates its host as a being that feeds on the blood of its own species. Does that sound familiar to you?"* The interviewer respectfully nodded. *"And even though the host is technically no longer alive, by feeding off other human blood, it is able to continue hosting the micro-organism that dwells inside of him."*

The student remained respectful, although I sensed a

smirk being repressed. *"Do the hosts have any recollection of who they are or what happened to them?"*

"It's very interesting that you ask that," replied the doctor. *"I have found that there were humans that had a genetic resistance towards complete transformation. There has been a small amount of cases where victims retained a consciousness of who they were when they were alive, therefore carrying the characteristics, memories, intelligence and emotions that they've always had. Those are the ones that suffer the real horror, the horror of losing everything and everyone that they've ever loved."*

"What about the others?" the student asked.

"Their consciousness stems from the organism within. They have the capability to interact with society, but they are strictly predatory with no consciousness of the life the host had before."

Again the student wanted to carefully select his next words. *"Just so we can be clear, what you're stating is that you can scientifically prove the existence of vampires."*

"No, that is not what I am stating," replied the doctor.

"Then what is it that you are stating?"

"I am stating that I already have."

20

Juanita runs past me in tears.

"Juanita, que pasa?"

No answer.

There's a lot of commotion in the ER, more than usual. It appears chaotic over there. Jimmy can use some help.

Generally, there isn't much that happens here that would stir us outside the norm. We get everything here; shooting victims, knifing victims, domestic violence, hell, sometimes a skirmish will break out right in there in the ER (which is quite convenient for whoever comes up on the short end). But working in a hospital, one tends to get used to the pandemonium.

Unless it's personal.

The doctors, nurses, and aides are doing their best to clear a path as onlookers crowd the area. Between me and Jimmy, normally just one of us is stationed in the ER while the other patrols the hospital, but when something like this happens, it becomes more of a two-man job. "Jimmy, what's going on?"

"Oh shit!" Not exactly the way to welcome a helping hand. In fact, he's breaking from the crowd to intercept me. "Stay here, my man. Stay here."

"Stay here? What do you mean, stay here? I'm here to help."

He looks shaken. "Nah, man, it's okay, I got it. Just take it easy."

"What do you mean, take it easy? What the hell is happening here?"

A blood-spattered gurney bursts through the doors. Normally, to get through I'd have no problem flinging Jimmy across the ER like a rolled up newspaper but that hardly seems necessary. From the blood all over the gurney I can tell something happened to somebody, but—

The scent! The blood!

"Jimmy, get out of the way!"

"No, man, don't," pleads Jimmy as I effortlessly shove past him and follow the gurney.

"Georgie, step aside!" orders Dr. Roehning as I try to get a view. I push him aside, too.

Adam, a tall, muscular orderly tries to intervene, but he is no match for someone who has seen his share of death, including his own.

The gurney stops, not because the EMT's have stopped pushing, but because *I* stopped it.

The face is unrecognizable. Her once full, sensuous lips are split in four different places, exposing a row of teeth that's been almost completely knocked out. The swelling of her blackened eyes forces them completely shut. Her face is deformed into a shape that I never imagined possible. A genetically resistant whisper seeps through my barely clinging projection. "Veronica?" Blood pours freely from a large open wound exposing her skull, but it activates no hunger, only the intensifying tone of *Los Ruidos*. She lays motionless, barely alive. I whisper her name again. I was there for her a couple of nights ago. I wasn't tonight.

"Dammit Georgie get out of the way!"

Adam pushes me aside and takes the gurney. From behind, a hand takes me firmly by the shoulder. It's Jimmy. No need to shove him aside this time. I've seen what I needed to see.

What in the world was I thinking? I am not alive. I do not have the right to interact with others. I do not have the right to experience friendship nor do I have the right to love. I am dead. The more I love, the more I try to be a part of the lives of humans around me, the more death I bring. Death brings more death.

In Veronica's case, she's still alive—barely. How she will come out of this remains to be seen. On the other hand, there is one thing that be counted on, one thing that is certain. *Orquesta La Luna* is going to very soon have to find themselves a new trombone player.

21

The Raiders, Scarsdale High School's baseball team, had a pretty bad stretch in the early 1990's. It had been quite a while since they'd enjoyed a winning season. But when scrappy second baseman Davey Negrón made the Senior Varsity in his freshman year, their record quickly turned around. His soft hands on the field and his quick bat not only delighted those who were sitting in the bleachers but it also caught the eyes of major league scouts throughout the country.

Uncle Dominic accompanied his sister Stefanie to watch Davey play whenever he could and there was no way he was going to miss the big game against the New Rochelle Huguenots. It was for a final playoff spot.

Davey's recently deceased dad was also there, sitting in the row above Dominic and Stefanie casually eavesdropping in on their conversation. I had gotten there in the seventh inning because I had to wait for the sun to come down. As always, it was bittersweet sitting together with the family and of course I had to resist the urge to stand up and cheer Davey on. As far as Dominic and Stefanie were concerned, the space behind them was unoccupied.

At the top of the seventh, Davey smoothly fielded a routine grounder to end the inning for the Huguenots. It would now be the bottom of the seventh with the Raiders' last chance to come from behind. The score was 7-4. If they strung a couple of hits together, Davey would have a chance to be the hero of the game. He was scheduled to bat fifth.

As the teams changed sides, Dominic took the opportunity to quiz Stefanie about her personal life. "So you really like this guy, huh?"

"He's very nice," answered my widow.

"So, what's his name again, Bill?" He observed her like he was questioning a perp. Stefanie just nodded without turning away from the field. Big brother persisted. "Nice guy, huh?" I couldn't see from behind, but I'm sure Stefanie was rolling her eyes at her overprotective brother. "So, he's a teacher?"

"He's a college professor."

"Yeah, so, like, what does this guy profess?"

"Calculus." Stefanie shook her head, smiling, though I'm not sure she was amused.

"Calculus, huh?"

"Will you stop?"

"What? What? I can't ask my sister a couple of questions about some guy she's seeing?"

"Just watch the game. This is their last chance," she said, redirecting his attention.

The hometown crowd cheered on, trying to charge up a Scarsdale rally as the first batter approached the plate.

Dominic clapped his hands rhythmically, beaming at his nephew on the bench. "Come on guys, you can do it!"

This would have been one of our moments; Stefanie, Dominic and me together rooting for our boy, me holding Stefanie's hand and me breaking Dominic's balls about something, anything (I didn't need much). Instead I sat quietly behind them and reflected on how many moments like this I'd missed.

"Davey looks good, don't he?" said Dominic, nudging his, sister. "Even better than his father." Was that necessary, dumb ass, bringing me into the conversation? "And it's unbelievable how much better he is than all these seniors that are bigger and older than him. I can see him in the majors someday."

Stefanie didn't reply, keeping her focus on the game. Dominic then caught on that maybe bringing me up wasn't the smartest thing to do. He apologetically took his sister's hand. "I'm sorry, I shouldn't have said that. You probably still miss him a lot."

"Dominic, don't," replied Stefanie as the first batter popped out to short.

"Hey, I miss him, too. He was my buddy."

I miss you too, you fat bastard.

Stefanie didn't want to hear it. "Stop," she ordered.

"Come on, sis, you know there's no way he would have done those things they said in the paper. He loved you. Believe me, I know."

"You know?" She almost laughed in his face. "Tell me, how do *you* know?"

"Stef, all he ever talked about was you and how much he loved you. You know that. That whole thing was some kind of set up. I'm telling you—"

"Set up?" Their voices rose but the roar from the bleachers drowned them out as the Raiders first baseman ripped into a fastball and drove it over the fence. The score was now 7-5. "I'm a grown woman, Dominic. There was no set up. It's a fact of life. I know he loved me, but that's what men do."

"No, sis, that's not true."

"Of course it's true. After a few years of marriage, you get a little bored. Some other woman gives you attention..."

"No, Stef, it's not like that at all."

"Sure it is, Dominic. Even you—"

Stefanie cut herself off.

They were temporarily distracted as the Raiders catcher hit a liner back to the pitcher for the second out. The next batter had to get on base for Davey to have a chance at bat.

The distraction was only momentary. Dominic's eyes narrowed. "Even me? What do you mean by that?"

Stefanie backed down. "Forget it."

"No, no, tell me," he prodded.

"No, forget it!"

"No, sis, I want to know what you meant by that."

Stefanie gave in. "Dominic, you don't think everyone knew about Colleen?"

Dominic turned pale. "Colleen!"

"Yes, Colleen Ryan, your old partner's wife, you don't think I knew? You don't think Patti knew?"

Holy shit! *I* didn't know! Who says women can't keep a secret? Dominic was fucking Colleen Ryan??? Dominic, you animal!!!

Usually, he was quick with an answer, but not this time. All he could mutter after a moment of stunned silence was, "It wasn't like that..."

"Oh, no? Then tell me what it was like? Was that a set up, too?"

A welcome change of the subject came when the Raiders third baseman was hit by a pitch. Davey was now going to get a chance to hit. As the tying run, he had a chance to be a hero. On the other side of the coin, if Davey made an out, the Scarsdale High School baseball season would be over.

Dominic and Stefanie cheered.

"Come on, Davey!"

"You can do it, Davey!"

Davey wasted no time. He drilled the first pitch into the right centerfield alley past the outfielders. They chased desperately after the ball as Davey rounded first and headed towards second. By the time the right fielder got to the ball, the runner ahead of Davey crossed the plate to make it 7-6. In the meantime, the bleachers were shaking with excitement as Davey sped towards third. When the cutoff throw reached the first baseman in shallow right, the Raiders third base coach signaled Davey to stop.

He didn't listen. Thick-headed, just like his father.

The first baseman's throw to the plate was perfect and the catcher blocked the plate beautifully, absorbing Davey's hard slide. The catcher fell over but he had already received the throw and made the tag. The only question was whether he held on to the ball.

The crowd's cheerful roar became a somber quiet as they waited for the umpire to make his call.

He looked down at the catcher.

The ball was still in his mitt.

The umpire threw his fist in the air.

"OUT!"

The season was over. No playoffs.

Davey got up in a rage, throwing his helmet and kicking it. (*Deja-fucking-Vu*) The umpire warned Davey to stop, prompting the Raiders coach to run over to calm him. Dominic also ran down from the bleachers to soothe his nephew. Stefanie slowly followed.

By the time they were out in the parking lot to head home, Davey's tantrum subsided. Stefanie and Dominic didn't say a word. They knew a consolation speech would only set him off again so they just walked together towards their cars. Dominic was parked next to Stefanie. Davey had ridden in with his mother.

Dominic patted Davey on the shoulder, who grunted goodbye to his uncle before going into the car and slamming the door shut. Stefanie's eyes welled up with tears.

"Hey, don't worry, sis. It's only a game," said Dominic. He then shot his nephew an angry look and spoke loud enough to be heard inside the car. "He'll get over it!"

Stefanie shook her head and hugged her brother, kissing him on the cheek. "I'm sorry I said that."

"Nah, it's in the past. What's happened, happened. Don't worry about it."

"But, to answer your question, I do. I do miss him," she said, barely getting the words out. "I miss him every day of my life."

Dominic hugged his sister tightly and watched her as she got into her car and drove off.

His eyes were red.

He hadn't been sleeping much. I could see that his mind was in a jumble. But why? What was going on in that fat bastard's head?

He then took a sudden turn and looked squarely, right into my eyes. It startled me enough to take a step back. I looked at my hands to make sure my I wasn't exposed.

Nothing.

I looked to the ground to see if a shadow was cast from lights in the ball park. The only shadow was Dominic's. So why did he turn and look right at me?

It was almost as if... he knew I was there.

22

Who else would live here but a nice, hard-working family? The cement steps leading up to the porch of this semi-attached duplex in the Rego Park section of Queens, have a few cracks in them, but as a whole, the house looks pretty well maintained.

Through the front window of the living room I see three lovely Puerto Rican ladies from different generations watching Telemundo on a Sony 42" flat screen. I've been meaning to get one of those. The bulky rear-projection monster I have is taking up way too much space in my apartment.

Two little ones are seated on the floor in front of the television, a boy and a girl. On screen is a *Sabado Gigante*-type variety show like Don Francisco used to have. The host on screen is ogling the tits of the salsa dancer he's introducing about as subtly as Benny Hill used to during his skits back in the seventies.

The little girl has a broken Barbie doll. It's the Puerto Rican Dolls of the World Collector's Edition from about twenty years ago. From the wear and tear I figure it belonged to the girl's mom once. The dark-haired doll is wearing a white almost bridal-like dress with a pink cummerbund belt and a matching flower in her hair. This is apparently how Mattel pictured Puerto Rican girls in the late nineties. I guess someone forgot to do their research and actually *go* to Puerto Rico. The boy looks like he's about the same age as what I presume is his sister. Maybe they're twins. He's got a toy truck in his hands and is totally undistracted by the dark-haired salsa singer and her impossibly tight body suit. Just wait a few years, bud. You won't be playing with trucks anymore.

The music kicks in and the singer starts gyrating. It reminds me of when I was fifteen years old and I had a little portable twelve-inch TV in my room. We had trouble getting UHF in the Bronx and I had to move the TV antenna around the room to get Channel 47 so I could rub one out while watching Iris Chacón shake that giant ass of hers.

On the couch, the youngest lady looks no older than sixteen. She's probably the older sister sitting with *Mami* and *abuelita*—a lovely innocent family quietly enjoying a peaceful Saturday evening at home. I almost hate to disturb them.

Like any smart family in New York they have the front door locked. Fortunately, the loud salsa blaring from the TV will drown out the sound of me turning the doorknob past its breaking point. During my living years, I used to go around with comfortable L.L. Beans on my feet, but these days I find Reeboks (which I have on now) or Nikes to be much quieter.

The wall in the foyer is decorated with achievement plaques from the New York City Police Department. It looks like the daddy of the household is Julio Miguel Rodriguez, a respected officer of the law. I wonder if he knows Dominic.

Thankfully, Officer Rodriguez doesn't appear to be home. Having had a policeman in the family that was also my best friend, I always had great admiration for the police and wouldn't want one to get in my way. I don't like to hurt the good guys. He probably does know that his trombone-playing younger brother is a lowlife, but what he probably *doesn't* know is that Mr. Roberto beat the mother of two young boys into a coma a couple of nights ago.

Hello.

The collective gasp from three ladies on the couch is an expected reaction to spotting a strange man standing in their living room doorway. What I don't want is any unexpected reactions, which is why I quickly raise my hand and calm them. I don't really need to raise my hand, taking over their minds doesn't require that, but I remember Obi-Wan Kanobi doing it in Star Wars and I always thought it was kind of cool.

Strangely enough, the boy with the truck and the little girl with the doll don't seem frightened. Is it a regular occurrence for unexpected strangers to just walk in here? Anyway, it's not my problem. But rather than take a chance of any sudden change in reaction I'll take over their minds as well, something I normally don't like to do to children. Extended mind control can cause permanent brain damage, but if I get this done quick I should be able to release them with no harm done.

"Everyone please just relax. I will be out of your way in just a few minutes and you can continue to watch Telemundo." Having to step over the toys on the floor brings back memories of our living room back at our house thirty years ago. I must have stepped on a hundred Hot Wheels cars back then yelling, "Davey, pick your shit up off the floor!".

I kneel in front of the ladies on the couch to look less threatening. Again, isn't really necessary but it does make for easier eye contact.

I address the children's mother first. *"Hola Señora,* I take it the man of the house isn't home?" Her eyes are blank, even as she nods. "A couple of Roberto's friends said he might be staying here tonight. Is Roberto home?"

"Bobby?"

Oh, how sweet, they call him Bobby. "Yes, Bobby."

Her eyes drift up towards the ceiling. "Bobby's upstairs."

A thunderous bang!

A jolt in my temple!

Almost simultaneous!

The force of the bullet crashing through my skull and burrowing into my brain sends me flying towards the flat screen, shattering the image of the sexy salsa singer into an infinite amount of pieces.

Why didn't I hear him? Was it the salsa? My heightened sense of hearing should be at its peak after my Buffalo Johnny session with Veronica less than a week ago. How was I not aware of his presence? Did my genetic resistance allow my pent up rage to distract me to the point of carelessness?

The horrified screams of the Rodriguez family indicate that their minds are free of my control, not surprising considering a slug has tunneled through my cerebrum and exited through my cheekbone. This is the kind of encumbrance that comes with my genetic handicap. Another of my kind would have just fed on everyone before searching the house. Me, I can't bring myself to harm an innocent family. Why should they pay for Uncle Bobby's barbarities? They probably don't even want him there.

"Die, you fucking freak!" Uncle Bobby, that ship has sailed a long time ago.

How stupid can I be? A cop's house! Cop. Gun. Simple math, what's the matter with me? Not that the bullet's going to kill me, but I should have considered the fact that there could have been firearms on the premises. I also should have considered that, even with the entire living room having been in a trance, someone else in another room might not have been under my control.

If I was alive, the bullet obviously would have killed me. If that didn't do the trick, the electrical current from the circuitry of the smashed television would have been the finishing touch. If somehow I managed to survive even that, at the very least, I would have ended up with permanent brain damage. But alas I am dead. And there's nothing more permanent than that. And right now this dead man wants blood—Puerto Rican trombone player blood!

The shock of the bullet has not only cut off the spell I had cast in the room but it also knocked out my projection, which means now Bobby and the family are treated to the sight of broken fragments of cheekbone hanging from the torn flesh below my right eye. These wounds won't heal magically the way they do in those movies you see on TV. They'll heal somewhat but dead skin does not regenerate the same way it does among the living. When my projection is back intact, the unsightliness will be covered up, but for now it is all out for everyone to see.

"*Demonio!*" shrieks *abuelita*. Every superstition she probably grew up with has now been confirmed. The ladies pick up the kids and flee out into street screaming.

Roberto continues to still hold out his gun, petrified as he witnesses the freak he just shot rising after taking a bullet through the brain. From the smell of the room, I think he just shit himself.

That doesn't stop him from taking another shot.

This time I'm hit in the forehead right above the left eye. For a musician, this fucker can shoot. Shoot all you want, you son of a bitch. Do your best, or do your worst, whatever that fucking saying is. Your life is ending tonight and there's nothing you can do about it.

Too bad I can only kill you once.

Roberto fires two more panicked shots—one hits me in the neck and another gets me in the thigh just below my balls. The impact from the bullets sets me back a couple of steps but it doesn't stop me from moving forward, to which Roberto reacts with a helpless whimper.

That's right, buddy, the salsa party is over.

Roberto darts out of the house, following the rest of his brother's screaming family out into the street. If the crap from the movies were true, right now I'd transform into a bat and fly past the frightened shitbag scrambling down the block. I'd then land in front of him and turn back to human form in front of his eyes.

Like I said before, I would fucking love that!

Too bad. Instead I just have to go run after him. And we don't have super speed, either. In fact, we don't run any faster than humans do. Our advantage is that we don't tire. So a human can run from us all he wants but eventually he'll get winded. We don't. With our non-functioning lungs, that's never a problem. If it weren't for the daylight, I could run straight to California without breaking stride.

The only problem I *do* have right now is that all of the screaming has alerted the entire neighborhood. Curious neighbors are now in front of the house and a gang of young, Latino punks with baseball bats is approaching me with harmful intent.

Are you kidding me, guys?

They must be stoned out of their minds because I haven't yet regained my human projection and they're not even flinching at the sight of me. Maybe they think I'm made up for some kind of costume party.

What they *don't* realize is that the real monster, the woman-beating trombone player, is down at the end of the street running his ass off. But looking the way I do right now, I don't think they're going to listen and help me with my chase, so it looks like I'm going to have to engage and kick some young Latino ass.

The first punk charges in swinging a stickball bat, which I easily catch and pull from his hands. This cues the rest of the gang to blitz and start pounding me. A couple of others, standing outside the melee, hold up their smartphones, recording the fracas on video. That's going to be a problem. My projection still isn't up. Even if my face is distorted to the point that it is unrecognizable as anything human, my clothes may be recognized as something that was seen worn by Jorge Sangría.

Usually pricks like these are looking for any excuse to get into some kind of free-for-all (I doubt if this is the neighborhood watch group), but tonight since I have my eyes on a different prize, I'll give them the benefit of the doubt and assume their community spirit is sincere, which means I won't kill them. That being said, at this moment I don't have the time to reason or be gentle. *That* means some of these punks are going to get hurt.

My tightened grip on two of my attackers' necks enables me to throw them from the pile as the rest continue to pummel me, not realizing that their punches and kicks are having no effect other than keeping me from my prey. A flurry of blows connects with each punk's jaws sending them reeling back and knocking over one of those jackasses with the smartphone. Record *that*, ass wipe. I think now they're getting idea that they're dealing with something unusual. That's right, fuckers, you want to take me on? Let's go.

They haven't exactly retreated, but it seems like they're not too eager jump back in. Good, back off, punks. Consider yourselves lucky that—

Are you kidding me?

There's always that one. And here he comes charging me with a yell. I never understood that. What is that supposed to do, scare me? Did you get a good look at me, idiot? The blitzing punk's momentum is halted by my grabbing his arm and twisting it around his back, past breaking point. His tortured scream as I throw him face first against a parked car sets another punk off in our direction.

Man, these fuckers are dense!

The roaring yell of my antagonist shakes me up so badly that I take him by his shirt and guide his head into a parked car window, letting the shattered pieces of glass sprinkle around him.

Like I said, someone's going to hurt.

Throwing the bleeding-from-the-head unconscious yeller to the street, I step towards the gang inviting any additional comers.

Anyone?

I didn't think so.

Good.

Now let me go after my prey.

#

I smell his fear. I hear him hyperventilating. My senses are not yet as strong as I need them to be, but they're slowly coming back. Roberto's bullet had knocked the crap out of me and whatever was left was exhausted by my tangling with the neighborhood goon squad. And from the sound of it, they apparently didn't get the message because I can hear them regrouping with intentions of chasing me down like the villagers in *Frankenstein*. The fact that they're still a couple of blocks away will give me a little time, but I'd rather not have to scuffle with those imbeciles again.

My death face is still out for everyone to see. I can see it reflected on the window of a parked car. In order to kill that reflection, or to get myself out of sight I need to feed.

Now!

There's a string of apartment buildings and alleys on both sides of the street. More often than not someone fleeing in fear like Roberto would probably duck into an alley, looking to break the trail. Instead I'm tracing his scent to the building in front of me.

But I'm weak. I'm losing focus. I can smell him but I can't pinpoint where. Damn that fucking bullet.

Blood. I smell blood, sweet, fresh blood, of the quality I rarely get to enjoy. And it smells so fucking good.

I want it.

I got to have it.

I don't care whose it is.

Through a window of the tenement in front of me, on the first floor, a lovely young mother, rocking her precious little newborn in her arms.

A young mother, the blood of a young mother.

Even more potent, the blood of a freshly born child.

So sad.

Wrong place, wrong time.

In the ongoing struggle between the monster and his genetic resistance, sometimes the monster wins.

The inside door of a tenement like this is usually locked. To get in you need a key or someone to buzz you in through the intercom. But many times in certain neighborhoods of New York, these doors, like this one, are broken by vandals. It's a nice building, though, well kept. The lobby's clean, well maintained. They'll probably have that lock fixed in twenty-four hours.

The apartment that offers me the fuel I need to re-emerge is to my left. Inside, the mother sings softly to her child. The baby coos at the comfort of her voice. My shadow casts a looming specter in the otherwise empty hall outside her door, evidence that Death still lurks (we are not supposed to cast shadows).

The monster is exposed.

The monster must feed.

The door to the apartment is locked, but again I am able to force it open. Thanks to the Rebooks, no sounds are coming from my footsteps, only the sound of a nurturing mother and her angelic, dependent child.

It isn't a large apartment. It's more of a warm, cozy nest for a nice couple whose family just had an addition. The child's bedroom has charming pink decorations on the wall. It's a baby girl.

Mommy sets her little princess down in her nicely crafted Cinderella-themed crib. Sweet young mother, innocent child, you do not deserve this. But I hold no responsibility over what I am. I am Death. And I—

The slam of a door—five flights up, on the roof! It wasn't vandals that had busted the door in the front of the building. It was Roberto! He had no keys so he threw his body against it to get through.

A grunt of anticipation escapes me.

The mother turns.

Her scream rattles the Disney decorations on the wall above the crib.

No way the neighbors in the building won't hear that. I gotta get the fuck out. My real prey is upstairs, on the roof. The faster I get out and feast on the salsa playing brute upstairs, the better chance for me to avoid causing more trouble than I already have.

Fuck! What did I almost do? Never have I come even close to doing something like that! But then again I never had a bullet bounce around in my brain like a pinball before. I can't believe what I was just thinking. What about my genetic resistance? Could a bullet through the brain have damaged me that much? As for you, sweet lady, make it a point never to miss another Sunday at Church. God just intervened for you in a very big way.

Leaping up the steps three or four at a time, I can already taste Roberto's *cerveza*-soaked blood pouring down my throat. It reminds me of the feeling I used to get when I passed the Outback Steakhouse on my way home from work.

Too bad dead guys can't participate in the Olympics. I must have made it up these flights in record time. The door to the roof has a sign that says open only in the case of an emergency. I think it's a safe bet that for Roberto this qualifies as one.

The crisp, cool air of a New York City night kisses my ashen face as I step out on the roof. There is no hostess to lead me to my table but the whimper coming from the opposite end of the roof tells me Outback's is serving *cowardly woman batterer a la carte*.

He's winded, shivering on the roof's tar surface in the fetal position. It actually surprises me a little bit, I expected him to have a bit more stamina. I've seen trombone players blow those things for hours without even taking a break.

Anyway, it's not my problem. He's got no breath left

to run which means his only choice as he sees me approaching, is to beg for his life.

"Oh God, no, please. I'm so sorry. Please." The last word barely gets out as he breaks into a pathetic sob. It is such fulfillment witnessing the fright of your prey before you feed, knowing that his body will be lifeless within the next few seconds. Genetic resistance or not, when filth like Roberto is about to become your next victim, it's easier to understand the joy of the kill.

Roberto clasps his trembling hands together in prayer as I kneel before him. "Ay, *Jesus Crísto, Santa Maria. Ayudame, Dios, por favor, ayudame.*"

It shouldn't bother me since God and I aren't exactly on the same team these days, but it does. God steps in to protect young, innocent mothers and babies like the ones downstairs, not a worthless piece of shit like you, you fuck. You have no idea what I almost did because of you.

"Stop praying. You have no right!" He's not hearing me. His hands are still together, eyes closed, lips moving. "Stop it, I said. Stop praying, now!" He tapers off a little, but not completely. "NOW!"

This time I got his attention.

The prayers stop.

Good.

Say goodbye, fucker.

The sickening wail of the fallen abuser resonates through the rooftops of Rego Park as his unearthly executioner gnaws like a rabid Rottweiler. Below on the street, the Rego Park vigilantes arrive, wondering aloud where the scream is coming from. The whole neighborhood in itself is already in a stir, having heard the scream of a young mother, fearing for her life and that of her child.

Heads pop out of the windows looking at the

commotion forming on the street.

A vigilante punk wanders in circles, waving his arms maniacally. "Anybody see anything?" Surely somebody did. It's not like the street was empty. But being New Yorkers, some crazed guy running away from another is probably nothing out of the ordinary (assuming they didn't get a good look at my face).

"Where did he go, where did he go?" he asks to anyone who will listen.

The answer arrives in a splattered thud on the street, twenty feet behind him.

"Holy shit!"

The gang members gape at the gored, headless torso before looking up and spotting their targeted subject on the roof. "Get that motherfucker!"

Like the Keystone Cops, they charge the entrance of the building seeking another round with the Rego Park *demonio*.

When they finally make it up here, they won't find him. Instead they'll find the head of a woman-beating trombone player with his mouth wide open, paralyzed in fright.

Okay, so it was reckless kill on my part, no question about it. And it was in New York, out of my territory. Nonetheless, it had to be done.

No doubt Travis and Donny will be pissed. They will have sensed this one as it happened and they'll know it was me. And if that's not enough, there are going to be smartphone videos all over the ten o'clock news tonight showing a street brawl with some young punks and a guy that looks like he's auditioning for a Bruce Campbell movie.

It's the second ruckus I've caused in their territory in less than a week. Yeah, Travis and Donny are going to rip me a new one for sure.

23

What was she supposed to do, spend the rest of her life mourning for a husband who spent his last night in bed with another woman?

We all deserve a second chance at happiness. I got mine when Stefanie put a twenty year hold on the punishing song of *Los Ruidos*. She deserved a second chance, too. So did Jessie, and so did Davey. My boy was eighteen, looking handsome in his sharp, black dress suit, and his big sister, who had turned twenty-one, was already a clone of her mom, wearing a modest but very charming bridesmaid's gown. Their mother, the forty-eight-year-old bride, was wearing a cream-colored dress that fit very nicely over her still shapely figure. It was July 1998, ten years after life was sucked out of me by a serpentine redhead at the Ritz-Carlton.

Stefanie's side of the family filled up most of the banquet room at the Ardsley Hilton, but friends were there too, along with members of Rippey's family and his college professor associates. All were there to celebrate the happy bride and groom. The late July sunset and the drive from Newark got me there a little after 10:00 so I could feed my masochistic habit of watching Stefanie become happy again with someone who wasn't me. Somehow I kidded myself into thinking that the reality in front of my eyes would help me let go. That foolishness went out the window the second I saw the love in Stefanie's eyes as she danced with her new groom.

The kids too, had taken to Rippey. He brought a sense of sanity back in their lives. The suffering and embarrassment from my scandalous death was at last beginning to subside. I was an unpleasant distant memory.

Dominic, Artie and Ramona helped maintain a strong presence for the kids during their growing years, applauding at Jessie's dance recitals and celebrating Davey's victories on the baseball field. They were also there to congratulate them for their good grades and beamed proudly as a family at their graduations. Now they were all sharing this special moment together. It was time to say goodbye to the tears and escape the ugly cloud that had followed them for most of the past decade.

Grandpa Artie and Grandma Ramona looked sprite and energetic at their table, even healthier than their son Dominic, who had by then let himself go considerably. He reminded me of that cop Dennis Franz played on NYPD Blue. By the time I got to the reception everyone had already eaten, had a few too many drinks and was dancing to some really bad disco being played by an overpriced DJ. The more reserved guests were off to the sides having their little chats, like this tipsy group of wine-drinking hens I passed. They were colleagues of Stefanie's from Fordham University, sharing thoughts of how happy they were that she had found somebody new.

"Especially after that first son of a bitch left her so humiliated," said an over-perfumed fish-face whose glass of cabernet mysteriously tipped over on her lavender dress.

I was then treated to the sight of Rippey and Stefanie playfully dancing to that mind-numbing *Macarena*. Artie and Ramona also watched happily, enjoying the sight of their daughter smiling again. When that record mercifully ended, the DJ softened the mood with some slow-dance numbers. It seemed to be the preferred music of the evening as the guests filled the dance floor, enjoying the sensual air set by the lush tunes.

For me the music was drowned out by *Los Ruidos*, and *they* picked up a few decibels when Rippey and Stefanie again held each other tightly and looked into each other's eyes. The room then broke into a large round of applause as they went into a long, deep kiss that hammered a crack in my heart no smaller than the San Andreas fault. But hey, what did I expect? It was a wedding. Was I expecting them to sign a contract and shake hands?

Torturous as it was, I was still compelled to look. Maybe I thought I could get used to the idea and make it hurt less.

Boy was I off.

The first notes of the next tune were vaguely familiar. When the bass came in to flesh out the mood, it became a little more familiar. But when Roberta Flack breathed out the first line of the romantic tune, it then became unbearably familiar.

Bad move, DJ. You should do your research before taking a job.

The female guests on the dance floor gasped as a loud sob broke out above the music. When the bride turned away from her husband and ran out of the room in tears, the ladies followed her, leaving their dance partners to wonder what was going on.

"ARE YOU FUCKING KIDDING ME?"

Dominic was incensed, both startling and confusing the puzzled guests, who didn't know where he was venting his anger at.

Dominic stomped his way towards the DJ. "ARE YOU FUCKING KIDDING ME?" I wanted to say the same thing but obviously couldn't without turning the reception into a fright fest. "Give me that CD!" ordered Dominic. The DJ was as shaken as the guests who stood nervously on the dance floor. "I said, give me that goddamn CD," he warned.

The terrified DJ hit the stop button, bringing the room to a sudden silence. He then handed the CD to the seething 260 lb. beast, who promptly broke it in half and threw it back at him. Without offering any explanation, Dominic marched towards the hallway outside the banquet room where his family was trying to comfort Stefanie. She was sitting on a bench with Ramona and Jessie by her side. Artie and Davey were also there lending support while Rippey knelt in front of her and stroked her hair.

In the banquet room, the bewildered DJ was still looking for a clue as to what just transpired. Rippey's friends had no answers and neither did some of Stefanie's friends. They all shared the same quizzed expression. But not the Torres side of the family. They knew. And they probably even had a little sympathy for the DJ who didn't understand that he had just played the wedding song that Stefanie and I danced to back in 1972. It was an unexpected, hurtful jolt to Stefanie at a time she was supposed to be celebrating the start of a new life.

"It's okay, baby," said Ramona, stroking her

daughter's back.

Dominic knelt beside Rippey in front of his sister. "You okay, sis?"

Stefanie responded to no one. She just kept on crying. Artie shook his head, frustrated he could do nothing to soothe his daughter. He settled on taking her hand and giving her what was meant to be a reassuring smile. Instead it made her cry more.

Dominic rose and turned back towards the banquet room cursing under his breath, not realizing that yet again, like back in the ball park, he was looking right at me—right at the center of my forehead. If I were visible, it would have looked like he was cursing at me.

Again I checked.

I was still out of sight, but for how long? The high emotions from hearing that song and seeing Stefanie break down had the potential to weaken me. I was still in there. I was still in there, somewhere in her memory, somewhere in her heart.

I had to get out. The last thing that needed to happen was for her dead husband to make a sudden grisly appearance. Afraid of knocking something over and creating some sort of poltergeist moment, I restrained myself from bolting out that very second. But to reassure myself, I checked the mirror across the hall. The reflection was still of just Dominic and the rest of the family. When I turned to face him again, I then saw him squint, slightly tilting his head, looking side to side before zeroing in right back at me.

He was concentrating. Again I resisted moving, for fear that he might hear the rustle of my clothes—and it definitely looked like he was trying to hear something.

I checked the mirror again—still unseen.

Dominic's eyes continued to wander, now roaming above my head as if he were following a fly that he was going to swat with a rolled-up newspaper.

Suddenly there was no one and nothing else in the hall. Stefanie's cries had drifted off to the distance. Everyone consoling her had faded from Dominic's line of vision. His mind was no longer at the Ardsley Hilton sharing space and time with those attending the wedding. He was now focusing at a vague area just below my hairline.

I remained motionless. His calmness unnerved me.

Dominic took a deep breath and nodded. He had returned to Earth. The family had soothed his sister while he was away. Not that they'd noticed he was gone, but gone he was. Where? I didn't know.

I slowly edged away and backed the hell out of there. For me, this party was over.

24

Will her eyes ever again flash that twinkle the way they did whenever she passed her undead friend in the hallways at work? I doubt it. They're now blackened and swollen shut on a misshapen face that is almost completely purple. Her busted nose is flattened and spread to the sides while her cracked lips hold a loose grip on the respirator that is trying to compensate for her collapsed lungs.

My distance from Irene, the new third-shift nurse that is monitoring her from the other side of the bed, should be enough that I don't interfere with the observation of her patient. I haven't formally met Irene yet, just polite nods when we pass each other in the halls. For all I know, she probably doesn't really know Veronica either. But whether she does or not doesn't mean she can't be shaken by the sight of a co-worker being assaulted to such a level of disfigurement. This is a mother who worked endlessly to support her two boys. What happens to them now? The reality is Veronica Rojas is probably never going to rise from this bed again, which only underscores the fruitlessness of revenge. Even the surge of energy I received from the sanguine geyser that sprung from Roberto's arteries is now dissipated.

Never seek satisfaction from an act of retribution.

Vengeance is a terrible lay.

Irene has done all she can to make Veronica comfortable—which is really a joke. In Veronica's current world there is no such thing as comfort or discomfort. She just lays in a constant state of nothing, which means there's nothing I can do either.

When Travis lost Donny eighty years ago, he took a shot at turning him so they could stay together. To each his own. I'm sure as hell not going to do that. I wouldn't wish this curse on anyone. And let's say I did. Let's say I did and she turned out to be genetically resistant. With what's left of her brain after the battering that lowlife gave her, she wouldn't have any cognizance. On the other side, if she weren't genetically resistant, then she would be completely consumed by the venom that would make her a reckless predator, feeding on her neighbors in Newark.

Not exactly the best Mommy material.

I may as well follow Irene out of ICU. At least there I can come back into view and stop draining myself.

Looks like another visit to the blood bank is in order.

#

"Hey man, you okay?" It's fitting the first face I see out of ICU is Jimmy. He's the closest one that can fall into the category of friend for me, even if it's through no effort of my own. Sometimes I feel bad blowing him off as much as I do, but it's hard to explain that dead guys aren't the greatest company.

"Thanks Jimmy, I'm good. But it's bad, man. It looks

really bad."

"I know, brother, but listen. There's nothing you can do here. Just go home. Get some rest. If anything changes, I'll give you a call."

#

My apartment has only the bare necessities; a couch, a small dining table, and an outdated 40" rear-projection TV. I've been meaning to get one of those new 70" plasmas but those have to be mounted on the wall, which means I need service installers. Why is that a problem? Well, how many TV installers do you know that would do that job late at night?

The Branch Brook Park section where I live in Newark is a busy, vibrant community and the view from my 15th floor balcony almost makes me nostalgic for my metro days back at the Big Apple. For the most part though, I keep my blinds shut, especially in the bedroom. There, I even cover the windows with aluminum foil and duct tape. I got that idea from a documentary I saw about Elvis. He did that to keep the sun out while he slept during the day. Think about *that* one, fans. He *was* still looking pretty young before he went apeshit with the cheeseburgers.

Loud banging on my door.

This time of night?

Who the hell could *that* be? It's not like I entertain up here. Hell, I don't think anybody even knows my address.

"Open the damn door, young man!"

"Travis?" I knew he and Donny wouldn't be pleased with me, but to come all the way out to Newark? "I said, open the door!"

"Travis, calm down!" Donny, too?

Just what I need, a pair of loud gay guys loitering outside my apartment at 2:30 a.m. Better I just open the door and let them in before they wake anyone up. "All right, wait a second, and keep it down. I got—"

Before I can even turn the second latch Travis pushes the door open, slamming me in the face.

Donny's pleads to keep things level headed. "Travis, take it easy!"

His paramour isn't listening, clutching my throat and forcing me against the wall of my kitchenette.

Maybe I should remind him that he isn't thinking too straight. "Hey, you dumb fuck! You can't choke me. I'm dead, remember?" He's not letting go. "Travis, take your hands off my throat before I grab you by your pants and throw your ass out the balcony."

Donny's wedges himself between us. "Stop it, you two."

Travis still isn't letting go. "What are you doing feeding on our side of the Hudson? Who do you think you are?"

"Travis, listen to your sweetheart and calm down."

"Are you with her?"

"Am I with her? What does *that* mean? What are you talking about?"

"Don't you play games with me, young man."

"Travis, one last warning, take your hands off me."

"Stop it, I said!" Donny finally manages to make it between us but his mate isn't letting up.

Travis circles around Donny pointing his finger at me. "Are you with her?"

"With her? What does that mean?" I ask Donny, since he's the more clearheaded one right now. "What is he talking about?" Donny's look is one I haven't seen before—at least towards me. I guess an apology is in order. "Look guys, I'm sorry about last night, but that guy killed a friend of mine."

"What about last week in Brooklyn?" Donny with the follow up question, I didn't expect that.

"Hey, that fucker threatened my boy's life."

Travis shakes his head. "You're still stalking your family?" He looks back at Donny. "You believe that? He's still stalking his family."

"I'm not stalking them!"

Travis snorts with his usual disdain.

"So then you're not with her?" Donny the interrogator, I'm not used to this.

"With who? What are you two talking about?"

They exchange glances again. They're not sure they believe me. "Okay, young man, have it your way. Now, we've told you in the past that every couple of decades or so, she comes back to create more havoc."

"No fucking way!"

"And this time," says Donny. "We're sensing others feeding along with her."

Travis adds, "And since you and our redheaded friend have a little history and you've been having these little feasting parties in our outer boroughs..."

I can't believe what these fuckers are thinking. "She's here? And you two dumb asses thought I was *with* her?"

Travis points at me, accusingly. "Listen, young man, you know about her capabilities. She can control anyone of us given the opportunity."

My fangs are ready to burst through my rotted gums. The one that took my life from me is within reach, somewhere where I can find her. "Where is she?"

"If we knew, sonny, we wouldn't be here trying to draw it out of you," says Travis.

"We do know she fed three times last week in Long Island," adds Donny. "We also think she turned three teenagers and that they are now following her around."

"How do you know they're teenagers?" Our ability to sense others feeding in our area doesn't extend to identity-unless we've gotten to know them. It's sort of like when dogs recognize each other's scents after sniffing each other's asses.

"Look at this." Travis hands me a newspaper article.

"VAMPIRE CULT TEENS REPORTED MISSING".

I've read about these *Goth* morons before, dumbass kids dressing up to make themselves out to be vampires. They get caught up in all this *Twilight, Buffy* and *Vampire Diaries* bullshit and wear black gothic clothes, eyeliner and blood-red lipstick. They also discolor their faces with chalky white makeup. Some even drink each other's blood, not stopping to think of the diseases they could bring upon themselves. With the tainted blood that I've come across over the years that's something I am too painfully aware of, but being dead I can benefit from the nutrients without suffering any infections my victims might carry.

The New York Post says these dumb kids were last seen in the company of a "tall red-haired woman", bringing speculation that their cheesy-named Scarlet Widow is back! There are even pictures of me and Ronnie Gunder in a side column. Since the Scarlet Widow deaths have spanned a couple of decades, speculation now is that it could be some kind of cult.

I crumble the article and throw it at Travis. "How can you think that I could be with her?

"Now you listen to me, young man. When Simone is involved, we take nothing for granted. All we know is that you and she are feeding in our territory at the same time. If what you say is true and you've been running around our city like some vampire vigilante, then you need to redirect your energy." Travis signals to Donny it's time to leave. I couldn't agree more. "We'll see ourselves out."

"Oh please, do stay in touch."

"Oh, you'll be hearing from us all right."

"Fuck off, asshole. Don't let the door hit you on the way out."

It's been a while but we've spoken about it in the past. Simone's been long overdue for one of her returns. I was starting to think that maybe she'd been staked or had woken up to a little sunlight. But now she's here! She's here and we have an actual chance of putting an end to her. Well, so we hope.

The reality of trying to destroy one of our own is problematic enough, never mind one that has superior capabilities. Sure, in the past they've had some measure of success in fighting her off. In fact, even Ronnie Gunder put up a decent showing against her. But if time has proven anything it's that Simone is like an undead Energizer Bunny. She just keeps on coming until she gets what she wants, stronger and more evolved with each return.

Her most distinguishable trait is that she can control others like us. None of us know of anyone else that can do that. She's an undead queen bee. And she's now forming her own little army.

How do we go about taking her on? Who the fuck knows? We can't expose her to daylight 'cause obviously we'll fry too. As for staking, sure it's possible, but most of us are more than capable of defending ourselves. Our fights usually end up in frustrating draws, with both sides scattering to their respective coffins before the sun rises. Now let's take that and consider that Simone is the savviest, most ferocious and relentless predator that anyone of us has ever heard of. *And* she can control our minds.

Sure we can go out there and find her.

But what happens then?

#

Again, with the loud, obnoxious banging on my door!

So much for winding down quietly with some ESPN, a little on-demand porn and maybe an episode of Seinfeld (that Kramer guy never fails to crack me up).

"Dammit, what is it now?"

25

My body already is cold so I can't say a chill has run up my spine. And since I don't breathe, it wouldn't make much sense to say that the air's been knocked out of me.

I can only *imagine* the emotions on the other side of the doorway. "I knew it, but still, I can't believe it." The world he knew; all the laws of logic, reality and proper order have just been flipped over like a table on the Real Housewives of New Jersey. Across the doorway from Dominic is the brother-in-law that mysteriously disappeared more than two-and-a-half decades ago. "You—you look the same. It's..." How do I respond? What could possibly come out of my mouth that would make any sense to him?

"Demonio!"

"DOMINIC, NO!" The large pewter crucifix knocks me back into my apartment, sending me crawling back towards the living room. "Put that away!"

"Stay down!"

There's little chance of him listening as he follows with the crucifix in one hand and his NYPD service Glock in the other.

"Dominic, stop!"

"*Cayate, Diablo!*"

"Dominic, it's me, Nicky!"

"Bullshit! You're not Nicky. You're the thing that killed him. That's why you can't even face the cross."

"Dominic, stop! You're family. I'm not going to hurt you."

"*Embustero.*"

Cowering into the fetal position, I hold up my hand defensively, facing away from the cross. I don't know how much less of a threat I can be. "Dominic, I'm telling you the truth."

"You don't know the meaning of the word."

"Please put the crucifix away."

"The Nicky I knew loved God."

"Oh bullshit, Dominic, you know I hated going to Church." *Mami* might have instilled into me the fear of God, but Church still bored the shit out of me.

Dominic lowers his gun, but keeps the crucifix in sight. "You sure talk like he did." I might have struck a chord of recognition.

"That's because I *am* him, fuckhead." I can't turn to face him while he holds up that cross but I can still get up.

The only shadow on the floor is Dominic's. It shows him raising the gun up again. "Slowly." Poor bastard, this isn't the easiest shit to try and wrap your mind around. Believe me, *I* know. Holding his pistol pointed at me, Dominic scouts the area. Considering the high-end apartment building I live in, my personal space can be called humble at best "You live here?"

"Well, I don't know if I'd use the word *live*. How

about we just say I reside here?"

Dominic marches angrily towards me, talking into my ear like the drill sergeant from Full Metal Jacket. "You think this funny? Do you know what your family's been through?"

I'm trying to be patient but my prick brother-in-law is really pushing it. "Hey, you fat fuck, what about me? What about what *I've* been through?" I turn to face him but have to turn back. Again, that cross!

I can't see him but I imagine he's shaking his head. "*Jesus Cristo,* you sound just like him."

"Dammit, Dominic, I *am* him! Now put that damn crucifix away. I'm not going to hurt you."

"Okay, turn around slowly. I want to look at you."

"Did you put it away?"

"Yes, I put it away. Now turn around." He did put it away but he's still pointing his gun at me. "I'm holding on to this."

"Dominic, you know that can't hurt me."

I shouldn't have said that.

The crack of a gunshot can sound especially explosive inside a small apartment. I didn't really get the full resonance of the shot from Roberto back in New York because, by the time the sound travelled to my ears, the bullet was already dancing around in my brain, which made his follow up shots barely audible as well. Not so with Dominic's shot, which bored through my chest and knocked me on my ass.

"Dominic, what the fuck, man?"

He shakes his head at the bullet hole in my shirt as he watches me rise. "I guess I just had to see for myself."

"Dammit, man! I have neighbors!" Not to mention that I'm tired of being target practice. His eyes are glazing; he looks like might throw up. "Dominic, go sit on the couch, man. You look sick."

I reach out to help but he pulls away. "Don't touch me."

Dominic takes a seat on the couch and places his head between his knees.

I take a seat beside him. "How'd you find me?"

Dominic raises his head. "Are you kidding me? That whole scene in Queens, the brother of a cop wanted for assault and battery, this freak in the news fighting the local gangs, terrorizing the neighborhood, beheading the cop's brother."

"It was those smartphone videos, wasn't it?"

"*¡Que, ní smartphones, ní smartphones!* Those videos were useless. I just followed the trail which led to a case of battery in Newark where a woman was left barely alive. It turns out she has another boyfriend. He's a co-worker and his name is Jorge Sangría. In his employee folder at personnel I see this picture." My Atlantic Indemnity picture from the eighties! Not being photographable, I hypnotized the woman at Human Resources into using that old picture for the hospital files. That explains the unfortunate haircut. "I'm a detective," exhales Dominic. "I get paid to detect." He tucks his gun in the shoulder holster inside his jacket.

No use beating around the bush, I'll just come out with it. "Dominic, what's going on with you and Teresa Gunder?"

He nods. "So what, you've been spying on me all this time?"

"Well, I wouldn't call it spying. You know, I miss all of you. And it's hard to stay away. But obviously I can't be there all of the time, so there's plenty that I don't know. So while we're on the topic of things that I don't know, tell me, Dominic, please. What's wrong with Stefanie?"

His face sinks. His eyes moisten. "So *that* you don't

know?"

I'm afraid of the answer, but I have to insist. "Dominic, what is it?" *Los Ruidos* make an uninvited entrance. They huddle to eavesdrop in on the conversation.

Dominic closes his eyes. A tear squeezes out. "She's... she's got a tumor. It's inoperable..."

No! No! Not Stefanie!

"... and it's terminal."

What?

I did help myself to a serving of plasma when I left the hospital the other night so I should be able to hold on. The last thing I need right now is to freak Dominic out with my death face. "How... how long does she have?"

Dominic's tears are now falling liberally from his eyes. "The doctors told her she had about nine months." "That was a year-and-a-half ago.

26

It would have been a stretch to have imagined five-year-old Nicky Negrón becoming the nocturnal predator he is today. In *Papi's* eyes I was *un ñoño*—a whiny little mama's boy that was afraid of the night. And actually, that was understating it. To put it more accurately, I was scared shitless of the night.

Mami, on the other hand, was the enabler. Not only was I still sucking my thumb at that age, I was also still drinking out of a baby bottle. Bullies quickly caught on and pushed little Nicky around until he would run to *Mami* in tears. It was several years before Dani would come into the family, so it was all me at that time. *Mami* was happy to give me all the attention I needed and I was even happier to be on the receiving end. So, me trying to fall asleep alone in my bedroom? Yeah, right. I would high tail it at the first shadow outside my window or the first creak behind the walls.

At first *Mami* and *Papi* tried helping me through the shivers by leaving my bedroom door open. The light would shine in from the living room while they were watching TV, and I would fall asleep to the sounds of Ed Sullivan, Jackie Gleason or Lucille Ball. But then there were other nights when I was still awake after they went to bed. Those sucked. Sometimes I'd whine out loud to let them know I was scared. Other nights, if I heard a sound I didn't like, I'd run to their bedroom and jump in their bed, wedging myself between them.

That really tested *Papi's* patience. It kept them from rocking that headboard against the wall, something they used to like to do a lot. If it wasn't every night, it had to be close. I still don't know how I wound up with only one sister.

To try and *macho* me up, *Papi* would ride me, telling me I had to toughen up if I was to grow up to be *un hombre*. But *Mami,* she was no help. She would tell him I was just a baby and let me fall asleep in her arms as I took in the scent of her hair, which brought me comfort and made me feel safe. She was more patient in that way than *Papi*.

"Never be afraid of the night," she said. "Do you feel safe in my arms, baby?"

"*Sí, Mami*."

"Good, then always let the night remind you of how you feel in my arms and you will never fear the night again. If you can always remember that feeling, you will learn to love the night and you will always feel safe."

It was a nice try but it didn't work. The more *Mami* protected me, the more I wanted to be near her—especially at night. It took the eventual concealed threat of *Papi's chancla*, the slipper he used to whoop my ass with. Now *that* worked. That resolved the problem of *el ñoño* raiding their bedroom.

Years later when I was a teenager, in the aftermath of Dani's death tearing our family apart, the night was no longer a threat to me. The horror that I had experienced—the worst horror imaginable—occurred during the day. And it was far worse than any possible boogey man I might have envisioned creeping out of the dark. The night had now become a reminder of the love, safety, and comfort of my mother's arms, just as she said it would. It was a feeling I would never come across again.

It was only at night that I could remember the *Mami* that cradled me in her arms instead of the one that could barely stand the sight of me. I fell asleep longing to have that love again, hoping that someday I could find a way to earn it back.

When morning came around, everything seemed harsh again. I felt exposed; that everyone I passed knew of my failure, the older brother whose sister died a horrible death under his care. I felt it in the streets, and I felt it in the hallways at school. The evening couldn't come fast enough. I wanted to be alone.

Alone in the comfort of the night.

And I wasn't even dead yet.

27

As much as I'd like to give credit to those who are putting such an effort into rebuilding Newark, really, who the fuck are they kidding? It's still a shithole. Ever since those race riots back when Martin Luther King was murdered, decent, hardworking families abandoned Newark for safer ground in other parts of the state. The city still hasn't recovered.

Sure, they've tried. Several committees over the past 35 years brought urban renewal projects to the table that worked in other parts of the country. But here, any positive-minded plans were diverted by crooked politicians and self-serving mob types, blocking any hint of progress outside of the Ironbound district. And it's been that ongoing cycle of politics and corruption that has prevented Newark from becoming a place for sane human beings to raise a family.

Are there nice, decent families living a safe, law-abiding life in Newark? Absolutely. Has crime dropped dramatically in recent years after the city built a cultural center with an entertainment arena and a professional baseball stadium? Again, yes. Are there well-lit, residential areas where someone can walk safely from his car to his residence without being confronted by a knife-wielding heroin addict? Affirmative—as a matter of fact, I live in one. Yes, there are some truly, wonderful people here in the primarily Black and Hispanic population of Newark. In fact, when I think about it, of all the Newark residents that I work with in the hospital, I can't think of one that I can say anything negative about.

So why do I feel the way I do?

Easy, I snack a lot.

Decent folks in Newark know that there are surrounding areas you don't go wandering into without putting your life at risk. I know those areas, too. But for me there's no life to put at risk. They're just places I go when I get a little nighttime craving; a nice little serving of junkie street scum followed by a half-dozen sliders at White Castle. Like those little square burgers, their drug-tainted blood has little nutritional value, but also like the sliders, they hit the spot when you have that little hankering. It's my little contribution towards urban renewal. The more I feed, the better the hope for the future of the city.

The nighttime view from my balcony is accentuated by the lights of the Blue Cross Blue Shield building, the Prudential offices and the new cultural center. On a late night like this, it actually looks quite impressive. Maybe someday this city *will* have some potential. But no one that's alive right now will ever see it. I, on the other hand... Well, let's put it this way, there will be lots of things that I'll see that no one else around me ever will, including Stefanie and the kids. I may be only sixty-three now, but I have an eternity of undead existence ahead of me. I will witness the death of my children, their children, and the children after that. But it all starts now with Stefanie.

Dominic stands beside me on the balcony as I gaze blankly into the Newark city skyline. It's almost as if he's forgotten what I am. For the last ten minutes we haven't exchanged a word. I wish I could say the silence is allowing me to reflect, but for me there is no silence, only the raging buzz of *Los Ruidos*.

In the stillness, Dominic observes me with genuine curiosity—a concern for me, since my thoughts of Stefanie's condition could force a genetically resistant slip that might come into view, a luxury I don't have at the moment. One look at my death face and Dominic will surely pull that cross out again.

Dominic breaks the silence. "You better not be thinking what I think you're thinking."

"And what do you think I'm thinking, brother-in-law?"

"You know."

"Dominic, knowing me, how can you even think that?

"Hey, I *don't* know who you are or *what* you are."

"Well, know this then, you stupid fuck. Turning Stefanie into the abomination that I am is not an option that I would even consider, okay? So rest easy on that and get that ridiculous thought out of your fat head."

Dominic's eyes narrow. My presence confuses the shit out of him. Even with the discussions he's been having about our existence with Dr. Gunder, seeing one of us before him (especially one that he was related to) has got to be something different altogether. "Tell me, what was it like?"

"What was *what* like?"

"You know, when you died. What was that like?"

How do you possibly explain death to someone who is alive?

"I had no control, Dominic." That doesn't even begin

to describe it. "I wanted to get away, but her power was too strong. She willed me into wanting to stay. And when she fed on me, the pain was the worst I had ever felt in my life." Physical that is, the pain of losing Stefanie and the kids exceeds that by leaps and bounds. "And yet I didn't try to fight her off or even move. I couldn't even cry out in pain." Dominic's stone face shows little sign of sympathy—not that I expected any. "Do you really want to know what it's like, Dominic? Do you really want to know what it's like to be helpless as your life slips away from you, knowing that you could never be with your wife again or be there to watch your children grow?"

"Bullshit, you things have no soul. You're just trying to make me believe you're Nicky."

"Oh, cut the shit, Dominic. You've been communicating with Teresa Gunder for what, over twenty years now? You're going to tell me you don't know about genetic resistance? You know almost as much about us as she does."

"This is too unreal."

"Yeah, Dominic, it *is* too unreal. But it is also real. I am dead. And I am genetically resistant. And believe me, it is a curse. I wish that when I died, I stayed dead and never rose. But I didn't. I rose. And I am here."

Dominic does the sign of the cross. The flicker of my humanity has him struggling inside. "What about those two *maricóns*? Are they like you?"

That came out of nowhere.

"How'd you know about *them*?"

"What, that they're gay, or that they're freaks like you? 'Cause either way, it doesn't take a genius."

No, there's something going on. I can't quite pinpoint what it is but there's something going on here besides good old-fashioned detective work. Holy shit! The emails to Dr. Gunder!

"Dominic, you crazy fuck. Please tell me you didn't let her put that shit in you."

Teresa Gunder's MV-12 was a serum composed of elements found in the fossilized meteorite and the blood from her son's death scene—the micro-organism that alters our genetics. Apparently, when injected in humans, it enables the sensing of our presence within a forty-mile radius, just like we sense others when they feed in our area. The problem is that it also effectively injects terminal cancer to its human recipients. The fact that she injected herself with MV-12 over twenty years ago and that she's still alive could indicate that she's come up with a treatment or is in remission. Or maybe she made some modifications. Who knows? I just hope this isn't something Dominic decided to mess with.

Too late. The look on Dominic's face tells me all I need to know.

"Shit, Dominic! I don't believe you! Are you crazy? That's like putting cancer into your body! How did you let her do that to you?"

"She didn't. She refused. So I stole some from her laboratory."

"What!"

"What do you mean *what?* You all need to be stopped. You can't go on taking lives whenever you want and expect us to sit back and do nothing about it." He seems almost embarrassed, and perhaps, a little defensive. "Besides, she's made improvements on the serum. I'll be fine."

"How fine?"

He scoffs with the wave of a hand. "I won't suffer any effects for another ten years, or something like that. It's no big deal. I'm sure I'll be dead by then anyway."

"Well, how is *she* alive? Didn't she once say she had

only, like, a short time to live?"

"She did. She got seriously sick and went into treatment, got chemo and all that shit. At the same time, she was working on her own remedies and somehow, between what the doctors did and the treatment she gave herself, she went into remission."

"Remission? For what, twenty years? Bullshit! Did you ever see her in the daylight?"

Dominic rolls his eyes. "She's not one of you." His attention is drawn back to the apartment. There standing are Travis and Donny with murderous eyes aimed at my brother-in-law.

Travis slowly approaches. "So, detective, you're friends with the doctor." Dominic pulls out his gun, making Travis almost smile. Almost is as close as it gets with Travis. "Really, detective, you tried that already on your brother-in-law."

I step in his path. "Travis, he's family."

His cold eyes meet mine. "You have no family, young man. You are dead."

"I think he can help us find Simone."

Travis looks over my shoulder at Dominic, laughing. He's laughing without smiling. How does he do that? "Boy, where is your head? Forget our little redhead. From what I heard, he can help us find the good doctor."

"Never mind that. What are you doing here, anyway? Why'd you come back?"

"We smelled the pork in the hall when we came in and we smelled pork on the way out."

Hold everything.

I turn to Dominic and he immediately does not like the way I'm looking at him. "You knew they were in here before I did, didn't you?"

Travis' eyes light up. "That's true isn't it? He sensed us while we weren't feeding!" We can only sense each other when we feed. If Dominic can sense us when we're not feeding, that is a major game changer. Travis smells blood—Dominic's. He makes an effort to circumvent me. "Tell us detective, how did you manage that?"

Dominic pulls out his cross. "Back off, faggot, you don't scare me!"

"Dominic, no!"

I fall ass backwards onto my living room carpet, giving Travis a chance to charge Dominic and yank the cross from his hand.

Travis throws the crucifix over the balcony out into the street and puts his hands around Dominic's thick neck.

With the cross out of sight I am able to jump between them and push Travis back. Donny steps forward. Even *he's* ready to rumble.

"Donny, stop," I say. "I can *talk* to you."

"There's nothing to talk about," says Donny. "Your brother-in-law is working with Teresa Gunder and she can destroy all of us." Man, Donny's really been *Travis-ized*. I gotta talk some reason into these boys. "First things first, guys. Right now, Simone is the bigger threat."

Travis disagrees. "We can handle Simone."

"Bullshit! She's been coming in and out of here for eighty years now. And she has the ability to control others like us, which means she can control *you*. How is that *handling her*?" I turn to Dominic, who's rubbing his neck, still trying to catch his breath. "Dominic, tell me. Is it true? You can sense us even when we're not feeding?"

The three of us surround him, making him more uncomfortable and afraid than he's willing to admit. To sense one of us when we're not feeding? That creates a whole other world of possibilities. We rely on not being able to be detected. If humans can detect us, they can defend themselves against us. And if humans can defend themselves against us, who will we feed from? And if they can sense us when we're not feeding, can they sense us when we're resting in the daylight? Will they be able to find us and destroy us when we are at our most vulnerable?

Dominic clams up. I need to remind him we are waiting for an answer. "Dominic?"

He knows he's not getting out of here without answering. "This is why you all need to be destroyed."

"Dominic. Answers. Now."

"With humans, that's the way the serum works. With you things, it's territorial. You only sense those that feed in your area. But the injection, it lets us sense you even when you're not feeding. Once we find out where you are, we can find your coffins in the daylight, bring them outdoors and open them up."

Travis is speechless. Well, maybe not. "This fat boy needs to die."

"You're not killing anybody, Travis. He's my wife's brother."

"Go ahead, kill me," says Dominic. "The process has already started. You can't stop it. They'll eventually catch up to all of you."

"They?" asks Donny.

Yeah, Dominic what do you mean *they*.

"She's got a lot more support now. More than she's ever had. And she's looking for one of you that will cooperate with her. As soon as she does, she'll be able to refine the serum and gain enough credibility to get this plague the attention it needs."

Travis seems offended. "She's treating this as a plague?"

"It *is* a plague. You're all carrying communicable micro-organisms. What do you think a plague is?"

Donny brings the subject back on course. "Well, if that serum works the way you say it does, then you *can* help us find Simone."

"Who, the redhead?"

I nod.

"You guys don't stand a chance. She and those kids she killed already know where to find you. I've been sensing them around that club you're always at down in the village. They're staking you out." Tread carefully, brother-in-law, you're getting a little too ballsy. "Your only chance is to help me and the doctor. If you do that, I can see to it that you get human blood without having to kill." Travis is ready to jump out of his shoes. It's getting harder for me to restrain him. "Yeah, I know that killing is something that all of you enjoy." Dominic's really picking up the bravado but unfortunately for him, we bloodsuckers also have a built-in bullshit detector— his tough-guy act is a façade, and so is his little bargaining chip. Human blood without having to kill? Really, Dominic, we're not some junkie perps you picked up at the Bowery.

I have to knock him off his bullshit stool. "Dominic, you're lying. We can tell."

His poker face fades.

He knows he's going to have to be straight with us. "Nicky, you have to do what's right." Oh, so now I'm Nicky.

"Really, Dominic, and why is that?"

"Don't you want to finally be at peace?"

"Dominic, you *have* to know about our self-preserving instincts. Even genetic resistance won't stop me from killing Dr. Gunder in order to protect myself."

"Not if I'm there with you."

"But you won't be. Not if I don't want you to be. If I am of mind to stop Dr. Gunder, you will not be there to try and stop me."

"Then why should I help you find that redhead?"

Travis slowly steps in front of Dominic and looks him in the eyes (I knew that was coming). "Because, detective, right now, *that* and your brother-in-law are the only things that are keeping you alive."

That's right, Dominic. You are alone—alone in a room with three aberrations of nature. Aberrations that prey on people like you. But then again, you already know that.

28

With my Achilles Heel of genetic resistance, you could say that my transition into Nosferatu had its share of hiccups— especially when Travis and Donny first set me free onto the unsuspecting public. No longer able to come home to Stefanie's *arróz y habichuelas con chuleta,* I had to learn to adjust my palate for a steady diet of *sángre víva.* And the blood had to be human since the thing that lives in us can only be fed with the blood of its host species.

Travis assured me that killing was something I would learn to enjoy. But not having done that yet, it was difficult at first to imagine that being possible. It was not until later that I found my *niche* in disposing of those that I felt wouldn't be missed by society. Once I did, it admittedly became a little easier and sometimes quite pleasurable. For this, I will burn someday. Neither my loathing of what I've become, nor the nights I've spent wrestling with guilt, will excuse me. My destiny is eternal damnation. And with that lovely offering waiting at the other end, you can understand how permanent termination has little appeal for us.

No longer being spoon fed by Travis and Donny, I spent my first dreadful nights suffering an insatiable hunger. I also found Buffalo Johnny's solution unpalatable because Travis mentioned it was difficult to control their minds. That meant having to develop a relationship where a woman would be comfortable with my face between her legs during that time of the month. Not an easy task without hypnosis being involved. Also, my face was all over the newspapers so I had to keep a low profile. I was already getting curious looks from strangers on the sidewalks.

So, what to do? I didn't want to take innocent lives and I also didn't want to roam the nights auditioning for kinky porn videos. There was also the question of where. Travis and Donny already had claims to the Big Apple. Where could I conduct my new nocturnal existence without being somewhere that was totally unfamiliar?

I contemplated my future one night while having a Whopper at Burger King. Reading the *Daily News*, I came across an article about a Wisconsin mother that drowned her kids in a bathtub (not all monsters have fangs). The case was being compared to one in North Jersey from five years before, where a woman claimed that her two-year-old son drowned in their swimming pool. The distraught father of the child had serious doubts about her story since she had shown signs of mental instability and was undergoing treatment for postpartum depression. When the investigation turned up traces of soapy water in the boy's lungs, his suspicions were confirmed and it led towards proof that she had drowned their child in the bathtub. The woman's name was Melissa Traynor, also known as "Missy".

Missy was sentenced to be held at Blackwood State Hospital in West Orange, New Jersey after being declared legally insane. Local citizens were up in arms over the injustice. New Jersey is a death penalty state and in the eyes of the local residents, that was the more fitting punishment for the atrocity she committed.

I remembered watching the news report the night the trial ended. It was the ten o'clock news where the announcer would say before the broadcast. "It's ten o'clock. Do you know where your children are?" Both of our children were home safe in bed while my head rested comfortably on Stefanie's lap, watching the appalling newscast. How could even an insane person do that to her own child? Not that anyone believed her plea. The general consensus was that her claim of being *possessed by evil spirits* was designed to avoid the death penalty.

Missy was a petite blonde-haired woman, just out of her teens, that was actually kind of cute. It was impossible to believe that such a fragile-looking young woman could commit such an act.

The Whopper and the fries weren't doing it. I had to do something before I lost the remaining nutrients from Travis and Donny's leftovers. Surely someone capable of committing such an atrocity as Missy Traynor's could be considered expendable by the general population.

A stolen taxi and a few trances later, I found myself at Blackwood in padded solitary confinement with sweet little Missy. When the entranced security guard allowed me in and closed the door to give us our privacy, she remained reactionless, just sitting on her bed, staring at the wall opposite her. I detected nothing on the wall that was visible to someone from this world so, to test her cognizance, I blocked it by stepping in front of her. Again no reaction, completely catatonic, to put her in a trance would have been redundant.

Not having killed yet, I was still having trouble mustering up the necessary venom. I had to focus. I had to imagine the frightened cries of the child that trusted his mommy and couldn't understand what she was doing to him.

Why, mommy, why?

I sat beside Missy and looked at her profile. She really was pretty, although incredibly skinny. Would her blood be good enough—especially in that sedated state? What the hell kind of drugs did they put in this girl? I had learned later that sedatives were necessitated by frequent, unpredictable outbursts in which she'd violently attack other patients.

Oh, well, no need for formalities.

I gently took her by the hand and laid her head on my lap—two tender lovers on a Central Park bench. Her expressionless eyes gazed at the molded ceiling while I fixated mine on the freckled flesh above her shoulder.

The current of her blood pulsed through my fingers.

The scent of her willowy flesh...

the involuntary extension of unhesitating fangs...

...the loss of my humanlike projection...

...hello Missy, Death is here.

Not a flinch! Nor a gasp. Nor a scream. Nothing. Holy crap, woman, did you get a look at this face?

I raised her to me like Rudolph Valentino preparing to engage in a long, passionate kiss with his leading lady.

Sorry Missy, no kiss. Instead my incisors spiked through her neck as I lustfully swallowed every surge of her life that gushed into my mouth. It was my first feeding—the first time I ever did it on my own. I felt a sick air of pride while guzzling on Missy but there was no one around to pat me on the back—not that Travis was the pat-on-the-back type anyway—maybe Donny. It was too bad. I could have used the coaching, especially after what transpired next.

For the first time Missy started to move. Her head, which I had been holding in my hand, turned towards me as she softly moaned and started kissing my shoulder! And if that wasn't weird enough, she then started to bite me back! Okay, no one prepared me for this one. I lifted my blood-covered face to look at her. What the hell, woman? Do you have any idea what's happening here? Her eyes lit up! It was a look I'd recognize anywhere. Missy was turned on! Here she was, her life spilling away onto her shoulders, dripping down to her bed, and the crazy little hellcat was horny!

I roared. I have no idea why, it just felt like something I should do before throwing my head down and devouring Missy in reckless delight. She gasped and grunted—not in pain, not in fear, but with pleasure, biting back with equal aggression. Her jaws were not strong enough to break my dead skin, but I was confounded. I had to stop and take a look at her again. She was disappointed. Why did I stop? She wanted more.

Missy then arched her eyebrows and gave me a demented smile. I bulged. I couldn't hold back.

I pulled Missy's face to mine and engaged in a forceful kiss (better than Valentino's). Both of our tongues swirled in her blood as we tore off each other's clothes. Her blood, still flowing, coated our skin as I pressed her down to the bed, alternately kissing her and feeding from her neck. Missy reached down, bringing me inside. Our bodies then slammed at each other's with violent thrusts as her life continued to drift into the next world. Through it all, Missy never screamed once. She just moaned with pleasure as her blood poured generously, covering our entire bodies.

Did she know she was dying? Honestly I had no idea, nor did I care. I was having a great time enjoying my first kill. As for Missy, she couldn't have been more cooperative. She was enjoying it like it was the best lay she ever had, licking and sucking ravenously at my shoulders, growling with delight, taking in her own blood as I thrust my hips into her.

Minutes later, Missy's wiry frame was limp and unresponsive. Her life had drained away with her eyes remaining opened, staring blankly at the ceiling—just as they were when I came in.

I closed Missy's eyes with my blood-drenched hand and climbed off her. Her pale, naked corpse lay back peacefully on her bed with chunks of flesh dangling from her neck.

I had actually done it. I killed. And I didn't hate it. Maybe I could do this killing thing. If I could dispose of worthless trash like Missy, maybe I could turn my need to feed into something positive—something I could do, guilt free.

Well, not quite. If you are a human being that was conscious of the fact that actions could result in consequences, genetic resistance will not allow rationalization to come so easily.

In the days that followed, reality set in. The next morning, when daylight broke through, Missy went up in flames—another unexplained case of spontaneous combustion. And though the afternoon newspapers showed little or no sympathy for the child murderer, reports came out that Missy's mother was demanding an explanation for the mysterious death of her daughter. Months passed, investigations ensued. The end result? Missy's mother sued the hospital and several employees lost their jobs, including the security guard whose brain I scrambled so I could get in. I then realized that no matter who dies, good or bad, productive to society or general waste of human flesh, death will have its collateral effect on the people who are left behind. Sure Missy was a child murderer, the lowest form of criminal around, but she was also someone's daughter.

Missy's mother took action against those that were responsible for the care of her daughter; administrators, nurses, security guards, etc. And all of them had families; parents, children, spouses and even friends that would suffer the after-effects of this one death.

One feeding, one death, yet so many lives affected.

Do the undead normally care? Not in the least, unless you are cursed with genetic resistance like I am. Then every feeding becomes a struggle with your remaining humanity. You are not even free to be the monster that you are.

I have been a night predator now for over twenty-seven years. That's a lot of feeding. How many people have I killed? How many lives of survivors were affected by my need for self-preservation? For me, guilt-free killing is nothing but a fantasy. Yes, there are times I enjoy it. Roberto is a good example. But in most other cases, guilt eventually creeps in to make my eternity miserable.

Well, Nicky, if killing makes you so miserable why not just end it?

That's easy.

Never underestimate our innate need to remain walking among the living. What waits for us in the next world is motivation enough. So if killing is the only way for me to go on, then the choice is clear. Although I may *be* a product of Hell, it certainly doesn't mean I wish to reside there.

29

With its thumping bass and hammering beat constantly pounding you in the head, the term "club music" couldn't be more perfect. The assault on the senses is even worse when you're in a crowd of gyrating tarts and sweaty metrosexuals. But if it leads me to the red-haired demoness looking to cause irreversible destruction to the big city and her undead teen minions, it is a price I am willing to pay. I'll just cleanse my senses at the apartment later with some Motown vinyl.

I opened my casket a couple of hours earlier to the sound of my cell buzzing on the night stand. The caller ID read Dominic, but I picked it up a second too late and the voicemail kicked in. The screen on the phone indicated that it was Dominic's fourth attempt to reach me, making me immediately fear the worst—Stefanie!

I didn't even bother checking the voicemail. I just dialed back. Dominic picked up halfway through the first ring. "Where are you? I've been trying to call you."

"Hey dumb ass," I snapped back. "The sun just went down. Dead guy, remember?" I then asked the dreaded question. "Is it Stefanie?"

"No, no, it's not that. It's your redhead. I sensed her early this morning before daybreak. She's in the Soho area!"

"Soho! That's where Travis and Donny's club is. She's coming right at them. Why didn't you call me before the sun came up?"

"My battery was dead. I called as soon as I got back and charged it." Dammit, he did. His calls were at 6:42, 6:47, 6:52 and 6:58, all a.m.

"Shit! I must have been in the shower when you called."

"You shower?"

"What do think, because we're dead, we're slobs? Of course, I shower! I shower every night just before sunlight." This week, the sun's been coming up around 7:00 a.m.

"All right, never mind that. I feel her close by. She's definitely in Soho right now and she's got two others with her."

"Two? There are supposed to be three, aren't there?"

"Who knows? Who cares? Just get your dead ass down here."

I reached for my jacket. It's a mid-length, dark brown, suede one that I bought in the eighties. It has a deep enough pocket to conceal my Filipino blade. "Okay, I'm coming. Meet me at The Hindquarters."

"I'm already here," said Dominic.

"What! Dominic, don't you dare try anything stupid if you see her. She *will* kill you."

"I can protect myself. Just get your ass over here."

Thankfully by the time I arrived, Simone still hadn't materialized. Otherwise my dumb ass brother-in-law's high-cholesterol blood might have already been layering the Hindquarters' dance floor. Instead he's now beside me suffering today's latest beats while maneuvering through this horde of hip-thrusting airheads.

To be heard I have to yell over the auto-tuned muck playing overhead from some singer whose better known for the size of her ass than her voice. "Anything?" Dominic shakes his head, yelling back that it's hard to hear with all this shit playing so loud. "Well, she's got to be somewhere around here if you sensed her in the area."

Dominic gestures to the far corner of the dance floor where the kitchen is. "Let's go in there for a minute."

Communicating out here isn't as much of a problem for me as it is for Dominic. Years of sorting out sounds picked up by my hypersensitive hearing enables me to make out what he's saying over the techno thumpety-thump. It is he who can't take in anything that I say back.

That being said, a moment in the kitchen does bring a much welcome break from the anarchy out on the dance floor. Only the sound of the workers defrosting and microwaving what will soon become overpriced "fresh" Buffalo wings and burgers, clanks around in there. The occasional profanity-laced hip-hop only bleeds in when the swinging doors open.

Dominic's uncomfortable about something. He's led me in here because he wants to get something off his chest. "We gotta talk."

"Okay, what's up?"

He points his finger at my chest. "If I do this for you, you gotta do the right thing."

"Uh, Dominic, we've already had this discussion."

"Bullshit! You're telling me you're not like them, right? That you're genetically resistant and that you're still Nicky, right?"

"That's right."

"Well, the Nicky I remember, my brother-in-law, my best friend, he's a Christian."

"Not anymore, Dominic. I'm dead. If I stop walking this Earth, you *know* where I'm spending my eternity. And it sure as hell ain't with Christ."

"How do you know? This could be your way to seek forgiveness and repentance."

"Forgiveness and repentance? Listen to you. There is no forgiveness for what I am or what I've done. If your Dr. Gunder needs help, she ain't getting it from me."

He grabs me by the collar. Is this fucking guy nuts? "*Mira maricón!* You know what's right. You know what the right thing to do is. It's the least you can do given the way you died."

Low blow, fucker.

Now it's my turn to grab Dominic by the collar and push him against the kitchen wall. "What is that supposed to mean? Who are you to tell me what's right, huh?" Perhaps Mr. Righteous needs a little reminder. "What about you and Colleen Ryan? Was that the right thing to do? Banging your partner's wife?"

An entire spectrum of colors rainbows through Dominic's face, he's a breathing Peter Max print. It finally settles on a very pale white. What's the matter, buddy? See a ghost? "Y-you-you knew? *¿C-c-como tu sabiste eso?*"

I let go of his collar. He doesn't move. It looks like he's still pinned against the wall. "I *didn't* know, Dominic. I found out after I was dead. What's wrong with you? Not only were you cheating on Patti, but damn, your partner's wife? Really, man."

"Hey, fuck you, what about you and that redhead!"

"Hey, don't you go there! You know that wasn't my fault!"

"Really? Are you sure about that? Because, you know,

even though I defended you all these years, it was because I didn't want to believe you could do something like that. You know how screwed up it was between me and Patti. But you, you and Stef, I looked at you guys like you were perfect. It was everything I wanted me and Patti to be. So when that shit happened, it made no sense to me 'cause all you did was talk about Sis and how much you loved her. So then what happens? You're downtown with two friends that *know* how much you love your wife, and you go disappear with some redhead? No, no, there was no way. It made no sense. That's why I defended you. I went out and I checked around, asked around, looking for answers. But the truth? You wanna know the truth? The truth is I have no idea what happened. I have no idea why you died in bed with some redhead after being married all those years to my little sister. So why don't you tell me?"

The silence in the kitchen is paralyzing, cold. Only the drumbeat from outside the swinging doors brings any indication that there is anything going on outside of the staring showdown between me and Dominic. He's crossed a line and he knows it. Instinctively he remains stoic, but by now he probably knows that I can smell fear. What stands before him is not his brother-in-law but an anomaly that has no place in God's world.

"Okay Dominic, pick up that big knife on the table behind you and bring it here." The Hindquarters' kitchen employees, paying no mind to the brotherly spat, ignore the sight of Dominic lifting the chef's knife that was sitting on the kitchen island. "Good. Now take the pointed edge and press it against your neck." Without a second of hesitancy, Dominic agreeably pushes the sharp edge to the right of his Adams Apple. "Press it a little harder." With no fear or indication of any pain, the knife presses forward, breaking skin. A burst of blood colors the tip of the blade. "Okay, stop."

Blood oozes a path down my brother-in-law's neck as he stands quietly, knife in hand. Conveniently, there is a First Aid cabinet on the wall where I can access a Band-Aid. Before the blood reaches the white collar of his shirt, I intercept it with my finger.

No reason to let it go to waste.

Rather than wipe it off with one of the nearby napkins I lick the blood off my fingertip. The taste settles on my tongue as I tear open the Band-Aid. "Ugh, Dominic, you really need to cut down on your drinking."

Dominic shakes the haze out of his head and looks at the chef's knife in his hand as I place the Band-Aid over the puncture wound. He reaches for his neck with his other hand and feels the bandage over the wound.

"Any more questions about that night, Dominic?"

His expression is one of raw disgust. "You sick fuck."

"No, Dominic, not sick. Dead."

How can his mind even process this? I keep trying to imagine what this must be like from the other side; a dead brother-in-law standing before him, a dead brother-in-law that feeds off of humans, something that people dress up as for Halloween. A ridiculous figure of fantasy facing him as a horrifying reality—one that has taken a tragic toll on all the lives around him.

The thumping bass seeps back through the swinging doors as Dominic storms back out to the dance floor. Before they swing back shut, Travis passes Dominic and notices the wound on his neck.

Travis approaches me with an expression that almost passes as a laugh. "Did you just...?"

"Don't be ridiculous."

"Okay, if you weren't feeding off the detective, did he at least offer some intel about our friend, the doctor?"

"No, we were discussing family matters."

"Family matters?" Travis reverts to his sour demeanor. "Listen, amigo, you have got to reevaluate your priorities."

"I know, I know."

The hip-hop beat blasts its way back into the kitchen as Dominic bursts through the door. "She's here!"

"What?" Butterflies! I actually have butterflies! Are they dead, I wonder? "How do you know?"

Travis eyes light up. "Did you see her?" This is a man who loves confrontation.

"No," says Dominic. "But she's here, with two others."

"Just two? Where is the other?"

"All I know is what's here right now," says Dominic. "There are six of you freaks right here, right now, in this building." Dominic nods towards Travis. "There's you and your sweetheart, the thing that calls himself my brother-in-law, the redhead, and two others."

We have to bring Travis' mate up to speed. "Dominic, does Donny know?"

"No, I didn't see him."

"Donny's up on the balcony watching the floor," says Travis. "Let's go tell him."

30

The dance floor is packed so tight that it's almost impossible to move, let alone flail around to the noises excreting out of the house system's woofers. To a human, if he or she had the heightened sense of smell that I carry, the stench of the sweaty armpits and bodily fluids coming from the patrons might be nauseating. For me it heightens my anticipation, my hunger. Hand inside my jacket, ready to clash, I hold tightly onto the handle of my concealed Filipino. I also brought a wooden stake, as did Travis. Dominic's weapon is his serum-induced ability to sniff out the undead—much more useful than his service pistol, unless he wants to snuff out a dancer or the DJ (which I would welcome).

A stunning red-haired woman in a crimson dress would probably stand out under normal circumstances— especially if she's accompanied by a pair of Goth freaks. But in this crowd, any given night could resemble a Halloween party with the dissonance of questionable fashions bopping to the brain-mashing beats on the dance floor. Add to that the colored lights flickering all around us and, hell, a T-Rex could stomp through this throng without getting a second look.

The tune changes again. Fittingly, this one has a gothic echo-like feel with crunching guitars and an industrial tech beat. I kind of like it. It feels angry, like we are. The light show changes with the tune, flashing strobes that make the arms and heads rhythmically flailing about look like dismemberments. Even the faces of the dancers are taking a *Carnival of Souls*-like appearance.

Death is stalking. We know it is here somewhere. But where?

I call out. "Travis!" No response-despite his being only a few steps ahead of me. He's either extra focused or his hearing isn't as sensitive as mine. I take hold of his arm to get his attention. "TRAVIS!!!" His swift turn, with stake in hand, is thankfully caught by Dominic, who grasps Travis wrist before he could put a hole in what used to be his brother-in-law. There was no mistaking it—there was deadly intention in Travis' eyes.

"WHAT?" He is clearly in no mood for distractions or conversations.

"WHY DON'T WE TURN ON THE HOUSE LIGHTS AND SHUT OFF THE MUSIC?" My suggestion might frustrate the crowd for a moment, but who gives a shit? Combined with Dominic's sensory ability, the house lights and the lack of noise might give us a chance to spot Simone and her *hench-teens*.

Travis nods. He likes the idea. Suggesting that we could get a better view, Travis gestures towards the balcony. Dominic and I follow as the music continues to pound. Halfway up the steps, Travis stops to look down at the dance floor. I stop beside him and turn to Dominic, who's two steps behind me. "Anything?"

Dominic shakes his head. "I don't see her but she's

definitely here!"

"Dammit, Dominic! Where?"

Travis signals Donny, who's looking down from the balcony. Donny, not knowing what I recommended, seems perplexed. Of no temperament to explain, Travis repeats his gesture with more emphasis. Donny shakes his head. It's a good night at The Hindquarters, why stop the party? Travis' cold stare conveys that the topic is not up for discussion. Donny shrugs and heads towards the control room.

Below us, unaware of the danger lurking amongst them, the crowd continues frolicking happily. Until the music stops. A disappointed moan rises. The patrons look around, trying to figure out what happened. Donny turns on the house lights, blinding everyone as their pupils struggle to adjust. The roar of disapproval grows louder. It might not be the best way to run a dance club but, right now, Travis doesn't give a shit. He is in predator mode-not businessman.

Travis, Dominic and I scope the dance floor from the steps. Neither of us sees anything. Below, the patrons are turning testy. Some are even heading towards the exit.

A feeding!

It bolts through us like a charge of electricity.

Two feedings!

When someone feeds within a close distance from where we stand, our senses pick it up instantly. Travis felt it, too. I can tell by the way he just looked at me. He sways his head, searching frantically throughout the dance floor. Below us the clubbers are still buzzing in frustration. Thankfully they're completely unaware of what's going on. Otherwise there would be a riot on the dance floor with frightened patrons clawing over one another. For now, only Travis and I know the horror that's happening somewhere below.

A piercing scream! Well, so much for just Travis and me knowing.

A second scream! The unintelligible grumble below turns into a collective panic with a sea of confused torsos slamming into one another. Dominic barrels down the steps towards the direction of the screams. Travis and I trail him, trying to crane our necks above the crowd to pinpoint the center of the chaos.

The screams are multiplying. They appear to be coming from the far corner near the back exit as we wade against the fleeing crowd. Blood! There's blood on the dance floor. No surprise there.

Some freaked-out burly dude in a buzz cut tries to overcompensate for his diminished macho façade by attempting to grab me by the shoulders and forcibly shove me away. Sorry buddy, but I am just as determined to get to the scene you're running away from as you are to get away from it. I lift him by his pants and throw him aside, probably turning his world upside down even more.

Our field of vision is clear. The evidence of what Travis and I sensed stands right before us. They're kids! They're just kids! They can't be older than seventeen, one male, the other female. Both are dressed in black leather and studs, openly feeding on a pair of young clubbers in miniskirts and high heels. The pretty legs of the victims hang limply, blood streaming down the calves of their nylons, forming puddles on the dance floor. Their heads hang back lifelessly as the teens continue to gorge themselves.

Travis is stricken in disbelief. Why such a senseless, haphazard attack in such an open venue? What could this possibly accomplish? This isn't the way we feed. Not in public. Not out in the open. We are not supposed to exist. What is the purpose of causing this panic? Why make our presence known? If no one believes we exist, no one is out to stop us. Why do this?

Dominic pulls up beside me, having puffed his way through the crowd. The young Goth male lifts his head and looks right at us. Now the female picks up her head, licking the blood from her lips.

Before I can stop him, Dominic instinctively pulls out his gun and squeezes off a shot, ironically striking the girl in the neck. The bullet knocks her back and her victim falls to the floor. The male decides to get chivalrous, dropping his victim to charge at Dominic with fangs aimed at his neck.

The male teen takes down my brother-in-law but I am able to knock him away with a flying tackle, leaving us rolling on the floor like a sheriff and an outlaw in a Dodge City saloon. I reach for my stake but the female joins in on the scuffle and starts biting my arm.

Their energy is fierce. They're hyper-powered with no capability of forming any calculated thought, feeding and fighting with aimless abandon. I don't think they even realize I'm one of their own. These little fuckers are definitely *not* genetically resistant.

With the young male Goth kid firmly under my control in a headlock, I struggle to shake off the female, who pulls on my head as if trying to rip it from my shoulders. It's almost funny how completely vacuous they are, thoughtlessly focused on me while completely ignoring Travis, who calmly steps over and plunges his stake through the young male's back, into his heart.

The female Goth doesn't even notice, continuing to wrestle blindly with my head. Travis drives his stake through her back, also, but he misses her heart. Her attention shifts, and with a hideous growl she turns and attacks him. Not that Travis can't hold his own against her, but rather than waste time that can be put towards finding Simone, I take my out my blade and carve through girl's neck until her head is completely severed.

Her body falls to the dance floor, leaving me holding her detached head by the hair. I raise it to look at her heavily made up face, eyes and wide open mouth. Fucking morons, you dumb little shits know nothing about Goth.

Fuck it. No time for pity, we've got problems of our own. Dominic stands couple of steps away, dazed, blankly staring at everyone that's fighting to get to the exits. His hand over his neck, blood seeps between the fingers. The Goth kid got to him before I could intercept. He broke skin.

Dominic's reads my sunken expression. "Like I said before, I'm half dead anyway." Gunder's MV-12 poison was bad enough. Now he has a bite that has breached his flesh. The venom is in him. It's just a matter of time. It might take days, a couple of weeks, maybe even a month. But the venom will kill him and turn him into one of us. "At least I'll have the decency to stay dead."

If I had the time to mourn the inevitable, I would. But time is a luxury we don't have. Simone is lurking. We might not see her but she is here. And she's orchestrated this chaos for a reason. Why?

Travis looks up to the loft area to bark an order out to Donny. His mouth freezes. I look up to see what could possibly paralyze him in such a way.

That face—the face I haven't since in twenty-seven years, yet its image is burned in my brain like branded cattle.

And that red dress!

Simone calmly looks down at us, proudly admiring the destruction below her. Her eyes beam while her wine-colored lips form a disgustingly satisfied smile.

Travis seethes. He's fixed and poised to attack but his hatred appears to have him almost in stasis.

That's all right, Travis. Sit back, buddy. She's mine. This is the first time I've seen this soulless *puta de la madre* since she took my life away and I want it to be the last. I wonder if she recognizes me. I wonder if she even gives a shit.

Travis and I both know that the second we make a move she will disappear into nowhere just to enjoy our frustration. So what's the plan? What can we do to change that? She stands there so smugly, feeding off the hatred emanating from us, two night walkers that she sired. Dammit, what's the plan? How do we attack?

Dominic is also game. But this is a confrontation that he has no business being involved in. He is grossly overmatched, no matter how much he wants in.

Simone's taunting smile takes an unsettling turn. Her eyes widen into a crazed glare. It shakes me. Shit, even Travis is shaken. I never thought I'd see Travis shaken. Her right arm rises teasingly. She's got something hidden behind the wall of the balcony. A fistful of blond hair comes into view.

NO!

A pale, bluish forehead. The darkened eyes of someone who's been dead for well over 75 years. Travis cries out. His heart has been ripped from his chest. The head Simone boastfully displays is almost completely detached from the body. Only the vertebrae are holding them together. Not only has Simone staked Donny, but she has almost completely decapitated him!

"DONNY!" cries Travis. His projection is fractured, his death face exposed. I've never seen it before. His demonic features somehow seem more pained than a human's ever could.

Now past boiling point, I charge towards the steps

leading up to the balcony. Simone watches, unimpressed. Three steps up, I hit a wall as Simone looks down towards me from the top of the stairs. Oh, she remembers me all right.

Simone licks her lips, seductively. Damn, what a sexy woman! She's only a few steps above me, almost within touching distance, the unmerciful daughter of Satan that took my life away, the one that made Stefanie a widow and took me away from my kids.

I want her crushed.

I want her in flames.

I want her destroyed.

And I want to fuck her so bad.

Travis' cries are distant echoes. I'm lost in another place, another time. I'm at the Ritz-Carlton. Travis roars with rage but it only slightly jostles me from my trance, even as he darts towards the steps where I stand motionlessly, visualizing Simone's red silk panties clenched between my teeth.

A loud bang rings out, snapping me back into consciousness.

Thick blood oozes from a fresh bullet hole in Simone's right temple as her body collapses into the hallway leading towards the management offices.

Dominic waves his gun indignantly towards the balcony. "Get her!"

Travis shoves past me as I inch my way back towards the here and now. I slowly follow, shaking the cobwebs, reaching the top of the steps to find Travis on his knees besides Donny's butchered body.

But where is Simone?

The bullet wouldn't have killed her but her reaction time should have been slowed enough for us to catch up with her.

I can see inside the management office. The door is

open. She's not there. Neither is she down the hallway. The only other room is the bathroom. A dozen feet or so, at the other end of the balcony, is an emergency exit. But surely Travis or Dominic would have seen her go there. The only place to check is the bathroom. Admittedly, I'm having second thoughts on confronting our maker alone, but Travis right now isn't in any shape to face her.

Simone won't be as easy for me to decapitate as the Goth girl so I'm better off having my stake ready as I step towards the bathroom door and slowly push the door open.

I can see through the small crack between the door and the frame that it's dark inside. My hand holding the stake shakes as I open it wider. There's nothing I want more than to destroy Simone, but if there is anything that my heightened senses can do, it's separate the bullshit from the bravado. They know that there's a big part of me that will be relieved if Simone is not behind that door. No sign. She's gone. We lost her.

Back at the balcony Travis' face is helplessly crumpled as he cradles Donny's headless body in his arms.

Dominic, finally making it up the steps, is startled by Travis' death face and agonized howl.

Travis leaps towards my brother-in-law. "You worthless, wretched mortal, why didn't you find her?"

Dominic has never seen one of us with our death face exposed and it's evident by his shaken demeanor. He has seen the unholy in the flesh. His stoic demeanor is gone.

"Travis, stop!" Again I have to step in to keep him from ripping into Dominic's throat.

Dominic backs away. He's worked many crime scenes where he's had to wait out the irrational anger of a murder victim's survivors, but this is no grieving human. It is a blood-driven predator to whom the only good Dominic is a dead one.

Travis wrestles to get past me. "You said you could stop her!"

I can hold off Travis a bit, but not forever. "Dominic, you better go."

He stubbornly refuses, clenching his lips in frustration. "I *will* find her!"

What?

Dammit, Dominic, wrong thing to say. In fact, right now anything would be the wrong thing to say, which Travis makes clear by overpowering me and grabbing hold of Dominic's arm. "You powerless fool, what are you going to do? What do you think you're going to do?"

Don't say anything stupid, Dominic.

"And you," says Travis, turning his anger towards me. "What were you doing just standing there?"

"I'm sorry, Travis. She—"

"Sorry? Sorry?" Travis falls to his knees again, beside Donny. This time his uncontrollable grieving resembles unearthly moans echoing in a cave. Against my better judgment I place a hand on his heaving shoulder. Surprisingly, he doesn't flip out. Instead he leans his face towards my hand appreciatively.

A teardrop trails down Travis' cheek, spilling onto my hand.

A teardrop! Tears are actually streaming down Travis' face!

This contradicts everything I ever thought I knew about us. All this time I thought that the dead could not produce tears. I thought we didn't have the capability. But now as they pour from my grieving friend, I realize that it's not the dead. It's just me.

Whether I was alive or dead, I have no recollection of ever producing a tear—not through my mother's death, not through my father's abandonment, nor after the accident that killed Dani. I wanted to, but maybe the horror of seeing Dani's life end right in front of my eyes, sucked my life along with it. And if the shock was too much for me to react in tears, surely the pounding my mother gave me should have left me crying. Instead I just lost control of my bladder.

Every morning I rose after that day, the shame of my failure to protect Dani was a weight that crushed me through my entire existence, living or dead. But yet it never produced one tear. And then there was *Papi*, a man that I idolized, suddenly disappearing from our lives, someone I wanted so much to have been proud of me. But how could he? The one time he needed me to be there to protect his little girl, I wasn't.

If ever there was ever a time I needed all the love I could possibly get, it was then. But somehow, everyone around me forgot that I lost Dani, too. She was my little sister and it was my fault. All it took was a few seconds. And in those few seconds that I lost sight of her, my life changed forever.

I guess *Mami* later tried her best to do the right thing and raise me as her child. But in the end she was just going through the motions. I knew that she would never forgive me. The protected feeling I had when *Mami* spoiled me with her love would be a distant memory. Still I tried. Throughout high school and college when it was just me and her, I turned the tables and did my best to spoil her. I cooked, I took care of the house, hell, I even did the shopping. Through it all, she remained numb, never again to show any sign of love for her firstborn. Did I want to cry? Hell yeah. I just didn't know how.

Not knowing my history, Travis can't be expected to understand my shock at seeing him crying. He squints his cracked, blackened eyes at me, wondering why he needs to explain. "He was everything to me."

"I'll bring you her ashes in a jar," says Dominic.

Travis grits his teeth. He's a kettle of rage, seconds from boiling over. I hold his shoulder a little firmer. "Easy, Travis." My brother-in-law's stubbornness is even starting to piss me off. "Dominic, I told you to get out of here."

"No, screw that," he insists. "I can do what you two can't."

"And what exactly is that?" snaps Travis.

"I can get to her in the daylight."

"Well, she's long gone by now," says Travis, holding back, but probably not for long. "That opportunity is gone."

"No," says Dominic, looking down at the destruction on the dance floor. "She's done her damage. Any second now the police are going to pull in here. She's made it impossible for you to stay around and keep this place open. And since you things are territorial, she did this because she's making plans to stay, which means she's not going far."

Dominic, this is not a good time. Go home. You're really testing my patience. "So what, Dominic? Look at what's happened here. What makes you think you can find her?"

"I've been a detective for forty years. That's how I'm going to find her."

"POLICE!"

The cops have arrived, inching their way into the club with their guns drawn.

Dominic heads towards the back exit. "I can't be seen here." He stops for a moment, looking back at us, shaking his head in irony. "You two better...disappear."

31

She's Puerto Rican. That much is a fact. Even though she was born in New York, her parents Artie and Ramona were childhood sweethearts in Rio Piedras, so Stefanie is one hundred percent Puerto Rican. That's why I could never figure out her infatuation with the whole English literature thing. *"Tu eres una Boricua. Why do you give a crap about all this Shakespeare shit?"*

It didn't end there. She loved all that Charles and Diana *bochinche* and she used to get weak between the knees over Michael Caine. "Mmm, his accent is sooo sexy," she'd drool.

Michael Caine?

According to Ramona, her fascination began as a little girl when she saw a Popeye cartoon where he was a Medieval Knight defending Olive Oyl's honor against the lecherous Bluto. It blossomed from there. Anything with knights, princesses, kings and queens, she just ate that shit up.

Whatever.

At least she got me through those required literature classes that I had no chance of staying awake in.

One year, when we were married, we even went on a vacation in England.

England!

I busted my ass collecting insurance premiums in the most dangerous projects in the South Bronx and Harlem to spend two weeks "relaxing" in the grey skies of London walking in and out of ancient castles with no air conditioning and no Piña Coladas.

"Ooh, isn't this exciting?" squealed Stefanie.

"" Yeah, babe, this is great," I lied, wondering where the fucking beach was.

After the kids were born, she began the annual tradition of dragging all of us—and I mean all of us; the kids, Dominic, Patti, the twins, Artie and Ramona—to the Renaissance Festival in Upstate New York. None of us wanted to go, but Stefanie insisted that the kids would love the costumes, the accents, and the jousting. "They'll have a great time," she'd say. "And it'll be educational too."

Of course when they were babies, the kids had no choice. But once they got older, they'd always try to find a way out of it. Davey suddenly had a "big game" he had to participate in and Jessie planned sleepovers at her friend's house in White Plains, with hopes of being too out of the way and inconvenient to pick up. Nice try, Jessie. "Don't worry," said Stefanie. "We'll pick you up bright and early, so be ready." You didn't think you were going to get off *that* easy, did you, Jessie?

On the morning of our Renaissance excursions, Dominic and I would load up our station wagons while Artie and Ramona would board his car and the twins would go in mine so the cousins could all be together. When Davey, being the only boy cousin, found himself being the brunt of the girls' constant teasing and giggling, he started riding with Uncle Dom.

That whole Renaissance Fair thing still goes on to this day. They hold it in Tuxedo, New York, which back then was a foreign country to me, like everything else outside of the Bronx and Manhattan. That's why Dominic's car led the way with me following close behind.

The first time we went, I remembered seeing signs that said "Sterling Forest". Something about the name bounced around my head like the logo in a Windows screensaver and I repeated it to myself to see if I could jar something loose out of my memory.

Sterling Forest.

Sterling Forest.

Nothing came to mind, even as we arrived.

The kids were still babies so Dominic, Patti, Stefanie and I were all pushing strollers as we entered the park. Jessie was around three, Davey was a newborn. Dominic and Patti's twins, Aida and Penny, were turning two.

Upon walking in it became quickly apparent that whatever Sterling Forest was before, it wasn't anymore. And while the knights, wenches, Robin Hoods and Merry Men all did their best in welcoming us and creating a festive atmosphere, to me, something about the park was a little unsettling. Directional signs pointed towards attractions that were long gone and the park's benches had weeds growing through the seats. Yet, in my mind, the park remained eerily familiar.

"What was this place?" I asked Dominic.

"It used to be some kind of like botanical gardens in the sixties," he replied.

Stefanie observed as I studied the area, searching through my memories. "There's something about this place," I said.

To my right was a big pond, abandoned, just like everything else around us. It had a small wooden bridge going over it, but it probably wasn't sturdy enough so a barrier blocked the entrance to prevent anyone from crossing. Below the bridge, weeds grew out of the water and brushed against the bottom. I paced a couple of steps, observing the park's state of disrepair before stopping cold. Aha!

"What's wrong?" asked Stefanie.

"I *was* here."

"When?"

I stepped away from the stroller towards the pond, leaving Jessie with her grandparents. Davey, in the other stroller, started crying so Stefanie picked him up and followed me to the edge of the pond.

I sang under my breath, staring into the water. *"Oh, Dani, oh Dani, ohhh..."*

I was weirding Stefanie out. "Nicky?"

I nodded my head. "The paddle boats."

"What paddle boats?"

"Oh, Dani, oh, Dani ohh..."

Those weren't the real words that the Four Seasons sang. That was *Papi's* version. He was sitting in the paddle boat with my three-year old sister on his lap, singing his own words along with Frankie Valli. *"Oh Dani, oh Dani, ohh..."* He was a beaming, proud *Papi, un hombre bien orgulloso,* smiling, holding his chin up high, nodding hello to everyone in the paddle boats that passed.

"How you doing there, Nicky?" he called out. I was a few yards away paddling in another boat with *Mami*.

"*Mami*'s letting me steer," I answered.

Stefanie's voice brought me back to the abandoned pond of the present. "Honey, what's wrong?"

"Nothing," I said. "It's just that I was here a long time

ago with my family." Another lifetime ago was more like it. Another life that almost seemed like it wasn't mine. "It was so different then."

Stefanie asked nothing further. Some topics are better left alone. Later we sat in a quiet, grassy area while Stefanie fed Davey. The adults, Dominic, Patti, Artie and Ramona all sat together as the girls played beside us. Dominic was blowing smoke to me and Artie about how Dave Kingman of the Mets was a better hitter than Mike Schmidt of the Phillies. The ladies were fussing over cute little Davey. Giggles from Jesse, Aida and Penny echoed in the cool September air.

Hearing enough of Dominic's half-baked baseball analysis, I stepped away and sat beside Stefanie. *Papi* came to mind as I absorbed the harmonious sounds of our family. *Un hombre bien orgulloso*. Even the sound of Dominic grumbling, "Fuck Mike Schmidt!" was drowned out by the serenity of the voices surrounding me. All of us together, all of us happy. Even Dominic saying "Mike Schmidt can kiss my hairy ass" caressed my ears like the tune of a soft violin. Like *Papi* so many years before in the same place, I was enveloped in everything wonderful that life had to offer.

I leaned my head towards Stefanie, kissing her on the back of the neck, breathing in the fresh clean scent of her hair.

It smelled perfect.

32

It would probably be next to impossible for someone to identify with the sensation of a baseball bat smashing full-force against the back of your head. The most obvious reason being that if any mortal receives the thwack that I just did, it would be lights out—probably forever. At the very least, you would never recover to the point where you could say, "Man, that shit hurt!"

For me the sound is a dull eight-hundred-pound thud followed by the fizz of a champagne bottle after the cork pops. Or the static on the TV when you disconnect the cable. Being that I am *already* dead, my reaction is more like, "What the fuck!" while my wits are chased down by a centerfielder on the warning track. Yes, good old Nicky is still taking his lumps trying to be the good guy. You know, the good guy that also devours humans for survival.

At my insistence, Dominic's been calling every night so I can meet up with him to track Simone. I'm not comfortable letting him hunt by himself. Over the daytime, I have no control over Dominic no matter how much I try to discourage him. And that's when he runs the risk of exposing himself to a Renfield.

"What do you mean, Renfield," he asked. "You mean like that guy in *Dracula*?"

"That's exactly what I mean, Dominic, the guy from *Dracula*."

Like the Count, many of us use our mind control to employ *Renfields* to guard our coffins during the daylight. Many misinterpret the fictional Renfield as a character driven by loyalty. That's bullshit! The reason he protected old Vlad at all costs is because his mind was completely fucked by the Count. That's why they all wind up with permanent brain damage. And while Dominic might be armed with his NYPD Glock 22, if he gets caught off guard by a Renfield, he's as good as dead. Those loons are programmed to kill.

I've been staying at Travis' apartment because it takes some time off my commute to New York. Also, I honestly don't feel right leaving him alone with Donny gone. And though there isn't a chance in hell you'd ever get him to admit it, I think my being here actually brings Travis some comfort. The guy is completely broken. He can use a friend. These days, he can't even focus on trying to find Simone, especially since we've been starving ourselves to prevent her from sensing us. Me, I still have some reserve left from my last helping at the hospital. Travis, on the other hand, probably isn't in the best shape right now to face any sneak attacks.

I asked him if he wanted to join us tonight but he declined the same way he has every night since he lost Donny—by saying nothing. He just sits on the couch staring at the walls of his apartment, going through his database of memories. And that's all that he has. When you're dead there are no photos, videos, Facebook profiles, nothing. Memories are all Travis will have to remind himself of the times they had together. And he will be lost in them for quite a while.

In the meantime, there's a red-haired beast that needs to be slayed. For the past few weeks, Dominic and I have been focusing our efforts in the Long Island area where the Goth teens lived. We've broken into foreclosed homes, abandoned businesses, closed-down factories and other dark safe places where our nemesis might be hiding her coffin. Dominic felt her presence a couple of times over those nights but it was always from a distance. That allows plenty of time for her to be somewhere else by the time we arrive.

Dominic's determination to find Simone is taking its toll. Lack of sleep, combined with the venom that has penetrated his veins, has his face looking pale and gaunt despite his pudginess. But knowing him, he's never going to stop. Dominic thinks he has some kind of super-detective adrenaline that can get him through anything. Truthfully, the worst thing that can happen is that he finds her. He's no match for the demoness that made me what I am. He's just a 280-pound *happy meal* waiting to happen.

The current fucked-up economy adds to our workload by giving birth to an endless stream of boarded-up businesses, homes and factories—places where a nomad predator can crash during the day. It makes Simone a considerable needle in New York's urban and suburban haystacks. A short while ago at one of the less desirable neighborhoods in Nassau County, Dominic and I approached another of the dozens of foreclosed homes that we've combed through. This one had boarded windows with *cock, pussy* and other examples of eloquence spray-painted over them. There was also a collapsed wire fence that suggested some driver had one too many and made a left when he should have made a right.

I stepped over the fence lying on the unkempt grass and grabbed the corner of a plywood board with the intellectual scrawling, easily prying it from the front window.

While I placed the board on the grass, leaning against the house, Dominic tried to raise the window. "It's locked from the inside," he said.

"Let *me* try."

"It's no use," he insisted. "It's locked. Just smash the window."

Dominic scowled as I raised the window with minimal effort. It just needed a little undead *oomph*.

I stuck my head in to peep into the dark room. To the left there were no signs of life, nor any of the undead. But, like the car that took down the fence surrounding the house, I should have looked right.

The thunderous force of the baseball bat crashed against the back of my head, driving me face first on to the house's wooden floor. Hairline fracture. Again my skull has been breached, the fucker made perfect contact. Not expecting anyone that took such a wallop to remain conscious, the assailant with the Louisville Slugger was taken by surprise when the intruder leapt up and grabbed him by the throat.

Dominic swiftly pulled out his gun and shone his flashlight through the window. "Police!" Two screams wailed out from the far corner of the room, drawing the beam from Dominic's light.

Sitting on the floor, huddled against the wall was a trembling, young mother with a frightened little girl in her arms. Dominic shone the light back on the man with the bat, who was gasping for air under my grip. I set the man down. He was not a Renfield, just a dad. A dad doing what a dad does, protecting his family.

No further words were spoken. The only sound was that of the terrified girl sobbing in her mother's arms. I stepped aside and let the man walk over to his family to calm them. After he joined them, they looked back at the freak that was somehow still standing after taking that blow. They were squatters. People are going through difficult times these days. And through these difficult times, that little girl needs to know that she is safe under the watch of her father. He did what he was supposed to do. He protected his family. I did what I was supposed to do. I walked away. Daddy defeated the monster. They are now safe. Even with my head being smashed nearly open, my feeding from the hospital the other night is enough to keep my senses intact—no chance of a close call again like the other night at Rego Park with the young mother and her baby. I still don't know what the fuck that was all about. It's like I find new shit out about myself every night.

Dominic curses in frustration as I climb back out into the yard. He probably doesn't even give a shit that my head was just used as a piñata and that I have a few choice words of my own.

His cell phone vibrates in his pocket. Dominic pulls it and reads the caller ID. It's Jessie. His eyes meet mine. We're thinking the same thing.

Dominic answers. "Jess?"

"Uncle Dom?" There's heartache in my daughter's voice. I can sense the tears streaming down her face.

I don't need to hear anything more. Everything my little girl is saying can be made out from the film of tears welling up in Dominic's eyes. His voice cracks. "I'll be right there, honey." He places his cell back in his coat pocket.

Los Ruidos emerge. "I'm going with you."

The tears flow liberally from Dominic's reddened

eyes. "You can't."

"Dominic, she's my wife! I have a right."

"Right? You have a right? *Mira, este hijo de puta!* What right do *you* have? You're dead! You don't have any rights! You don't belong here! Don't you understand that? You're dead!" With revulsion, his eyes dissect the apparition that is me.

Do I understand?

Yes, Dominic, I do understand.

If you only knew how much I really do understand.

33

They're all here, family members I haven't seen in decades, all from Stefanie's side. Her uncle Tito, Ramona's perpetually unemployed younger brother, must have driven in from Connecticut. The last I heard about him was that he was living comfortably off a widow whose deceased husband's assets left her well taken care of. Claudia *la puta*, Stefanie's slutty cousin, is also here. Having fought over boys back in high school, they became close as adults, laughing about those days at family gatherings. She's about Stefanie's age, in her late sixties now, still wearing too much makeup and still assaulting my nostrils with her perfume.

She's crying hard.

This is goodbye.

Stefanie's room at ICU is more crowded than a bus terminal at rush hour. Jessie is at the doorway being comforted by Rippey, who's stroking her hair as she cries on his shoulder. He's doing his best to avoid weeping openly but it's not working, he's matching her tear for tear. What he *is* succeeding at is fulfilling his role as the comforting father—the role that should have been mine. If happiness, stability, and normalcy were all that I could wish my family after I had left them, Rippey was more than up to the task. For that reason, alone, I probably shouldn't hate him. But I do. And it's for the same reason.

Artie and Ramona are holding each other, suffering the unbearable sight of their motionless daughter being kept alive by some electronic contraption whose incessant rhythmic beeping is echoing throughout the room. Next to his *abuelita* is Davey, covering his face with his hands, crying louder than I've ever seen him, even as a child. *Abuelita* Ramona rubs his back softly. She has always been overprotective of Davey, having been a big part of his recovery when he fought off his demon of alcohol abuse.

When Dominic barreled into the room minutes ago, he unleashed a loud, gut-twisting bawl upon seeing his little sister breathing weakly with the aid of a ventilator. He didn't even notice that his daughters Aida and Penny were in the corner of the room, holding each other in tears. They've grown into two lovely young women who took on the best of Patti's features. Neither of them gets to see their father much these days. Aida's married to a car dealer in Philadelphia, and Penny's raising a family with her mortgage-broker husband upstate. But both are here to be with the family at this terrible hour. They always deeply loved their Aunt Steffy, and their hearts are shattered just like everyone else in the room.

The intangible curtain that shields me holds on as I stand at the foot of Stefanie's death bed, but barely. My incommodious tenants *Los Ruidos* are doing everything they can to break and expose me.

The only woman that has ever lived in this heart

for the thirty-eight years that it functioned will never rise again. She has fallen victim to a predator of another kind, a cancer that has taken over her brain. There is nothing else the doctors can do. For the last two and a half plus decades, Stefanie's last mental vision of her first husband was him spending his last living moments dishonoring her. To try and disprove that I would have had to expose her, and everyone else, to the horrors that make my current existence possible.

Stefanie was the one that saved *my* life, plain and simple. She was the answer to the prayers I made as a child, kneeling beside my mother at Church. On those Sundays, I prayed that the day would come when *Mami* would love me again the way she once did. Knowing that those chances were slim, I also prayed that if she didn't, someone else would. And now the woman that did bring that love back into my life, is lying before me, taking her last artificial breaths, thinking that seventeen years of her life were wasted on an unfaithful scumbag. But why flatter myself? She probably hasn't thought of me for years. She's been married to Rippey longer than she was to me. He saved her life the way she saved mine.

The song of *Los Ruidos* gets fierce and merciless, making the sobbing around me barely audible.

A woman's gasp breaks through—it might have been Ramona. The room turns silent. Everyone focuses on the bed. Was it a moan? Dominic brings himself closer to Stefanie. His head jolts back! This time several of the women in the room gasp. It was very slight but everyone saw it, a barely discernible twitch below Stefanie's left eye.

Her head makes a slight move to the left.

"Oh my God!" cries Jessie, choking in her tears. "Mommy?"

The relatives and friends outside the room, not having seen what happened, begin to buzz with curiosity. They're shushed by someone inside the room.

Stefanie's breathing turns erratic, as if she's fighting the ventilator that's keeping her alive. Her head moves more noticeably, jerking to the left and to the right.

"Get a nurse," calls Rippey to no one in particular.

Davey sobs helplessly in his grandmother's arms. The family members close in around the foot of the bed. I am still out of sight but any second now someone is going to feel the space my body is taking up.

Her movements stop. The beats of the life support system turn radically inconsistent. Family members clear a path for a nurse, entering the room.

There is rapid eye movement underneath Stefanie's eyelids.

The beeps grow farther apart.

A doctor comes in and places his stethoscope over Stefanie's heart.

The beats grow faint. She's fading.

Dominic is sweating so much his clothes look like he just came in from the rain. "Do something!"

Another moan from Stefanie. It brings the room to a stop.

Rippey's tears drip on to her pillow. "Honey, I'm right here," he whispers. "I'm right beside you."

"Sis?" Dominic is near convulsions. I've never seen him like this.

Stefanie's eyeballs continue to wander aimlessly under her fluttering lids. Is she trying to open her eyes? How is this possible? How can she—?

They're open! Her eyes are open! And she's looking straight ahead...

...fixated in horror...

...at me!

She closes her eyes, turning away from the frightful sight. Her hands shake. Rippey takes the one closest to him and holds it against his face.

This is much too painful for a woman of Ramona's age to have to see. *"¿Mi hija, que pasa?"*

Artie, whose cheerful air never failed to put a smile on anyone's face, does his best to soothe his wife, but he can use some comforting of his own.

The shaking stops. Stefanie's hands are now still.

The beep from the monitor turns in to a long dreadful tone, droning on in the same exact pitch, the same exact sound, as the noise I've been hearing in my head for over fifty years.

Combined, their force is overwhelming.

I have to leave.

Now.

34

How much pressure does it take for an egg to crack? Not much. How much does it take for the dead, or at least one cursed with genetic resistance? I just found out.

As much as I was able to hold out in the hospital room, once the tone from that monitor joined in unison with *Los Ruidos,* my presence risked exposure. Without consideration for any of its inevitable ramifications, I pushed my way out of ICU, leaving family members wondering what unseen force brushed up against them. Superstitious as some of them are, I'm sure they'll probably agree on some kind of spiritual explanation.

Miraculously, I managed to remain unexposed as I reeled out of the room into the hospital corridor. But the monitor and *Los Ruidos* were showing no mercy. The farther I got, the louder the tone. Halfway down the hall, I spotted a stairwell and ducked in, closing the door behind me. I had no fight left. The monster wanted to come out.

A harrowed wail escaped my deflated lungs, echoing

up and down the stairwell. Seconds later an orderly opened the stairway door to find Death sitting against the wall with tears streaming down the cracked paths of his pallid face. The sight knocked the shrieking young man back into the hospital corridor where he was unable to explain what he had just seen. Others had heard the haunted cry as well but when one of the other concerned coworkers opened the door again, there was nothing nor anyone to be found.

None of this mayhem mattered in and around the room where Stefanie had taken her last breath. Incognizant of the hysteria by the stairwell, Torres family members and friends grieved and consoled each other. In the days ahead they would continue to comfort one another and mourn together. They will share memories and promise to be there in time of need.

Lucky enough to get away from the hospital, just being seen by the faint-hearted orderly, I and my newfound tears stayed away from the wake in Scarsdale. No need to possibly create another scene there. As for the funeral, that was during the day so it wasn't even an option. What was the point, anyway? I couldn't mourn with everyone. To those who at one time loved and admired me, I was long gone. Dominic was right. I didn't belong. The living, mourn together as family and friends. The dead mourn alone.

#

Practically every possibility in Nassau County had been exhausted by Dominic in terms of abandoned factories and foreclosures with dank molded rooms and empty halls echoing memories that he never experienced. Repeated exposure also began having side effects on his psyche. He was starting to imagine the sounds of whispering voices from the past or movements stirring in the areas surrounding him. As a believer (in the Father, the Son and Holy Spirit) Dominic never before had any patience for anyone who spoke of any ghost or paranormal bullshit.

His tune has now changed.

How could it not?

Dominic has seen many deviations of late that would distort anyone's perception of reality. The impossible and the ridiculous have now stared him too many times in the face for him to deny their authenticity. If everything that he had recently witnessed was now possible, what now was *impossible*?

Dominic's serum-induced capabilities have had him targeting the Queens/Long Island border where he had last sensed Simone's presence, but none of his treks have been productive. Frustration was taking its toll. Still, Dominic remained relentless in his search despite working his regular shift, helping Rippey out with Stefanie's funeral, and of course, grieving—all this with infected blood. I don't know how the guy was even walking.

Dominic can be stubborn. His determination can sometimes drive him beyond his own physical capacity, but today even *he* had to concede that he was pushing himself too hard. He'd been running on fumes. His usually sharp deductive skills were starting to lag.

His weakened sixty-eight-year-old body, which could only take so much, was joining in with everyone else that had been telling him, "Go home, Dominic. Get your ass in bed and get some rest."

For a late December afternoon, it had been a relatively nice day with temperatures in the upper 40's, but he finally resisted the temptation to stay out any longer and picked up the entrance to the Meadowbrook Parkway.

Traffic was a little busier than usual for that time of day. He attributed that to holiday shoppers and moms picking up their kids from school. With the cruel string of events that had been crowding his mind over the past few weeks, Dominic hadn't even given any thoughts to the holidays. Normally it was his favorite time of the year, dressing up as Santa at the precinct, giving out gifts, and taking the suit home to celebrate Christmas with the family.

Not this year. With Aida, Penny, and Jessie scattered throughout Connecticut, Long Island and upstate New York, Stefanie and Rippey's house was always the central spot for the holidays for the grandkids to come and meet Santa. Future holidays will have to be celebrated elsewhere. And with the venom running through Dominic's system, they'll probably be needing a new Santa in the coming years, as well.

Heading home on the parkway Dominic saw the sign for the Greenwood Boulevard exit. It was a quarter mile ahead. He had passed it several times over the past couple of days but never paid it any mind until today when he recalled a documentary he had seen on Netflix. It was about a mental facility called Greenwood State Psychiatric Center that closed in 1995 after reports of patient abuse and neglect. Not having yet canvassed that area, Dominic wondered if the hospital was still there. Given our current horseshit economy, maybe there was no budget for any new projects or renovations in the area. If that were the case, the hospital could still be sitting there, boarded up, having gone decades without a soul walking inside its walls.

It was 3:30 p.m. with not a lot of daylight left. With only a second to make a snap decision, his detective's lack of will power won over. There'd be plenty of time to sleep later. Dominic swung over and took the

Greenwood Boulevard exit ramp.

The boarded-up stores and empty strip malls on Greenwood Boulevard confirmed Dominic's expectations, the post 2008 years have not been kind to the area. He made a mental note of all the additional spots he'd now have to come back to check on.

A half mile from the exit, approaching Garner Avenue, Dominic stopped at the traffic light. To his right was a distant campus, partially obscured by a forest of leafless trees. Behind them was a row of barren medical buildings.

So much for getting some rest.

The sign at the intersection said "NO TURN ON RED". "Fuck that, I'm a cop," said Dominic, making a quick right, searching for a road or an entrance that would take him past the trees. There were no residences down the stretch of road on Garner, nor any businesses, populace or other signs of civilized life—just trees. Less than a mile from the boulevard, the road bent towards the direction of the buildings. A broken gate materialized a couple of yards ahead with the arched iron sign above it reading:

"GREENWOOD STATE PSYCHIATRIC CENTER".

Oh yeah, definitely not getting any rest tonight. He took out his cell and sent a text to his undead brother-in-law. This search was definitely not going to be a one-man job.

Past the gate was a long solitary road through a forest that was deep enough to keep the crazies from straying too far. At the end of the road was a circular driveway that led towards the buildings. The disheveled grounds, the "NO TRESPASSING" signs, the boarded windows—how many of these has he seen over the past few weeks?

Dominic's senses stirred, but not from the injections.

This time it was the detective doing the sensing. The grisly publicized accounts of former patients and workers brought a cloud of eeriness to Greenwood State, a place most people of sound mind would prefer to stay away from. It was perfect. Not even junkies or squatters would be desperate enough to hole up in there.

Rather than start at the main center, Dominic chose to begin with one of the side buildings, cursing yet another board that he had to pry from a window. Once the board came off, Dominic looked into the room, which was partially lit by the late afternoon sun. Broken chairs, tables and desks were among the rubble. It appeared to have once been a group therapy room.

Upon climbing in, Dominic immediately gagged and fell into a coughing fit from the molded, rotted stench in the room, which overwhelmed the lungs he had already beaten down with decades of Marlboros and neglect. So much remained in the room from the days when the hospital was a functioning facility; file cabinets, shelves, books, bulletin boards, lamps, even clothes. It looked like somebody yelled fire, causing an immediate evacuation and no one bothered to come back. At the other side of the room, Dominic saw a doorway to the hall. The door itself was lying in the rubble. With the sunlight not reaching out into the hall, Dominic pulled a Maglite out of his coat pocket.

He also pulled out his gun.

The hall being completely black, Dominic flicked on his light, sending a litter of rats scrambling for cover towards a door with an "EXIT" sign. The door led to a stairway. He concluded that if there were going to be any night walkers in the building, they would be at the lowest possible level to avoid any trace of sunlight and any squatters with balls enough to seek shelter there.

Dominic navigated through the herd of rats and

opened the door to the stairway, following the beam of his flashlight downstairs with a firm grip on his Glock 22. He was ready to fire at any unwanted surprises. On the lower floor, a tilted "B" sign hung to the left side of a closed door. Another set of steps led to a level below. If this is the basement, what's below the basement?

Continuing downward, Dominic did his best to avoid contact with the molded peeling walls, webs, and all of the foulness around him, but once he got to the door at the lower level, he had to reluctantly give in and reach for the knob.

A hollow psychotic whale song echoed through the stairwell as Dominic opened the rusted door to an extensive cacophony of pipes on the other side. It was a utility area. A couple of yards away, a heavy iron door piqued his interest. Unnerved by the echo of his own footsteps, Dominic approached the door slowly, again brushing his *germaphobia* aside to turn the grimy latch.

It took about two or three tries, but Dominic eventually pulled the rusted door open to find an endless brick tunnel with larger pipes running along its sides. He had heard about these before but had never actually seen one. It was a steam tunnel.

During the years of the facility's operation, it was used to deliver heat generated from the nearby power plant to the buildings on the hospital grounds. It made more logistical sense in those days by offering an economic advantage over heating each building individually.

Below, on the surface of the tunnel, were pools of rusted water. Having already gone this far, Dominic forged ahead and sloshed through the scurrying rats on the tunnel floor, ruining his Oxfords and dampening the cuffs of his pants. After what seemed like a mile, he encountered another door. He had already covered some distance underneath the massive facility and he had had his fill of splashing through the muck. Dominic stepped through the door to see what was in the levels above. No longer in the shape of his prime, he cursed at the prospect of climbing more stairs.

Figuring he was probably underneath another one of the buildings in the complex, Dominic wondered how far he was from his car. It was 4:05 p.m. There was less than an hour of daylight left.

The first level was again the basement. This door was tougher to open than the ones in the utility room at the other building. After a few vigorous pulls, Dominic succeeded and climbed upstairs to the next level. A couple of puffs later, Dominic peered through the door on the first floor. His flashlight shone on some cheerful cartoon murals on the wall. It was the children's treatment center. Dominic opened the door and stepped into the hallway. All the favorites were there on the wall; Mickey Mouse, Dora the Explorer, SpongeBob, Ninja Turtles... Considering the hideousness he had been witness to in recent days, the childhood images shook him. Aida, Penny, Jessie, and Davey are all grown now, but with the suffering they've been sharing since the loss of Stefanie, he felt the pangs of wanting to be around the kids. Enough of this shit, he decided, it was time to go home.

It was too late.

Dominic would never get to see his family again.

35

He froze. Dominic never freezes. He's as cool as they come. But this time... he froze.

A hideous, guttural shout thundered from the children's therapy room. Dominic turned but couldn't react quickly enough to the pale, ghostlike face with blackened eyes charging at him with a fireman's axe.

The third Goth kid!

Barely dodging the weapon, Dominic threw himself to the floor, losing grip of his flashlight and gun. Seeing the overweight geezer in a prone position, the Goth kid dropped the axe and pounced, beating him with mallet-like blows.

The description of the third Goth kid from the Missing Persons reports said that he was six-foot-four and 310 pounds—bigger, stronger, and over fifty years younger than Dominic. But the kid was so blinded by his mission to kill, he took no notice that Dominic's gun was just a couple of feet away.

The driven rage was unmistakable. This kid was definitely a Renfield. Simone had to be close by.

Though barely conscious from the beating, Dominic *was* fully aware of the gun and was trying to reach it. The question was could he survive the attack long enough to get his hand on it.

With both hands, the Goth kid grabbed Dominic's head and started slamming it against the hallway floor, not realizing that his manhandling unintentionally brought Dominic within reach of the gun. With the hall so dark, in his barely operative state, Dominic couldn't detect if the room was spinning around him, but had enough awareness of the Glock's location to take hold and squeeze the trigger.

The bullet ricocheted aimlessly off the wall striking no one, but it did get the attention of the kid who easily pried the gun away and started fumbling with it. The Goth kid's inability to take proper hold of the gun served as enough of a distraction. Dominic pulled a stake out of his coat pocket, not because the kid was undead, but because it was the closest weapon within his reach. He thrust his arm upwards, driving the stake through the kid's neck.

With the pointed end lodged deeply in his esophagus, breathing became a priority for the Goth kid, enabling Dominic to reach for his gun, which had landed just beyond his fingertips. An inch of push was all Dominic needed to hook the gun into his palm with his forefinger, but he was so disoriented from the beating, he could only point the gun randomly upward and hope for the best.

The shot boomed through the gutted hall of Greenwood State.

Deafened by the reverberating bang and the subsequent ringing of the ears, Dominic was clueless to the results of his "Hail Mary" shot into the darkness. It was only when his attacker's 300-pound carcass collapsed onto him that Dominic knew he had hit his target.

His head still spinning, Dominic crawled from underneath the massive teen and spotted his still-lit Maglite a couple of feet away. He picked it up and pointed it at the Goth kid. The stake was still lodged in his throat, his face drenched with blood and no sign of any breathing.

Clean hit.

Dominic rose to his feet and pulled the stake from the kid's throat. He would be needing it.

The Maglite shone down the dark empty hall. She had to be around somewhere. The track of half-eaten rats littering the corridor attested to that. The Goth kid had been dutifully standing guard, feeding from the only available source of nourishment. There are no lunch breaks when you're a Renfield. The uncompromising invasion of your cerebrum vacuums any sense of self away. You belong to the one you are protecting. All you care about is that no one gets to the coffin. That means no visits to the local Burger King. You feed from the local rodent population. Renfields cannot be let out on an unsuspecting public. Their twisted behavior would send up all kinds of red flags that could result in local authorities being notified and a coffin being discovered.

Dominic checked his watch. It was only 4:08 p.m. That whole scuffle where he was almost beaten to death took only two minutes! Pitch black as it was in the halls, Dominic figured there was still at least forty minutes of daylight left outside.

The haze in his head lightened just a tad, but it was enough. An essence of death began to envelope him. The MV12 was kicking in. The evil bitch was close. She was definitely in the building. Knocking out some boards on the windows to let some light in was a thought, but Dominic didn't want to waste time. There were several rooms to check and he wanted to find the coffin fast so he could stake her and get the hell out.

About ten feet past the stairway exit, some chewed-up vermin peppered the entrance to one of the rooms. To free a hand for the Maglite, Dominic put the bloodied stake back in his coat. With his gun in the other hand, Dominic slowly pushed the door open.

His breath turned heavy.

There it was!

Three yards away, closed, undisturbed by the fracas that just occurred outside the room, lay Simone's coffin. It was hardboard, the kind they use for cremations. For nomads like her, those are more practical, lighter in weight and easier to move around.

Dominic holstered his gun and pulled out the stake. He had to raise the lid and stake her as fast as possible, allowing her no chance to react. Given a second of time, she could hypnotize him and stop him in his tracks before ripping him into a thousand unidentifiable pieces.

Grabbing hold of the lid, Dominic raised his stake, ready to swing it down into her chest. He took a deep breath and closed his eyes, whispering a prayer in Spanish. The prayer over, Dominic threw the lid open and furiously brought the stake down. The sharpened point plunged deeply into the soft cushioned bottom of a vacant casket. Startled by her absence, Dominic's panicked mind wondered, if she wasn't there, then where the hell was she? The answer came when two railroad spikes pierced through his neck, sending a harrowed shout into the halls of the forsaken institution.

Simone growled with gluttonous delight as the excruciation drilled through Dominic's spine, but she was so fixated on devouring her prey, that she failed to notice him pulling his gun out and pointing it at her face.

The first shot sent her back with a scream, landing somewhere behind him. But to Dominic the room was now teetering like a capsizing ship in a tropical storm. He looked desperately for the Maglite, which had fallen from his grip when she attacked him. He knew that the shot would only slow her down for a few seconds before she'd spring back and finish him off, but with no other answer in sight, he decided to randomly take shots around the room, hoping he'd hit something. There was no logic behind it. He could have hit her with a hundred bullets and it still wouldn't have stopped her. She might have had a lot of holes, but it still wouldn't have stopped her. But when the sound of broken glass was followed by a lacerating scream, Dominic turned.

He got her!

Not with a bullet, but with the sun. A shot had shattered the window across the hall, putting a hole through the board that was covering it.

Light had come in!

Fading, late afternoon light!

It wasn't a tropical day in the Bahamas, but it was enough light to turn the once captivating seductress into a cowering demon, crawling back to her coffin.

"Fuck that!" said Dominic.

With a second wind, he aimed at the boarded window and fired multiple shots with each bullet hole scorching more of Simone's dead flesh. But even with that, she was uncomfortably close to the protection of her coffin—a chance for her to put her mangled pieces back together.

Not if Dominic could help it.

He took whatever energy he had left and threw his considerable weight towards her, knocking her away like a linebacker. Unable to take any more of the burning, Simone speared out of the room, deep into the darkened hallway, shrieking in desperation.

The smell of burning flesh was not unfamiliar to Dominic. He was one of the first responders after the September 11th attacks. It was a smell he had tried hard to forget. But this time there was satisfaction, although he couldn't be sure the job was done since she ran off before he could see her go up in flames. Nonetheless, his part of the fight was over. He had done all he could as a human being. The rest would have to be done by something not human—something like her.

The light coming in from the bullet-riddled window was dimming. Dominic crawled to the nearest wall and sat against it. Pain was ruthlessly charging through his neck and his shoulder. He wasn't going to make it back to his car.

He pulled out his cell phone. The time on it read 4:13 p.m. He tried dialing for help but each button that he pressed brought him closer to losing consciousness.

#

At 8:18 p.m. Dominic opened his eyes again. He had nodded off. The light from the full moon came in through the bullet holes in the boarded window, shining on his cell phone, which had fallen a few inches from his hand. It might as well have been a mile. He was powerless to reach it. The lit screen showed that he had just missed a call, but his vision was so blurred he couldn't make out who it was. But he did see that there were multiple attempts.

Outside the room, the body lying in the hallway began to twitch. Apparently, the Goth kid was not only Simone's guard, but he was also a source of blood, meaning the undead venom was in him. Dominic, unaware of the kid's rising, was focusing on the phone which was out of reach from his shaking hand. He threw his body down so he could extend his hand and tap it a little closer. Good idea, but the substantially sized figure in the doorway was not about to allow it.

"Ah shit," moaned Dominic, seeing the Goth kid standing at the doorway. Freshly thrown into the ranks of the undead, the teen hadn't figured out how to activate his humanlike appearance yet, though in his case the difference would have hardly been distinguishable. But not activating his projection left the big hole in his neck and the blown off piece of forehead from his confrontation with Dominic in full view.

That's what you get for fuckin' with Dominic, kid.

Dominic dropped the phone and reached for the pewter crucifix in his jacket. The Goth kid was oddly still, thought Dominic, maybe he'd have time to pull out the cross and defend himself.

He didn't have to.

The Goth kid collapsed face forward into the room, exposing another, more slender, silhouette behind him. The dark-figure held a wooden stake dripping with blood. It was his brother-in-law, or at least the thing that claimed to be him.

36

The missed calls were from me.

It figures. The first night I decide to go back home so I could check on Veronica, this shit happens. I thought I'd start my night out checking in on her at ICU while keeping my cell phone handy in case Dominic tried to reach me. Rules say you're not supposed to bring cell phones into ICU but obviously that doesn't apply to me. Rules are for the living.

Not that I ever made it over there. I was barely out of my coffin when I saw Dominic's text. I rushed out, trying to make it over as soon as I could, but between the traffic on the Jersey Turnpike, the George Washington Bridge, the Cross Bronx, the Whitestone Bridge, and the Cross Island Parkway, fuck, I could have flown in from Hawaii and gotten there sooner.

I arrived at the abandoned hospital about two and a half hours after I got the text. Once I crossed the iron gate, I smelt the death bleeding through the bullet holes Dominic blew out through the boarded window. When I got inside, the kid was probably still adapting to his new undead state, standing at the doorway with eyes on Dominic. He never saw or heard me coming.

I stepped over the fallen Goth kid and knelt beside my brother-in-law, stroking what was left of his hair. "I have to take you to a hospital," I said.

Dominic shook his head. Logically, I knew he was right, but what was I going to do, just leave him there? I reached out to pick him up.

"Don't you put a fucking hand on me," he lashed out.

I insisted.

"NICK!"

It wasn't a shout of anger. It was a shout of horror. What caused such a reaction? I didn't know—not until I felt the axe, which nicked me between my neck and shoulder, sending me evasively scurrying across the room. Weakened from her exposure to the unfriendly rays of the late afternoon sun, the scorch-blackened figure struggled to maintain her balance as she attempted to raise the axe above her head. The charred skin on her face was sliding off her skull the way barbecued ribs come off the bone at Tony Roma's. Me? I had a nice, carved space between my neck and shoulder to go along with the holes in my head, face and chest, courtesy of Roberto and Dominic. It was all out to see after the axe knocked away my more human-like projection.

Simone's capabilities were pretty much cooked away by her encounter with the late afternoon sun. She blindly swung with the axe in the darkness, hoping the blade would find me. The first swing got some undead skin. But caught off guard as I was, I knew I had to recover fast to dodge the erratic hacks that followed.

This was not the controlled Scarlet Widow—the one that brought death and heartache with such predatory disregard. This was a frightened, cornered animal. She made a futile attempt to control my mind but all it did was help me sense her panic. The power wasn't there. She couldn't make me do what she wanted.

She swung again, high and hard, like an undisciplined minor leaguer trying to impress a scout. I caught it. I caught it with both hands and easily yanked it from her grasp.

I then sensed it! And saw it!

Fear!

Fear in the devil's eyes!

And then *she* saw it.

That's right, bitch. Now I'm *your* fucking predator.

The last time she was victimized by a predator had to be when she was sired, whenever that might have been. Allow me, you Satanic whore, to bring back the memories of being on the other side.

I swung the ax towards her midsection. It was a nice, smooth level swing that would have made Mike Piazza proud. The force sent Simone to the floor close enough for Dominic to offer a labored kick to her head. Not satisfied that it was over, I followed my first swing with a series of ferocious hacks, sending pieces of Simone flying in every direction.

For every life she ever took and every family she destroyed, I swung with a vigor built from every heart she had ever broken. There was no such thing as overkill in this case. I couldn't destroy her enough.

Incredibly, when I paused to see what was left of my hacks, I saw that her burnt eyelids were still fluttering, almost defiantly.

What the fuck?

The next series of hacks came down with such a tenacious fury that I didn't stop until I severed off the top half of her head, dividing it at the cheekbone. Still not satisfied, I followed her fractured cranium, which had rolled a few feet away. I then picked it up by its singed red hair and proceeded to smash it against the wall repeatedly, cursing each time. Only when fragments of her skull, face and brains were hanging from her hair like ornaments on a Christmas tree, did I decide it might have been okay to stop.

Dropping what was left of our redheaded tormentor, I looked back at Dominic. My projection had come back, making me look less like an extra from a George Romero movie. His head was off to the side; his eyes were closed. Damn it, Dominic, why couldn't you have just let it go? You didn't need to enter this world.

He took a short breath and exhaled. "Is she dead?"

I tried to hold back but I couldn't. I burst out laughing. He smiled too, that son of a bitch.

"Yeah, I think so," I replied.

I couldn't remember the last time I'd laughed that hard, but I'd been willing to bet that Dominic would have had something to have done with it. He opened his eyes, still smiling. Dominic hadn't smiled at me in over twenty-seven years.

"Do it," said Dominic.

I knew what he meant but I stalled. "Do what?"

His smile faded. "Do it, Nick."

"Dominic—"

The mood quickly turned. "*¡Mira, hijo de puta!* You think I want to be like you? Stake me, damn it!"

I knew he was right but couldn't wrap my mind around doing it—not to him. "No way, Dominic, I'm taking you to the hospital."

"For what?" he growled. "What are they going to do?"

Again, he was right. What was taking him to the hospital going to accomplish? What kind of questions would he have to answer? And what would happen if he died and turned right there in the hospital?

A tear crept out from the corner of my eye, a new, unfamiliar feeling. "Dominic, please..."

"*¡Empujalo en mi pecho, maricón!*" Like I said before, he now had the venom of two different members of our species in him. On top of that, there was also Gunder's serum, which has traces of the organism that lives in us. "Nicky, I want to be with God. Do this for me and maybe God will forgive you for what you've become."

No chance of that, Dominic. I've taken lives. Most of them were scumbags, but a few of them, like me, were just at the wrong place at the wrong time. They might have been tainted enough in my eyes that I could rationalize my feeding, but they were lives, and they weren't mine to take.

I pulled out my stake and tentatively pressed the pointed end against his heart. So now Aida and Penny are going to have to lose their father, too. And what about Artie and Ramona, they lived this long to see both of their children die within less than a month? You should have left it alone, Dominic. There was nothing to prove. I was dead. You should have left it that way. Now you're not going to see how awesome the Mets are going to be next year with that tremendous pitching staff, you fucking idiot.

After nodding his approval, Dominic took hold of my wrist. "I know you loved her, Nicky. She knew too."

It was all I needed. For that brief moment, he was talking to Nicky, his brother-in-law, not a child of Satan.

Dominic closed his eyes and went into prayer.

"*¡Dios mìo! ante el trono de tu adorable Majestad me postro pidiéndote la última de todas las gracias: una feliz hora de muerte. Muchas veces, en verdad, hice mal uso de la vida que me diste; pero a pesar de ello te* *ruego, me concedas la gracia de terminarla bien y—,"*

I didn't let him finish the prayer.

I thought it would be better doing it while his mind was distracted. His stunned gasp filled the barren corridors of Greenwood as I pushed the stake deep into his heart with both of my hands. His eyes then opened to see tears moistening the cracked flesh underneath my eyes. His chest heaving, Dominic struggled to take his last breath, with eyes fixed on the Filipino blade sticking out of my jacket.

He nodded.

I knew what I had to do.

37

The morning sun glaring in through the bathroom window highlights my tousled hair in the reflection on the mirror. Three years ago, I said, fuck it, and stopped dyeing it. Who do *I* need to impress anymore? I'm married to the same fantastic woman, the only one that I will ever love, for over forty years now. Let the white hair shine proudly.

Damn, I'm sixty-four today, just like the Beatles song. Will Stefanie still need me? Will she still feed me?

Stefanie calls from the kitchen downstairs. "Honey, are you dressed yet? The kids are already on their way."

Holy shit! The alarm clock on the night table reads 12:20 p.m. I never sleep this late. Even as a renewal-collecting, semi-retired regional manager that doesn't have to report somewhere every morning, I never get up past breakfast time. I guess I stayed up too late watching the Abbott and Costello marathon on the Nostalgia Channel.

Walking downstairs, the aroma of Stefanie's stew teasingly fondles my nasal passages. I wished she'd make it more often instead of just when family comes over. I asked her once if she'd teach me the recipe so I could make it myself and she refused.

"What?" I asked, thinking she was kidding.

"No," she said. "That is a recipe only to be shared with the women in the family."

"You're shitting me."

"No, *boca de caca*, Mami passed it on to me and I passed it on to Jessie."

"What about Davey? That's not fair to Davey."

"When he gets married, I'll teach it to his wife."

That could be a while. Davey's been enjoying the major-league lifestyle. And with the pretty good season he's had this year at Cleveland as a backup infielder, that day might not come too soon. His contract is up and he's a free agent, which means he might be able to land himself a nice little multi-year deal with another team.

Damn, that stew smells good! Happy Birthday to me! And though I love following that scent into the kitchen, there is another scent that I love so much more.

"Honey, I'm cooking," says Stefanie as I bury my face in her hair.

She's been working hard all morning preparing for our family, making me feel a tiny tinge of guilt for not helping her out. Very tiny. Still, I gotta try and fake it. "You should have woken me up. I could've helped."

She smiles that *knowing-I'm-full-of-shit* smile. "It's okay, Abbott. I'll give you a pass today. It's your birthday."

She's wearing her grey, wavy hair a little shorter these days. She's also put on a couple of pounds. But to me, she's still the girl I met at the college library.

"Well, you know I had to wait until they did *Niagara Falls*." That's my favorite Abbott and Costello routine. I still laugh my ass off when I see that.

"What are you talking about? You have that whole collection on DVD. You can watch that whenever you want."

"Yeah, I know but—"

The doorbell. I can hear the grandkids.

"Oh my God, they're already here. And look at you. You didn't even shave yet." Stefanie hands me a tray full of cold cuts, vegetables and dip. "Here, take this out to the living room and answer the door." Well, we all know who the boss around here is, may the festivities begin.

As soon as I dutifully carry out her orders and open that door, it's going to be like that Marx Brothers movie where all the people spill out of the closet. I wouldn't have it any other way.

"Happy birthday, Daddy!" says Jessie, throwing her arms around me and kissing my stubbly face. "Ew, Daddy! Shave!"

My ten-year-old grandson Pauly marches in right behind his mom so his grandpa can muss up his hair. I have no idea why I do that. It must be something grandpas do. "Hey, big guy!"

My granddaughter Jamie steps in, not even a teenager yet and already almost as tall as her mother. Man, they grow fast. At least she doesn't complain about kissing Grandpa's stubbly cheek. "Happy birthday, Grandpa!"

Jesse's husband Brad greets his former sales manager with a friendly hug. "How're you doing, Boss?" He was a cocky college graduate fifteen years ago when he started working with us at Atlantic Indemnity. He met Jessie at a company picnic and she fell head over heels. They've been together ever since.

"So, superstar, how are things back at the office?" Not that I really give a shit. All I care about are my renewals.

He was my top sales rep, though, when I brought him into the company—Leaders Conference every year.

"It's getting busy," says Brad. "Of course, if you'd show up more than two or three times a month, you'd know that."

"Hey, watch that fresh mouth of yours, kid. I can still get your ass fired."

Dominic's 2008 Ford Explorer pulls up to the driveway behind Jessie and Brad's car. He loves that SUV and still has the damn thing looking like it's brand new, even with it having, like, 240,000 miles on it.

"Get that old piece of crap out of my driveway." I love breaking his balls.

Patti steps out on the passenger side. "Happy birthday, Nicky!"

"You *wish* you could get the miles I get out this thing," says Dominic, stepping out from the driver's side to join me and Patti at the front of the car. They've been through a lot of ups and downs those two, but here they are, still together. "Hey Nick, your boy here yet?"

"Look behind you."

"How about that," says Dominic, as Davey's Mercury Cougar rolls in. "All you gotta do is mention him. Let's team up on him, Nick. Now that he's a free agent, maybe we can talk him into coming to the Mets."

"Damn right. He'd be closer to the family, too."

Davey steps out with a present in his hands. "Hey, Pop! Happy birthday!" He greets Aunt Patti with a kiss and Uncle Dom with a hug. Pop gets a big hug, too. "Come inside, Pop. I want to show you something."

"Never mind that," says Dominic. "You're gonna sign up with the Mets this year, right?"

Davey laughs. "Uncle Dom, you're starting already?"

"That's right, I'm starting," says Dominic. "The Mets were in the World Series this year. If you were with them, not only would you have been home, but you would have been in the World Series. I'm tired of having to wait until you play the Yankees to go see you."

What? I don't believe this.

"Dominic, are you serious?" Artie and Ramona's old Buick pulls up behind Davey's car.

Dominic gets defensive. "Hey man, I offered to drive them. But you know how stubborn that old prick is."

"It's true, he doesn't listen," says Patti. Wow, Patti defending Dominic? Now *that's* rare.

I shake my head at the two of them. "Jesus, he's 88 years old."

Stepping out on the driver's side, Artie's still got that spring in his step but on the passenger's side it a competition between me and Dominic to open the door for Ramona.

"Just one will do," laughs Ramona.

Dominic beats me to the car and helps his mother out. *"Como esta, Mami."*

All of us take turns receiving warm hugs and kisses from Mama Torres before stepping back into the house where the decibel level rises as everyone tries to talk over one another. Normally, the grandkids are the loudest, with the lady chatter running a close second. Today, I think the grand prize goes to Dominic, ranting that cheap bastard Met owner Fred Wilpon better offer Davey a contract. Davey nods, listening with only one ear as he works on connecting something to my stereo.

It's a good time to sneak upstairs and shave, although I'm enjoying watching the scene in the living room. Davey was just here this past September when the Indians played the Yankees, and Jessie only lives twenty minutes away in White Plains. As for Dominic and his folks, they live the next town over in Scarsdale, so it's not like we don't see each other that often. But it never gets old having everyone come together like this.

"Pop, come here, let me show you."

So much for me sneaking off to shave.

"Come on, honey." Stefanie accompanies me towards Davey at the stereo. I know they're now called home entertainment centers but to me they're still stereos.

"Is that—?" Antiquated as I might be, I recognize the device in Davey's hand.

"That's right, Pop, I'm bringing you out of the Stone Ages." Davey places a brand new I-pod in my hands.

"It looks like my iPhone."

"Similar, Pop, but here you can store your whole music collection."

"He's forcing you to join the rest of the world," says Stefanie. She already has one of those *Nano* things where she listens to reggaeton, bachata, and Marc Anthony.

The cord to the baseball-card-sized device is hooked up to the stereo. "You realize I have no idea how to work this thing, right?"

"Pop, it's easy. Check it out." Davey points to the screen. "You see that little arrow? Just press that."

"Okay."

Thick bass notes from a familiar tune drape over my shoulders like a warm blanket. Stefanie smiles with that little twinkle in her eye.

All these years and she still melts me. "May I have this dance, *Señora Negrón*?"

Together.

In each other's arms.

Our cheeks softly rubbing against one another.

Roberta Flack's voice.

The opening lines of our wedding song.

Swaying slowly with my wife, I recall the night, over forty years ago—the blonde singer in the sparkling, way-too-tight purple dress and her whiny monotone voice mangling the lyrics. Hey, what do you expect when you let Artie hire the band? Now he and Ramona are watching us, fondly remembering that night, as well—although Artie probably remembers the singer's ass a little *more* fondly.

Jessie tilts her head and makes that "aww..." sound women like to do.

"Forty-four years," says Artie. "Seems like such a long time ago."

"Forty-four years *was* a long time ago," cracks Brad.

"Shit, am I that old?" says Dominic.

I reply with a quick, "Yes!" Even during a moment like this I can't resist breaking his balls to get a laugh out of the room.

My laugh makes Stefanie back her head away. "Honey, you're laughing in my ear," she says, playfully hitting me on the chest.

I bring her to me again. "Get over here," I say, closing my eyes and resting my head on hers, moving slowly to the soft hum of the bass and taking in the peaceful scent of her hair.

We are all here, celebrating—celebrating me; Stefanie, my loving *esposa*, Davey, our son with the successful sports career, Jessie, who's juggling being a realtor along with motherhood, and the grandkids on the couch, already looking bored. Dominic's twins, Aida and Penny should be here soon, too. It always takes them a little longer, coming from Connecticut and upstate.

It all must bring such pride to Artie and Ramona, seeing that all this will continue on to another generation. And look how happy *Mami* is standing next to Ramona. *Papi* too—*un hombre bien orgulloso*—and little Dani in his arms, her tiny legs dangling above his belt as her head rests comfortably on his shoulder.

All these years, all these wonderful years and... wait... something's wrong... something's not making sense... this isn't right...

The music drifts into a hollow echo. The scent—the scent of Stefanie's hair, it's changed. The texture, it's frizzed, burnt. It smells like... death...

I pull back.

Her face.

It's blackened.

Charred flesh … melting off her cheekbones.

Her mouth, her fangs, they're ready to strike.

And that dress!

That fucking red dress!

38

I don't know how she did it or what it even means. So little is known about our species. Outside of a woman epidemiologist that the general public thinks is insane, no scientific research is being devoted towards what is believed to be folklore. But now, with the Hindquarters massacre and the reports of e*l mostro* terrorizing Rego Park, that tune is going to change.

And then there's that orderly, the one that saw me in the staircase at the hospital. Combine these all and we have way too many instances that are begging for an explanation. How long will it be before the general public catches on?

And I'm pretty sure this isn't going to be the last of it. More incidents will come. It's inevitable. And it's going to get harder and harder to keep sweeping them under the rug.

In her studies, Dr. Gunder suggests that our species is constantly evolving. How does something that's dead evolve? Her explanation is that the host human vessel is dead. The disease, venom, virus or whatever-the-fuck you want to call it—that's what's alive. And it survives on what drives its host—in our case, human blood. This keeps our little visitors feeding, growing and evolving. Our abilities, she says, suggest that we are other-worldly, enabling us to project human or invisible appearances and control the minds of others. What this means is, if whatever lives inside of us is indeed a species with other-worldly capabilities, then who knows what other traits we might develop or inherit? At least with my genetic resistance, I've been able to maintain some degree of control. But what about those who aren't genetically resistant and don't give a shit?

As far as any of us know, Simone was the only one to control others like us. I was fully intent on destroying her back at the Hindquarters. I was ready to attack. Instead she stopped me cold right where I stood, leaving me only wanting to attack what was six inches below her navel.

Okay, so what about what happened just now?

We are dead. We don't sleep. Even those of us with genetic resistance—we do not sleep. When I am in my coffin, there is nothing going on. I am dead. Completely dead. Not asleep. Dead. So if that's the case, then it goes to follow that we don't dream. If you don't sleep, then you don't dream.

So what was it, then?

What was this vision of me having aged, living a normal life with my family? I wasn't sleeping. I'm not even in my coffin. I'm miles away, sitting with my back against Stefanie's headstone in Nanuet.

It's 11:00 p.m. I'm alone. No one or nothing is in sight—just graves. There's only one possibility, just one that I can think of.

She's in my head!

I don't know how she did it but Simone is in my fucking head! Somehow in our last encounter, weak as she was, she was able to find residency in me. It's the only thing that makes any sense.

Simone was done. As a host, that ash-withered vessel was no longer going to serve. So what did she do? She hopped on board. She got into my head and stayed there. And that vision I had? It was her. It was Simone's way of saying, "Hello, honey, I'm home."

Great!

Just fucking great!

Finally, after over fifty years, I manage to have *Los Ruidos* leave my system only to have Simone fill the vacancy. What does it mean? If what I suspect is true, and I am carrying her around, what happens now? Can she take over me when she pleases? Will she control what I do? Will I no longer have control over my own actions?

It is nearly impossible for us to self-terminate. Otherwise, I would do it right now. My existence brings nothing but destruction to those around me. Even when my intentions are good, I bring misery to those I care about. I befriend Veronica, what happens? She's now in the hospital, pretty much a vegetable. Her kids must now face life without a mother.

My attempts to help Davey and Jesse also weren't stellar. With his past, if a witness places Davey where I killed Darryl Briggs, he could end up in a shitload of trouble, maybe even back in jail.

Nice going, Pops!

And Jessie, even though I got that shitbag Nemeth out of her life, my appearance in front of her car left her so shaken, she might never recover.

Dominic too, was a wakeup call. When he found me, his disgust reminded me of how I don't belong on this earth. Except for maybe his last few seconds, he never saw me as his brother-in-law. He only saw the product of Hell that I am. And in the end, I cost him his life, too.

My wife, the only love I've ever had, Stefanie, she's gone. I will never be able to see her again. The dream was to grow old together, die together, and spend eternity in Paradise. Instead it will be Rippey. He was a good husband. And it is *he* that will share eternity with my wife and my children.

My eternity will have me walking this Earth, preying on humans that I decide the general population can do without. It won't make me any less of a monster, but at the very least I will feel like I am doing something useful. When I was alive, no one at home ever wanted to take out the trash. It always wound up being me.

The tradition continues.

But this could only happen if I can maintain the power of my own free will. If I am unwillingly carrying a soulless guest with centuries of devastation marking her past, how could I know that any decision I ever make will be my own. Even now as I approach the door of a small cabin in the woods of Upstate New York, I am not sure if it is me or her that is doing the knocking. Who is it that is patiently watching as the door slowly creaks open? Who knows? Surely not the shocked and horrified woman that stands opposite me on the other side of the doorway. The smell of her fear is near irresistible, but I must have some degree of control because I am able to maintain my composure and patiently introduce myself. "Hello, Dr. Gunder. I'm Nicky Negrón."

The doctor stands frozen. She has opened her door to Death. And she knows all too well from her research, that unlike the fictional stories in books, movies or on TV, this real-life vampire standing outside her door does not need an invitation to come inside.

The End

And now, here's your opportunity to take an exclusive first look at the opening chapter of the much-anticipated sequel to Sángre: The Color of Dying...

Sángre:
The Wrong Side of Tomorrow

1

The rattled, pothole-ridden *Bx1* ride on the Grand Concourse always left me wondering why the fuck the New York City Transit Authority couldn't afford some shock absorbers for their buses. Like the crew members in *Voyage to the Bottom of the Sea,* all the standing passengers on the bus would rock from side to side, similar to when those sea monsters would grab hold of that show's submarine and shake it up like a bottle of Yoo-hoo.

I suppose I could have sat down, but the selection of seats weren't to my liking. Behind me, there was a seat between a pair of yakking housewives, but I wasn't keen about sitting in between their crossfire of gossip about Liz Taylor and Richard Burton. Shit, the whole bus could hear their conversation, which later shifted to their disgust at Jackie Kennedy, who was at the early stages of a relationship with some Greek billionaire only three years after her husband's assassination. In their minds, if she was not going to remain a widow for the rest of her life, at least she could have picked someone who was presentable looking, if not movie-star handsome like the late president.

There was another seat available that was next to some granny waving two knitting needles around like a samurai. She was making some scarf, sweater, or who knows what, but all I knew was that with the ragged journey jostling the bus around towards my stop at Fordham Road, there was no way I was going sit next to her and wind up with one of those needles in my eye.

There were also seats available above the wheels in the back. Nobody liked to sit on those. Any New Yorker could tell you that those seats used to bang up your ass like Desi Arnaz did with his conga drum during *Babalu.*

I also took a pass on the seat next to the geezer with the cane in front of me. The old guy not only stunk from the too-heavy-for-August sports jacket he was wearing, but he also had a series of Bronx cheers coming out of his ass that was threatening to melt the windows. As it was, the breeze that came in from those that were opened, provided little relief to the sticky, late summer Saturday that had everyone's shirts sporting large sweat patches below their armpits. The Transit Authority had yet to invest in the modern-day wonder known as air-conditioning. Perhaps there was no money left after the transit strike that crippled the city earlier in the year.

Next stop, Fordham Road.

Disembarking from the bus at the corner, across from Alexander's always brought a tinge of excitement. It might have just been a department store, but the large, broad sign across the rooftop always gave me the same cosmopolitan feel as the big Coke sign in Times Square. Hey, what the fuck do you want? I wasn't even sixteen yet. Alexander's also brought the promise of its crisp, clean air conditioning which would lift you in its arms and carry you towards the escalators before you're even halfway through the revolving doors.

It's not that we didn't have air conditioning at home. We still had the large window unit *Papi* bought when he was still with us, but since he had left and stopped sending checks over from Puerto Rico, *Mami* was strict about cutting back on expenses and only wanted it running at night when we went to bed. Besides, I think she liked sweating from the heat and losing the water weight. She had already shed about fifty pounds during the two-year period that followed the accident that killed my little sister, Dani. That, combined with the resignation that *Papi* was never going to come back, had stripped her of what used to be a sizable appetite, and her shape was returning to the hour glass that had caught *Papi's* eye back when they met at the garment district in the late 1940's.

But me, I wasn't about to spend my Saturdays collecting beads of sweat in the crack of my ass in of our grief-stricken apartment, so whenever I had a little change, I'd escape to the excitement of Fordham Road. That was the grand destination of the opposite end of the Concourse. At my end, it was Yankee Stadium, but being that I grew up rooting for the Mets (no matter how much they sucked), the House That Ruth Built held no attraction for me. But at the other end where Fordham was, there were stores like Alexander's and Sear s, along with palatial movie theaters like the RKO Fordham and the incredible Loew's Paradise.

Times Square? Who needed it?

Radio City Music Hall had nothing—and I mean nothing—on the Loew's Paradise. With its Venetian décor, Roman statues, and sparkling stars in the sky above the auditorium, you didn't know whether to watch the movie or just soak in the scenery around you. That afternoon, I was planning to go there to catch the matinee of *Fantastic Voyage*, a sci-fi movie where a medical crew is shrunk inside some type of submarine to the size of an atom. They are then injected into a dying patient to cure him. I had seen the commercials with Raquel Welch in her skin-tight diving suit and I wanted something nice to think about later that night when I would retire alone in my bedroom. But first I wanted to stop by at the record department on the second floor of Alexander's and pick up the new Percy Sledge single. I didn't care too much for the *white* music that was out in those days—especially those fab fuckers from Liverpool that provided the soundtrack for my sister's death. For me, it was soul—nothing but soul—which is exactly what was sucked out of our lives two years earlier.

There was also another reason I enjoyed going to the record department at Alexander's. She was tall, blond and about twelve years older than me. And though brunettes were more my type (like Raquel Welch), the blond cashier at the record department kept me company many nights when I was alone in my bedroom— although that night she would have to concede to Raquel (Man, that diving suit!).

She knew I was all gaga over her, too. But she was always pleasant and never embarrassed me about it. She easily could have laughed and made me feel like just some horny little kid. Instead, she did the opposite.

"Ooh, Percy Sledge. I love his voice." She'd always say something like that, which would send me skipping out of the store like a toddler with an ice cream pop.

"She talked to me! She talked to me! I think she likes me!" I'd say to myself. But before that, I would respond with some witty little banter like, "Um...yeah, like, um, yeah, he's good, yeah..." How could she resist a smooth talker like that?

Once I floated out of the store and landed on the balmy sidewalk, I crossed Fordham and picked up a blueberry Italian ice at the pizzeria next to the candy store. While licking along the rim of the paper cup, pretending it was the cashier, I spotted the latest issue of *World's Finest,* the comic book that always teamed up Batman and Superman. On the cover, it showed them going against Bizarro Batman, Bizarro Superman *and* the Joker! No way I wasn't going to get that!

In those days, the comics were only twelve cents. The problem was, after the Percy Sledge single and the Italian ice, if I bought the comic book, I wasn't going to have enough left to take the bus home after seeing the movie. But damn, Bizarro Batman *and* Superman, with the Joker! Fuck it, I said, I'll walk. I plunked down the quarter, pocketed the thirteen cents change and sat on the sidewalk to read the Caped Crusader and the Man of Steel's latest exploits.

About ten pages in, just as the Joker got his hands on some kryptonite, who came out of Alexander's? That's right; the beautiful blond cashier came through the revolving doors looking through her purse, presumably on her way to take a lunch break. And there *I* was sitting on the sidewalk with blue lips, an Italian ice in one hand and a comic book in the other. Ooh, she was bound to be turned on now!

I quickly rose off the concrete, picking up the Percy Sledge record, which I had laid on the sidewalk, and dusted myself off. Thankfully, she hadn't spotted me. But just on the chance, that she might come across the street where I was standing, I hid the comic book behind my back to try and maintain some cool points in front of her.

Once she got past the revolving doors, she pulled out a dollar (believe it or not, that was enough for lunch back then), but when she looked up from her purse to cross the street, some freckled, Irish-looking punk knocked her down and snatched her purse!

Oh, no you don't, fucker.

The turd dashed in my direction but there were passersby between us that slowed my attempt to intercept him. But once I navigated my way around an older woman to avoid blitzing into her, I dropped the comic book, the record, my Italian ice, and charged after him. The bastard was fast as hell, like an antelope being chased down by a cheetah. Unfortunately for him, this cheetah was the stolen base leader at junior high school.

With a flying leap, I caught up to the shit bag and tackled him right in front of a cardboard cutout of Raquel Welch wearing that diving suit, which was placed next to the box office at the Paradise Theater.

Not giving the punk a chance to react, I pulled the purse out of his hands, ready to square off. But before I could get up and take the punk on, a heavy, sharp blow across my back sent me down on the concrete sidewalk.

"STAY DOWN!" shouted the police officer, pointing his nightstick at me while the *white* thief got away. Stay down? After the crushing clout I had just taken, getting up wasn't even an option. I was too busy trying to learn how to breathe again.

"What is the matter with you?" cried the cashier from Alexander's, who had just caught up to us. And with an unfiltered fury, in front of a crowd of onlookers and ticket buyers waiting to get in the theater, she berated the officer mercilessly for brutally attacking the only one who didn't stand by to watch her assailant get away.

The cop couldn't believe it. He even had the balls to question her. "Are you sure?" That's right, fuckwad, the thief wasn't the *'porta-rican'*. Even after he learned the truth, the prick gave me no apology. In fact, he gave me a warning, instead. "Stay out of trouble, kid."

The cashier glared at the asshole cop before turning to me and rubbing her hand against my back. "Oh, my God, are you okay?" Still unable to speak, I nodded and handed her purse. She stroked the back of my head. "I'm Stacy. What's your name?"

"Nicky," I replied, the name barely crawling out of my throat.

Stacy smiled. Her high-wattage teeth and golden hair looked like something out of a shampoo commercial.

Raquel didn't stand a chance.

***

About the Author

Born in Spanish Harlem and raised by Puerto Rican parents in the South Bronx, Carlos Colón was a storyteller from the start. He began in his pre-teens by writing comic strips for his parents and continued throughout school writing dramatic short stories in his English classes. Teachers immediately took notice nicknaming him Hemingway and encouraging him to the point where he eventually graduated from Lehman College, CUNY with an English degree in Creative Writing. That same year, 1979, his play "Jerome" won Honorable Mention for the Jacob Hammer Memorial Prize. Since then he wrote several screenplays for Hollywood producers but unfortunately never saw one reach the big screen. Nowadays, Carlos is living out on Jersey Shore, serving as a singer/songwriter/front man for the retro rock n' roll Jersey Shore Roustabouts band, one of the most in-demand entertainment acts of the New Jersey/New York/Philadelphia area.

Sangre: The Color of Dying is Carlos Colón's first published novel, introducing readers to the foul-mouthed, urban-vampire vigilante , Nicky Negrón, a tragic anti-hero who is haunted by loss. Readers have already taken to the Nicky, who has alternately been described as haunting, hilarious, horrifying, and heartbreaking. As a result, Sangre: The Color of Dying, which was originally intended as a stand-alone tale, will now be followed up in late 2017/early 2018 with Sangre: The Wrong Side of Tomorrow, a sequel that will take readers deeper into the haunted psych and tormented afterlife of Nicky Negrón. Also being discussed are current plans to adapt Sangre as a feature film and television series

Other HellBound Books for your delectation

Available from www.hellboundbookspublishing.com

All available now in paperback and eBook from Amazon,
iBooks, Barnes & Noble, Kobo etc.
For full details, visit our official website

www.hellboundbookspublishing.com

Or
Download our App from iTunes / Google Play – or simply
scan the QR Code below

The Big Book of Bootleg Horror

Twenty tales of terror, darkness, the truly macabre and things most unpleasant from a delectably eclectic bunch of the very best independent horror authors on the scene today!

S.E. Rise, Kevin Wetmore, Paul Stansfield, Craig Stewart, Shaun Avery, Jeff Myers, Marc DeWit, Timothy Wilkie, Quinn Cunningham, Melanie Waghorne, Marc E. Fitch, Stanley B. Webb, Tim J. Finn, Ken Goldman, Ralph Greco Jr, Roger Leatherwood, Vincent Treewell, David Owain Hughes, J.J. Smith and the inimitable James H. Longmore

In this superlative tome, HellBound Books have embraced the taboo, gone all-out to horrify and have broken the flimsy boundaries of good taste to make The Big Book of Bootleg Horror the perfect anthology for those who take their horror like we take our coffee - insidiously dark and most definitely unsweetened

Shopping List

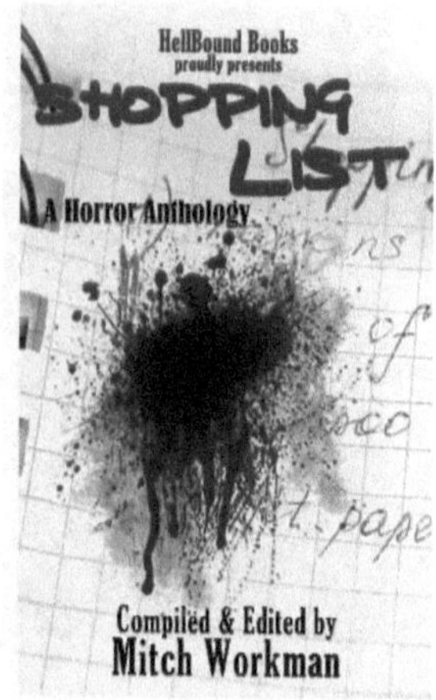

A simply superlative collection of spine-tingling horror from the very best minds in the business!

We decided upon the shopping list theme for this particular volume as an antithesis to those wildly successful writers (they know who they are) of whom it is often said *'we would read their damned shopping list if they published it!'*.

Well, we have given twenty-one of the hottest authors in the independent horror scene the unique opportunity to have their own shopping lists read by you - along with their most terrifying tales of course!

Stories of gut-wrenching terror from: Kathy Dinisi, Robert Over, Christopher O'Halloran, Eric W. Burgin, Russ Gartz, Mark Slada, Jeff Baker, Tim Miller, Nick Swain,JC Raye, Jovan Jones, Ben Stevens, David F. Gray, Brandon Cracraft, M.S. Swift, Kevin Holton, David Owain Hughes, Bertram Allan Mullin, Jeff C. Stevenson, Sebastian Crow and S.E. Rise

Man Eating F*cks
By
David Owain Hughes

A dark, incredibly entertaining excursion into the delightfully twisted imagination of David Owain Hughes....

An average teenage girl and her father find themselves caught up in a brutal nightmare at their local recreational centre, when an age-old enemy comes stumbling out of the woods to crash a heavy-metal gig; a gig that has all the promises of being killer. This is one blood-soaked gig you won't want to miss!

Praise for Man-Eating F*cks from Ty Schwamberger (author of The Fields, Deep Dark Woods & The Death of a Horror Writer.) "Man Eating F*cks is old school horror, but with a new, blood-soaked twist! David Owain Hughes effectively creates enjoyable and lethal characters in this tale that is sure to keep you up at night. This is the type of tale that you need to read with a light on...I'm serious. You better put your seatbelt on 'cause you're in for one helluva ride. Look out, Hughes might very well be headed to the major leagues after this twisted tale! Highly recommended!"

The Erotic Odyssey of Colton Forshay
By
James H Longmore

A stunningly imaginative bizarro tale in which Colton Forshay dreams himself into a bizarre sexual dystopia, a world in which nothing is as it should be. Sickening sex acts and sexual violence are the norm and in which the currency is deviant sexual acts.

At first disturbed, then intrigued - and aroused - by his dreams of this other world, Colton is drawn deeper in and begins to spend more and more time there; so much so that his wife forces him to visit a psychiatrist.

The psychiatrist encourages him to explore the dream world - and our hero goes on an odyssey with his dog/son, Eric, to discover the disturbing truth behind his dream world.

**A HellBound Books LLC
Publication**

www.hellboundbookspublishing.com

Printed in the United States of America

www.ingramcontent.com/pod-product-compliance
Lightning Source LLC
Chambersburg PA
CBHW030657120726
47905CB00001B/258